LARGE
PRINT
EDITION

RANDOM
HOUSE

The Waterworks

The Waterworks

E. L. Doctorow

Published by Random House Large Print
in association with Random House, Inc.
New York 1994

A signed first edition of this book has been
privately printed by The Franklin Library.

Library of Congress Cataloging-in-Publication Data
Doctorow, E. L., 1931–
    The waterworks / E. L. Doctorow. — 1st large print ed.
       p.   cm.
    ISBN 0-679-75441-5 (lg. print)
    1. City and town life—New York (N.Y.)—
History—19th century—Fiction.   2. Young
men—New York (N.Y.)—Fiction.
    3. Large type books.   I. Title.
    [PS3554.03W3   1994b]
    813′.54—dc20   94-5912
                                       CIP

Manufactured in the United States of America
FIRST LARGE PRINT EDITION

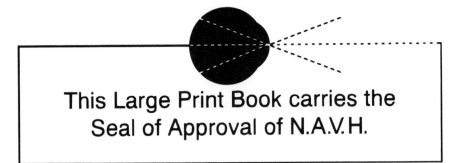

This Large Print Book carries the
Seal of Approval of N.A.V.H.

For
I. Doctorow
and
Philip Blair Rice

The Waterworks

One

PEOPLE wouldn't take what Martin Pemberton said as literal truth, he was much too melodramatic or too tormented to speak plainly. Women were attracted to him for this—they imagined him as something of a poet, though he was if anything a critic, a critic of his life and times. So when he went around muttering that his father was still alive, those of us who heard him, and remembered his father, felt he was speaking of the persistence of evil in general.

In those days the *Telegram* relied heavily on freelances. I always had my eye out for a good freelance and I kept a clutch of them on call. Martin Pemberton was the best of the lot, though I would never tell him that. I treated him as I treated them all. I was derisive because it was expected of me, I was funny so that I could be quoted in the saloons, and I was reasonably fair because that is the way I am . . . but I was also interested in the language and wanted all of them to write it for my approval . . . which, if it came at all, came barbed.

Of course, none of this was particularly effective with Martin Pemberton. He was a moody, distracted young fellow, and it was clear his own mind was more company to him than people were. He had light gray eyes which spasmodically widened from the slightest stimulus. His eyebrows would arch and then contract to a frown, and he would seem for a moment to be looking not at the world but into it. He suffered an intensity of awareness—seeming to live at some level so beyond you that you felt your own self fading in his presence, you felt your hollowness or fraudulence as a person. Most freelances are nervous craven creatures, it is such a tenuous living after all, but this one was prideful, he knew how well he wrote, and never deferred to my opinion. That alone would have set him apart.

He was slight, with a well-boned, clean-shaven face and pale thinning hair. He strode about the city with a stiff-legged gait, like a man much taller. He would walk down Broadway with his Union great-coat open, flowing behind him like a cape. Martin was of that postwar generation for whom the materials of the war were ironic objects of art or fashion. He and his friends made little social enclaves of irony. He once told me the war had not been between the Union and the Rebs but between two confederate states, and so a confederacy had to win. I am a man who will never be able to think of anyone but Abe Lincoln as president, so you can imagine how a remark like that stood with me. But I was intrigued by the worldview behind it. I was not myself exactly complacent about our modern industrial civilization.

Martin's best friend was an artist, a big, fleshy fellow named Harry Wheelwright. When not importuning dowagers for portrait commissions, Wheelwright drew mutilated veterans he picked up off the street . . . with pointed attention to their disfigurement. I thought his drawings were the equivalent of Martin's tactless but informed reviews and cultural critiques. As for me, my newsman's cilia were up and waving. The soul of the city was always my subject, and it was a roiling soul, twisting and turning over on itself, forming and re-forming, gathering into itself and opening out again like blown cloud. These young men were a wary generation, without illusions . . . revolutionaries of a sort . . . though perhaps too vulnerable ever to accomplish anything. Martin's defiant subjection to his own life and times was manifest . . . but you didn't know how long he could go on with it.

I did not usually care to know anything about the background of a freelance. But in this case I couldn't help knowing. Martin had come from wealth. His father was the late, notorious Augustus Pemberton, who had done enough to shame and mortify their line for generations to come, having made a fortune in the war supplying the Army of the North with boots that fell apart, blankets that dissolved in rain, tents that tore at the grommets, and uniform cloth that bled dye. Our name for this was ''shoddy,'' used as a noun. But shoddy wasn't the worst of old Pemberton's sins. He had made an even bigger fortune running slavers. You would think the slave trade was exclusive to the southern ports, but Augustus ran it from New York—even after the war had begun, as late as 'sixty-two. He had some Portuguese as partners, the Portuguese being specialists in the trade. They sailed ships to Africa right here from Fulton Street, and sailed them back across the ocean to Cuba, where the cargo was sold to the sugar plantations. The ships were scuttled because the stench could not be got rid of. But the profits were so enormous they could buy another ship. And another after that.

So that was Martin's father. You can understand why a son would choose, like a penance, the deprived life of a freelance. Martin had known everything the old man had done and at a still young age had arranged to be disinherited—how I will explain presently. Here I will point out that to run slavers out of New York, Augustus Pemberton had to have the port wardens in his pocket. A slaver's belowdecks were carpentered to pack in as many human beings as possible, there was no headroom—nobody could board a slaver and not know what she was. So it was hardly a surprise that when Augustus Pemberton died after a long illness, in 1870, and was buried from St. James Episcopal, on Laight Street, the city's leading dignitaries showed up at the funeral, led by Boss Tweed himself, along with members of the Ring—the comptroller, the mayor—several judges, dozens of Wall Street thieves . . . and that he was honored with major obituaries in every daily paper, including the *Telegram.* O my Manhattan! The great stone steles of the bridge to Brooklyn were rising on both shores of the river. Lighters, packets, and freighters sailed into port every hour of the day. The wharves groaned under the crates and barrels and bales of the world's goods. Standing on any corner I could swear I heard the telegraphy singing through the wires. Toward the end of the trading day on the Exchange the sound of the ticker tapes filled the air like crickets at twilight. We were in the postwar. Where you'll find mankind not shackled in history is Heaven, eventless Heaven.

I don't make any claims for myself as a seer of the future, but I remember what I sensed years before, when President Lincoln died. You will just have to trust that this, like everything I tell you, has a bearing on the story. They marched his catafalque up Broadway to the railroad depot and for weeks afterward remnants and tatters of the funeral muslin flapped from the windows along the parade route. Black dye stained the building fronts and blotted the awnings of the shops and restaurants. The city was unnaturally still. We weren't ourselves. The veterans who stood in front of A. T. Stewart's department store saw coins rain into their tin cups.

But I knew my city, and I waited for what had to come. After all, there were no soft voices. All speech was shouted, words flew like shot from our double-cylinder printing presses. I'd covered the riots when the price of flour went from seven to twenty dollars a barrel. I followed the armed bands of killers who fought with the army in the streets and torched the Colored Orphan Asylum after conscription was ordered. I'd seen gang riots and police riots and was there on Eighth Avenue when the Hibernians attacked the Orangemen on parade. I'm all for democracy but I'll tell you that I've lived through times in this town that have made me long for the stultifying peace of kings . . . the equanimity that comes of bowing and scraping in the dazzling light of regal authority.

So I knew some regnant purpose was enshrouded in Mr. Lincoln's death, but what was it? Some soulless social resolve had to work itself out of his grave and rise again. But I didn't anticipate . . . it would come through my young freelance, with his Union greatcoat lying on his shoulders heavy as sod, who stood in my office one rainy, wet afternoon and waited while I read his copy. I don't know why it always seemed to be raining when Martin came around. But this day . . . this day he was a mess. Trouser legs muddied and torn, the gaunt face all scraped and bruised. The ink on his copy had run, and the pages were blotted with mud and a palm print of something that looked like blood lay across the top page. But it was another contemptuous review, brilliantly written, and too good for readers of the *Telegram.*

"Some poor devil took a year of his life to write this book," I said.

"And I gave up a day of my life to read it."

"We should say that in a sidebar. The intelligentsia of this great city will be grateful to you for saving it from another Pierce Graham novel."

"There is no intelligentsia in this city," said Martin Pemberton. "There are only ministers and newspaper publishers."

He came behind my desk to stare out the window. My office looked over Printing House Square. The rain streamed down the pane so that everything out there, the schools of black umbrellas, the horse-cars, the plodding stages, seemed to be moving underwater. "If you want a favorable notice, why don't you give me something decent to read," Martin said. "Give me something for the lead essay. I'll show my appreciation."

"I can't believe that. The grandeur of your opinions stands in inverse ratio to the state of your wardrobe. Tell me what happened, Pemberton. Did you run into a train? Or shouldn't I ask?"

This was met with silence. Then Martin Pemberton in his reedy voice said: "He's alive."

"Who is alive?"

"My father, Augustus Pemberton. He is alive. He lives."

I pluck this scene from the stream of critical moments that made up the newspaper day. A second later, a cashier's voucher in his hand, Martin Pemberton was gone, his copy was on the dumbwaiter to the compositors' room, and I was looking to lock up the issue. I don't fault myself. It was an oblique answer to my question . . . as if whatever had happened was meaningful only as it evoked a moral judgment from him. I interpreted what he had said as metaphor, a poetic way of characterizing the wretched city that neither of us loved, but neither of us could leave.

Two

T HIS would have been sometime in April of 1871. I saw Martin Pemberton only once after that, and then he was gone. Before he disappeared he informed at least two other people—Emily Tisdale, and Charles Grimshaw, the rector of St. James, who had eulogized the old man—that Augustus Pemberton was still alive. I did not know this at the time, of course. Miss Tisdale was Martin's fiancée, though I found it hard to believe he'd give up his wild storms of soul for the haven of marriage. In this I was not far wrong: apparently he and Miss Tisdale were having a difficult time and their engagement, if that's what it was, was very much in question.

To a certain extent both she and Dr. Grimshaw assumed, as I did, that Martin could not have meant the statement to be taken literally. Miss Tisdale was so used to his dramatics that she merely added this startling example to her accumulated fears for their relationship. Grimshaw, taking it a step further, thought Martin's mind was at risk. I reasoned, by contrast, that Augustus Pemberton had been nothing if not a representative man. If you can imagine what

life was like in our city . . . The Augustus Pembertons among us were sustained by a culture.

We are in the realm of public life now—the
cheapest commonest realm, the realm of newsprint.
My realm.

I remind you William Marcy Tweed ran the city
as no one had before him. He was the messiah of the
ward politicians, the fulfillment of everything about
democracy they believed in. He had his own judges
in the state courts, his own mayor, Oakey Hall, in
City Hall, and even his own governor, John Hoff-
man, in Albany. He had a lawyer named Sweeny as
city chamberlain to watch over the judges, and he
had Slippery Dick Connolly to handle the books as
comptroller. This was his Ring. Beyond that maybe
ten thousand people depended on Tweed's largesse.
He gave jobs to the immigrants and they stuffed the
ballot boxes for him.

Tweed held directorships in banks, he owned
pieces of gasworks and of omnibus and street-rail
companies, he owned the presses that did the city's
printing, he owned the quarry that supplied marble
for her public buildings.

Everyone doing business with the city—every
contractor, carpenter, and chimney sweep, every
supplier, every manufacturer—paid from fifteen to
fifty percent of the cost of his service back to the
Ring. Everyone who wanted a job, from the school
janitor to the police commissioner, had to pay a fee

up front and then forever kick back a percentage of his salary to Boss Tweed.

I know what people of this generation think. You have your motorcars, your telephones, your electric lights . . . and you look back on Boss Tweed with affection, as a wonderful fraud, a legendary scoundrel of old New York. But what he accomplished was murderous in the very modern sense of the term. Manifestly murderous. Can you understand his enormous power, the fear he inspired? Can you imagine what it is like to live in a city of thieves, raucous in its dissembling, a city falling into ruin, a society in name only? What could Martin Pemberton have thought, as a boy, learning bit by bit the origins of his father's wealth, except that he had been sired from the urban grid? When he went around saying his father, Augustus, was still alive, he meant it. He meant he had seen him riding in a city stage up Broadway. In misunderstanding him, I found the greater truth, though I would not realize it until everything was over and done. It was one of those intuitive moments of revelation that suspend themselves in our minds until we come around to them by the ordinary means of knowing.

All this is by way of digression, I suppose. But it is important for you to know who is telling the story. I spent my life in the newspaper business, which makes the collective story of all of us. I knew Boss Tweed personally, I'd watched him for years. I fired more than one reporter whom he'd bribed. Those he couldn't bribe, he bullied. Everyone knew what he was up to and nobody could touch him. He would come into a restaurant with his entourage and you could literally feel his force . . . like a compression of air. He was a big ruddy son of a bitch, he ran about three hundred pounds. Bald and red-bearded, with a charming twinkle in his blue eyes. He bought the drinks and paid for the dinners. But in the odd moment when there was no hand to shake or toast to give, the eye went dead and you saw the soul of a savage.

You may think you are living in modern times, here and now, but that is the necessary illusion of every age. We did not conduct ourselves as if we were preparatory to your time. There was nothing quaint or colorful about us. I assure you, New York after the war was more creative, more deadly, more of a genius society than it is now. Our rotary presses put fifteen, twenty thousand newspapers on the street for a penny or two. Enormous steam engines powered the mills and factories. Gas lamps lit the streets at night. We were three quarters of a century into the Industrial Revolution.

As a people we practiced excess. Excess in everything—pleasure, gaudy display, endless toil, and death. Vagrant children slept in the alleys. Ragpicking was a profession. A conspicuously self-satisfied class of new wealth and weak intellect was all aglitter in a setting of mass misery. Out on the edges of town, along the North River or in Washington Heights or on the East River islands, behind stone walls and high hedges, were our institutions of charity, our orphanages, insane asylums, poorhouses, schools for the deaf and dumb, and mission homes for magdalens. They made a sort of Ringstrasse for our venerable civilization.

Walt Whitman was the city's bard, among other things, and not all that unknown. He went around dressed like a sailor in a peacoat and watch cap. A celebrant, a praise singer, and, in my opinion, something of a fool in what he chose to sing about. But he has these confessional lines about his city, less poetic than usual, like a breath he is taking before singing the next encomium:

> *Somehow I have been stunned. Stand back!*
> *Give me a little time beyond my cuffed head*
> *and slumbers and dreams and gaping . . .*

The War of Secession made us rich. When it was over there was nothing to stop progress—no classical ruins of ideas, no superstitions to retard civil republican ardor. Not so much had to be destroyed or overturned as in the European cultures of Roman towns and medieval guilds. A few Dutch farms were razed, villages melded into towns, towns burned into precincts, and all at once block and tackle were raising the marble and granite mansions of Fifth Avenue, and burly cops were wading through the stopped traffic on Broadway, slapping horses on the rumps, disengaging carriage wheels, and cursing the heedless entanglement of horsecars, stages, drays, and two-in-hands, by which we transported ourselves through the business day.

For years our tallest buildings were the fire towers. We had fires all the time, we burned as a matter of habit. The fire wardens telegraphed their sightings and the volunteers came at a gallop. When the sun was out, everything was blue, the light of our days was a blue suspension. At night the flaming stacks of the foundries along the river cast torchlight like seed over the old wharves and packing sheds. Cinderous locomotives rode right down the streets. Coal stoked the steamships and the ferries. The cookstoves in our homes burned coal, and on a winter morning without wind, black plumes rose from the chimneys in orderly rows, like the shimmering citizens of a necropolis.

Naturally it was the old city that tended to go up, the old saloons, the hovels, the stables, beer gardens, and halls of oratory. The old life, the past. So it was a pungent air we breathed—we rose in the morning and threw open the shutters, inhaled our draft of the sulfurous stuff, and our blood was roused to churning ambition. Almost a million people called New York home, everyone securing his needs in a state of cheerful degeneracy. Nowhere else in the world was there such an acceleration of energies. A mansion would appear in a field. The next day it stood on a city street with horse and carriage riding by.

Three

═══════════

IN one sense it's regrettable that I became personally involved in what I'll call, for the moment, this Pemberton matter. Professionally you try to get as close to things as possible, but never to the point of involvement. If journalism were a philosophy rather than a trade, it would say there is no order in the universe, no discernible meaning, without . . . the daily paper. So it's a monumental duty we wretches have who slug the chaos into sentences arranged in columns on a page of newsprint. If we're to see things as they are and make our deadlines, we had better not get involved.

The *Telegram* was an evening paper. By two or two-thirty in the afternoon the issue was set. The press run was over by four. At five I would go to Callaghan's around the corner and stand at the big oak bar with my stein and buy a copy from the lad who came in to hawk them. My greatest pleasure . . . reading my own paper as if I had not constructed it myself. Summoning the feelings of an ordinary reader getting the news, my construed news, as an *a priori* creation of a higher power—the objective thing-in-itself from heaven-poured type.

What else did I have to assure myself of a stable universe? Callaghan's oak bar? Above me was the dark patterned-tin ceiling, behind me the honest unpainted tables and chairs, and a floor of octagonal tiles with clean sawdust under my feet. But Callaghan himself, a florid man with a harsh wheezing breath, was an unfortunate patron of his own wares, and there had been more than one or two foreclosure notices in the window over the years. So much for solid oak. The newsboy, then? Piping his call at the door? But I lie if I say it was always the same one. Newsboys lived warring lives. They battled for their corners with fists and teeth and saps, they were cunning and brazen and brutal with one another. They made payoffs to get their papers early. They climbed stoops and rang doorbells, they muscled each other at the stage stops, they raced through the horsecars, and if they caught your eye, a folded edition was in your hand and the little palm under your chin before you could utter a word. In the trade it was said that newsboys were the statesmen and financiers and railroad magnates of the future. But no publisher wanted to admit that his weighty estate was carried on the small, rounded shoulders of an eight-year-old boy. If any financiers and statesmen were sprung from these urchins, they never made themselves known to me. A lot of them died of venereal and lung diseases. The ones who lived, lived to express the moral infirmities of their class.

I could have thought of Martin Pemberton, the self-impoverished son of a father he had disowned, or who had disowned him: I had come to appreciate his reliably tactless opinion—there was something assured! I wondered one afternoon, standing in Callaghan's and finding my culture page flat and uninteresting, where in hell he had been lately, Pemberton, because I hadn't seen him in several weeks. Almost at the same moment, at least I think so now, a messenger came through the door with a packet from my publisher. My publisher was always sending things around that he thought I ought to know. Today there were two items. The first was the latest issue of that organ of Brahmin culture, the *Atlantic Monthly*, in which he'd flagged an article by no less a personage than Oliver Wendell Holmes. Holmes was railing at certain ignorant New York critics who were not sufficiently in awe of his fellow trinomials of New England literary genius, James Russell Lowell, Henry Wadsworth Longfellow, and Thomas Wentworth Higginson. Though he didn't identify the offending critics, it was clear from his references that Martin Pemberton was one of them—I had run his piece on the subject early in the year, in which he had said of those men, and Mr. Holmes with them, that their names were too long for the work they produced.

Well, that was exhilarating but so was the second item, a letter from none other than Pierce Graham, the author of the novel Martin Pemberton had reviewed so thoroughly . . . the review I had published so promptly . . . that rainy day in April.

You would not know the name Pierce Graham; he had some brief notoriety as a literary figure who found his material in the territories, going among the frontier towns and mining camps or shooting Indians with the cavalry. He was a sporting man, a heavy drinker with a predilection for stripping to the waist in saloons and engaging in prizefight matches. Mr. Graham, writing from Chicago, advised that unless a printed apology was forthcoming in the *Telegram,* he would bring suit for defamation and, to round things off nicely, come to New York and thrash the writer of the review to within an inch of his life.

What a great day for the *Telegram*! Not before in my memory had we managed to offend both ends of the literary spectrum—bluebloods and redskins, the highborn and the low. Martin wrote his pieces and people were talking about them. Nothing else published in our paper had made anyone angry that I could remember.

Of course Martin Pemberton would never apologize for anything he had written, and as long as I was running things, neither would I. I looked up from my reading. Callaghan stood behind his bar, with his smile of blessing for the communion of good men on their bar stools before him. But I envisioned tables and chairs pushed aside, an overhead lamp shining on the sawdust, Callaghan holding the bell, and, surrounded by a crowd of shouting men, my freelance, stripped to the waist, his ribcage his most notable attribute, raising one fist before the other as his gray eyes widened in contemplation of the posturing idiot hopping up and down in front of him. The image was so ridiculous that I laughed out loud.

"Here, Callaghan," I called, "let's have another. And one for yourself!"

The next morning I sent a note to Pemberton's rooming house on Greene Street, asking him to come around to the paper. He did not appear or reply by letter, so after a day or two I took myself over there after work.

Greene Street was known for its prostitutes—a red-lamp street. I found the address—a small, clapboard house that was set back from the building line of ironfront machine shops on either side. It was badly in need of repair. The stoop leading to the front door was, in that way of grudging New York improvements, cast cement and without a handrail. A bent old woman, her whoring days long past, and with dugs hanging in her blouse to her waist and a pipe stuck in her jaw, answered my knock and pointed up the stairs with the slightest contemptuous gesture of the head, as if the person I had asked for deserved no more of anyone's attention than that.

Martin among the cyprians . . . I could imagine

him in his top-floor room articulating his contempts on paper, while below his window his neighbors strolled all night long, singly and in pairs, and called their lascivious greetings to approaching gents. Inside, I was nearly overcome with the rank smell of cooking cabbage, which became even worse as I went up the stairs. There was no landing, but a single door at the top. My own letter lay unopened across the door saddle. The door opened to my touch.

The son of Augustus Pemberton lived in a small attic room filled with the intolerable stink of someone else's cooking. I tried to open a window—there were two of them, set low to the floor and rising to waist level, and both stuck fast. The unmade bed was of the seaman's sort, set sideways in an alcove and without headboard but with a storage chest underneath. Some clothes on pegs. Muddied boots flung in the corner. Stacks of books piled everywhere . . . a writing table strewn with manuscript. In the hearth, stuck by their points into a bed of cold ashes, were three unopened letters in uniform-blue vellum—in the dim light they looked like distant sails at sea.

Here was a boxed-in life, careless of the things of the world. Martin was ascetic, yes, but without the ascetic's trim and tidy ways. Nothing I gazed at had been brought to the prim glory of the threadbare. The place was only a mess. Yet I saw his gallantry in the room. I saw the burden of an educated mind. I also saw that someone loved him. . . . I realized that I had come here without admitting to myself that I was magnetized by this wretch of a freelance. Here I was ready to put him on staff and give him a living wage ... and where was he! I would not sneak a look at his writings. Back down the stairs and outside, breathing again, I found the old woman putting her garbage in a can. I heard from her that Pemberton owed three weeks' rent and that if he didn't show up by tomorrow she was going to throw his things into the street.

''You have not seen him, in that time?''

''Not seen him, not heard him.''

''Has this ever happened before?''

''If it did, would I sit still for it again? Onc't is bad enough, ain't it? I live on this house, it's my living, and a poor bargain it is with the bank paper over me and the city marshal standin' in the shadows.''

She boasted that her rooms were highly sought-after, that she could rent his space for twice what she charged him. And he so high-and-mighty! Then her commercial cunning revived in her, and with one eyebrow cocked and the pipe pointed at me like a pistol, she asked if I wouldn't like to cover the young gentleman's obligation for the sake of his good name.

Of course I should have done just that to make sure the room was not disturbed. But this woman was offensive. She'd sent me upstairs knowing Martin was not there. I had no sympathy for her. And at the time, the premonition I felt was not a fully developed thing. It expressed itself as the faintest shadow on my own reasoning . . . that the moody young man, habitually in despair of the society in which he found himself, had finally cast me and the *Telegram* into municipal perdition. It was a measure of the powerful effect on me of his judgmental personality that I would read his abandoned room as, somehow, a comment on myself and my paper.

So I retreated in a disquieted state. It was small satisfaction that if I could not find him, neither would a drunk from Chicago, if it came to that.

My sense of Martin now was that the solitude in which he lived, as it brought him bruised and bloodied out of the rain, or broadcast itself in disdainful opinions, was inviolable. I found myself thinking that night of his remark about his father during my last conversation with him. I heard it again, in his reedy voice . . . that his father was still alive, still among us . . . and though the inflection did not change, I was no longer so sure I was hearing it the same way.

Martin would not let you settle your hopes on him, but neither would he be ignored. You can see how contradictory my feelings were . . . half the reporter's, half the editor's . . . the one's alertness to this strange young man and his visions . . . countermanded by the other's . . . sentiment that the same young man should establish himself comfortably in the newspaper business. I believed in ambition—

why couldn't he? At the same time I think, in the final analysis, I must have known that if there are people of such intense character as to call down on themselves a lurid fate, my freelance was one of them.

Four

NOW I think I have mentioned that I saw
Martin Pemberton once more before he disappeared
. . . though on that occasion I did not have the chance
to speak with him. You understand, of course, a freelance relies on several employers. In Martin's case
the assignments he got from the *Telegram* were
probably the best he could expect. More often he had
to demean himself by working for the weekly rags
. . . the *Tatler* or the *Gazette* . . . from which he would
get a couple of dollars for filling a column with the
inane social doings of the class of new wealth which
had once counted him a member. This had to be
more of an abuse of his sensibilities than the bad
novels I gave him to review.

At any rate, a few weeks after he turned in his
wet and blooded copy I saw him at a ball at the St.
Nicholas Hotel. I have to say . . . I detested balls.
They had them almost every night of the season . . .
presumably from the boundless need of arrivistes to
place themselves in the good graces of the earlier arrivistes. My publisher, Joseph Landry, felt it his duty
to subscribe . . . and then it was the duty of his luck-

less employees to stand in for him. And so on this occasion I came grumbling and muttering to what I remember was the annual fete of the New York Improvement Society. To make the best of a bad bargain, I believe I invited my sister, Maddie, a spinster who taught grade school, and who didn't get out often.

I'm sure it was the Improvement Society because behind the police cordons, aflame in the gaslight, a brilliant street assemblage of drunks, louts, and harridans made insulting remarks, some of them very funny, about each and every couple who stepped down from their carriage and walked into the hotel. Glorious laughter, hoots, jeers from the people in whose behalf the Improvers were sacrificing themselves! I held Maddie's elbow and steered her through the doors, feeling in spirit like one who belonged behind the cordon, and knowing I would be fully deserving if a rock came flying through the air and knocked my top hat off.

You wouldn't remember the old St. Nicholas on Broadway. It was about the best in town. They had the first elevators. And their grand ballroom was the length of the block.

Imagine the roar sent up by the conversation of fifty or sixty tables—something resembling a tropical volcano, with the clatter of dishes and the popping of corks like stones landing at one's feet. A chamber orchestra plays under the marble arch at one end of the room. The fiddlers saw away, and the harpist does her rolling hand gestures, but you can't hear a note, they could be lunatics from the asylum and no one would know the difference.

Our table companions were other editors and writers for the *Telegram,* men I saw all day and felt no desire to speak to. Like good newsmen everywhere, they knew what was important and homed in on their dinners. On the menu there would have been fresh oysters, inevitably, all of New York was crazy about oysters, they were served in hotels, in "oyster bars," in saloons, they were sold from pushcarts in the street . . . wonderful fresh oysters in abundance, cold, whole, alive, and dipped in a sharp red sauce. If we were a nation they were our national dish . . . And rack of lamb that you could rely on not to be served, as you understood the term, but, more nearly, thrown. The odor of the unwashed sommelier tinctured the bouquet of the wine he poured. But no matter. The newsmen were an island of quiet absorption in the roar.

Then I happened to see Pemberton in his limp black tie and dimmed shirt moving among the tables. As I say, the dailies didn't give an affair like this more than a paragraph, but the weeklies made it a momentous event. In the stifling heat of the ballroom my freelance looked peaked, wilted, almost greenish. Should I catch his eye or would it be kinder not to?

And then he was at the table behind me, where there sat a large woman in an extravagant gown about which my sister, Maddie, had earlier whispered in amazement. I heard Pemberton introduce himself and ask this woman if she would describe what she was wearing for the enlightenment of his readers.

"This is my rose satin," the woman shouted. "The brocade is white, with three flounces, quilled and tucked, in gradation one above the other, with headings of blond lace on top of each flounce." That is the precision with which such things were spoken of by our ladies.

"Your . . . rose . . . satin," Pemberton mumbled.

"The train is fringed in llama bordered by seed pearls, which go all up the skirt, you see, and around the Greek sleeves. Everything, bodice and skirt and train, is lined with white silk."

"Yes, the train of llama, thank you," Pemberton said, and attempting to disengage himself, he backed away.

I felt a jolt. The woman had risen abruptly, her chair banging into mine. "My shawl is Brussels lace," she said. "My fan is jade enamel. My handkerchief is point d'Alençon, and this stone," she said, lifting a pendant teardrop diamond from between her bosoms, "was presented to me on this occasion by my dear husband, Mr. Ortley."

She pointed to a beaming mustachioed gentleman across the table. ''Although it is of such considerable carat that I suppose you had better not
mention it. Shall I spell 'Ortley'?''

Pemberton caught sight of me, blushed, gave
me an angry look, and obliged himself with a glass of
champagne from the tray of a passing waiter. I could
not keep from laughing. I admit I was almost gratified to see how vulnerable he was in this life. Luck-
ily, Mrs. Ortley was diverted by the appearance of
the evening's baritone. The applause rose. The wait-
ers trimmed the lights. I told Maddie I was going for
a smoke and followed Pemberton, who had disappeared into the arcade encircling the ballroom.

In the shadow of a potted palm, I paused to light
my cigar . . . and heard him say: ''And which one is it
who's refusing immortality?''

A reply came from the rotund silhouette I rec-
ognized as his artist friend, Harry Wheelwright.
''That stupid manatee over there. Mrs. Van Reijn.
The one in blue.''

''Paint my Mrs. Ortley in her gown,'' Martin
said. ''You'll be our Goya.''

''I could do this whole damn ballroom and be
our Brueghel,'' said Harry Wheelwright.

They stood in contemplation of the scene. The
baritone sang lieder. Lieder were an obligatory taste
of the Improvers. . . . Was it Schubert's ''Erlkönig''?
''Du liebes Kind, komm, geh mit mir! Gar schöne

Spiele spiel ich mit dir'' . . . ''You lovely child, come, go with me, such pretty games we'll play . . .''

''To hell with art,'' Harry said. ''Let us find a decent God-fearing saloon.''

As they moved off Martin said: ''I think I'm losing my mind.''

''It is no less than I would expect.''

''You haven't spoken to anyone—''

''Why would I? I never want to think of it again. It's struck from the minutes. You're fortunate I even speak to you.''

This last exchange had dropped in tone to a conspiratorial mutter. Then they were out of hearing.

I had Maddie to take home or I would have followed them to their saloon. As to their two kinds of drinking, Martin's was the sort that turned him sodden and brooding with a single concerted intention, whereas Harry Wheelwright's was that of the voluptuary—assertive of its appetites, but easily disposed to laugh or cry or feel deeply whatever the moment called for. Wheelwright might have been rowdier and more full of bluster, as well as larger than his slightly built friend, but Martin had the stronger will. All this would become clear to me by and by. At that moment I felt only that sudden sensitivity to the unknown that makes it a . . . specific unknown . . . as if we discern in the darkness only the dim risen quality that draws us toward it. Nothing more. I would barely realize in the coming weeks that I was not seeing Pemberton in the office. I would notice that the books I wanted for his review had turned into a small stack . . . and then days later I would notice that the stack had risen. In modern city life you can conceivably experience revelation and in the next moment go on to something else. Christ could come to New York and I would still have a paper to get out.

So it was by the grace of the *Atlantic* and Pierce Graham that I had become concerned about my freelance. I didn't know why he was gone and I felt a certain urgency to find out. There might be a simple explanation, a dozen of them, in fact, though I couldn't finally persuade myself of that. The obvious thing for me to do was to track down the friend and sharer of his secrets, Harry Wheelwright. Yet I balked at the idea. I knew Harry Wheelwright and didn't trust him. He was a drinker, a chaser of women, and a society toady. Under his unkempt, curling mass of hair were the bloodshot eyes and fat cheeks and fleshy nose and mouth and double chin of someone who managed to feed and water himself quite well. But he liked to portray himself as a martyr to Art. He'd studied art at Yale. Quite early he'd made something of a name doing war engravings for *Harper's Weekly*. He took the rough sketches artists sent back from the field and made steel-points in his studio on Fourteenth Street. That in itself was no crime. But when people admired the engravings thinking that he'd done them under fire, he didn't tell them . . . that he had never been under fire from any-one but his creditors. He liked to fool people, Harry, he lied for sport. Wheelwrights having preached from their cold pulpits a hundred years before the Revolution, I couldn't believe, finally, that his pose of ironic superiority to those he made his living from was entirely uncorrupted by the snobbism of his New England lineage.

By contrast, my freelance's cold dissidence was the honest thing, purely and profoundly of his gener-ation. There was an integrity to Martin. His eyes sometimes took on a wounded expression which seemed at the same time hopeful that the world could in the very next moment fulfill his expectations of it. It seemed to me that if I was really concerned about him I should grant him his integrity and give re-newed thought to what he had said about his father. I would act privately on what I knew, on what he had told me, with due regard for the standards of the pro-fession we shared. To tell you the truth, apart from everything else, I smelled a story. If that is the case you do not, first thing, go to someone in whose inter-est it might be to see that you don't get it. So I chose not to speak to Harry at this point but to test the origi-nal hypothesis. And when you want to know if some-one is still alive, what do you do? You go to the morgue, of course.

Five

=====

OUR high-speed rotaries had come along around 1845, and from that moment the amount of news a paper could print, and the numbers of papers competing, suggested the need for a self-history of sorts, a memory file of our work. So that we would have at our disposal a library of our past inventions, and needn't always spin our words out of nothing. At the *Telegram* this enterprise was first put in charge of an old man down in the basement, whose genius it was to lay one day's edition on top of another, flat, in wide oak cabinet drawers, which he kept immaculately polished. Only when the war came, and it became apparent to the publisher that salable books could be made of collections of war pieces from the paper, did cross-reference filing begin in earnest. Now we had three or four young men sitting down there with scissors and paste pots who were never more than a month or two behind—fifteen New York dailies a day were dropped on their tables, after all— and I could go to a file drawer fully confident of finding a folder marked *Pemberton, Augustus*.

He'd first come to our attention as one of the

witnesses called before the Subcommittee on War Profiteering of the Senate Committee for the Army and the Navy. The item was dated from Washington in April of 1864. There was nothing on the story subsequent to this—what Augustus had in fact testified to, or what the outcome of his testimony was, or indeed if the subcommittee had ever again met for any purpose whatsoever, I would not learn from my dear *Telegram.*

A local item the same year afforded another glimpse of Pemberton's business affairs: One Eustace Simmons, former deputy chief clerk in the Office of the Port Wardens on South Street, had been arrested in the Southern District of New York, along with two Portuguese nationals, on a charge of violation of the slave laws. His bond was made by his employer, the well-known merchant Mr. Augustus Pemberton.

In this instance there was a following story, dated six months later: The case against Mr. Eustace Simmons and his two Portuguese partners for violation of the slave laws had been dismissed for insufficient evidence.

Our reporter was clearly irritated by the ruling. He described the proceedings as extraordinarily casual, given the seriousness of the charges. The defendant Simmons had not looked terribly concerned before the judge's decision, and not terribly elated afterward, and though the Portuguese gentlemen had embraced each other, Mr. Simmons had stood up with only the slightest smile to indicate his emotion . . . an angular man with a face marked by the pox . . . and barely nodded to the lawyers before he followed indolently after his employer, Augustus Pemberton, who was striding out of the courtroom, presumably to the next item of business on this ordinary business day.

Well, perhaps I embellish things a bit. But my impression of the reporter's feelings is accurate. We did not feel it so necessary to assume an objective tone in our reporting then. We were more honest and straightforward and did not make such a sanctimonious thing of objectivity, which is finally a way of constructing an opinion for the reader without letting him know that you are.

Simmons had been a deputy chief clerk in the Office of the Port Wardens when the Augustus Pemberton Trading Company hired him away. The port wardens did the onboard surveys of the condition of sailing vessels, inspected the cargoes on the wharves, and in general policed the maritime commerce of both rivers. It was a municipal office, of course, and the source of a reliable income for the Tweed Ring. Simmons would have shared in that and been assured of a long, profitable employment, which meant Augustus Pemberton's offer had to have been very attractive to lure him away.

I'll say here, this Simmons was the unwholesome fellow who was with Augustus Pemberton to the end, although now we tread on treacherous ground. I have occasionally to tell you things not in the order in which I learned them. But it was from the young widow Pemberton, Sarah, Augustus's second wife and the stepmother of Martin, that I would hear how much closer Eustace Simmons lived to the central affection of the man than either she or Augustus's first wife . . . and how Simmons knew it, and made it clear to her. ''No woman would feel right in the presence of Mr. Simmons,'' Sarah Pemberton told me when I had gained her confidence. She colored slightly speaking of the matter. ''It was nothing he actually said, he never spoke out of turn. But he had a tone of voice that I found suggestive. I don't think that's too strong a word. He made me feel . . . incidental. I assume he didn't have much regard for women in general.''

She told me this when Martin's disappearance was no longer an isolated matter but had compounded itself with others just as unsettling. While I had no pictures of the father and his factotum, I had their moral photographs clearly enough, from their relationship to each other, and the indicative choice we make of a right-hand man. And that the larger evil sustained them, I had in the numbers and quality of the municipal dignitaries who came to Augustus's funeral and, to be fair, in the obsequious tones of the *Telegram*'s account.

So: In black words on this white paper, Mr. Augustus Pemberton, merchant and patriot, had died at age sixty-nine of a blood ailment, in September of the year 1870, and was seen to his rest from St. James Episcopal. We celebrated the fact of his arrival in America as a penniless, unschooled Englishman who hired himself out as a house servant under a contract that required his labor for seven years. We admired him for never glossing over these humble beginnings. In his later years, as a member of the Surveyors Club, where he lunched frequently at the Long Table, a major conversational theme was the example of his life as a fulfillment of the American ideal. Christ, what a bore he must have been, in addition to everything else.

An obituary is no place to reflect that in domestic service you come to value *things,* and you learn all the refinements of taste and style that you can aspire to. But I could imagine Augustus's sentimental education in money and property. At the end of his indenture he became a coach builder's apprentice and subsequently bought out the business of the man who had hired him. Then he sold it and reinvested his profit in a ship's chandlery, thus establishing a pattern of loyalty not to any one business, but to the art of buying and selling them. These practices and other investments brought him in his late thirties into prominence as a merchant of the city. No mention of slave trading, of course. Only that he was brilliant at brokerage and was soon applying its principles to abstract materials—commercial debentures, stocks, bonds, and federal notes. He came into possession of a seat on the New York Exchange by default. We made out the old scoundrel as a kind of frugal, down-to-earth Yankee. He didn't advertise his place in the city's commercial life with elaborate or ostentatious business quarters and did not carry on his ledgers a large complement of employees. I'll bet he didn't. "It's all up here anyhow" was his famous line, delivered as he pointed his index finger at his head. "My own mind is my office, my warehouse, and my account book."

He would never have read Tom Paine, of course, who said, "My own mind is my church." But where deism, even in the 1870s, was a scandal, self-idolatry, if it left an estate of several millions, was an example to us all.

According to his eulogist, Dr. Charles Grimshaw, glory was bestowed on Augustus Pemberton in the War of Secession, when he put his skills to the service of his country, supplying the Union quartermaster with goods which he commissioned and delivered from mills as far away as Peking, China. Apparently, from their role as beggars, churchmen develop the same sympathies for the moneyed class as politicians do. Someone in Mr. Lincoln's administration was no less forbearing: I

sat in our morgue with the forlorn feeling of an orphan as I read that Augustus Pemberton was among
the select group of merchants given thanks by a
grateful nation in a dinner at the White House with
the president in 1864.

Six

I KNEW Charles Grimshaw, and to be fair to him, he was one of the abolitionist pastors in the 1850s of our copperhead city, and saw a chunk of his congregation fall away because of that. But he was in his prime then, and though never the orator and lacking the moral eminence of our more renowned preachers, he had the respect of his peers and the cozy devotion of his well-to-do parishioners. By the time of Augustus Pemberton's death, the rector and his church had both seen better days. The well-to-do had rushed northward, to the wider streets and sunnier neighborhoods north of Thirty-fourth Street—and then past the Forty-second Street reservoir. Commercial buildings replaced the homes, and where once St. James had towered over the city, it now stood in shadow half the day. Its solemn brownstone dignity had become quaint, its little parish graveyard, with its worn stones leaning just a little farther aslant in their inch-by-inch topple through the ages. . . . So the Augustan funeral was a remembrance of its glory, and for an hour or two St. James was restored to fashionable High Churchiness. It is not hard to understand why the pastor's eulogy was excessive.

I should have thought there were enough poor people you could find to fill your pews. But as the Reverend explained to me in his halting, high-pitched voice, poor people were not generally disposed to the Anglican communion. The new immigrants, for instance, were largely Irish and German Catholics. But Catholicism was not the problem. ''They have been here longer than we have,'' he said—here on earth, I supposed he meant. No, what made him clutch his crucifix and pace the floor of his study were the proselytizers abroad in the city—Adventists and Millerites, Shakers and Quakers, Swedenborgians, Perfectionists, and Mormons . . . ''There is no end to them, they come down from the burned-out district and parade along Broadway with their eschatology boards slung from their shoulders. They accost people in the beer gardens, they take over the street in front of the opera. They board the ferries. Do you know, yesterday I had to chase one away who stood on our doorstep to preach—before Christ's church, mind you! Speaking for God makes these people brazen. Christ forgive me, but do I need to doubt their sincerity to say, for all their invokings of the name of our Lord, they are plainly and simply not Christian?''

He had the fairest skin, the Reverend Grimshaw, the skin of a beautiful old woman . . . paper-thin and very white and dry . . . and very small regular features, with a nose barely sufficient to perch the pince-nez there, and bright birdy eyes still vigorous and alert, and thin waved silver hair through which you could see the pinkness of the pate. He was clean-shaven, and trim and small, everything from the little feet that marched him to and fro to the tiny flat ears was in proper proportion. It is a stature that wears clothes well, even clerical collars and shiny black bibs.

Here I will confess, if that's the appropriate word, I myself am a lapsed Presbyterian. It's the diction that did it, finally, the worn-thin, shabby, church-poor words, so overused they connote to me a poverty of spirit, not the richness of it. My own feeling about the street preachers from the burned-out district was . . . why not? To claim God, accept dispossession. He might even be truer unhoused, the property of the bearded maniacs with their eschatology boards. Why was he appropriately addressed inside a church, but outside in the gutter to speak of him with the carriages going by and the horses dropping their dung was clearly madness? I will say also that churches themselves, of whatever denomination—I can't speak as authoritatively for our temples and our mosques, but throw them in too—whether they are built Gothic, Romanesque, tiled oriental, or red brick, all smell the same inside. I think it's the smell of candlelight, or perhaps rectitude, or that sourness that comes of convened heated bodies condensing their glandular odors of piety against cold stone year after year. I don't know what it is, but it was here in Grimshaw's study as well, with its shelves upon shelves of the Book of Common Prayer . . . that must of sanctification.

As you might suspect, I confided nothing of these feelings. Grimshaw had received me, readily enough, the evening of the same day I'd sent a note to him. I waited patiently through his fulminations. When they were done, and he had got back in his chair and was quiet, I brought up Martin's name. I said nothing about my fears for him . . . only that he had one day said to me his father was still alive.

"Yes," Grimshaw said, "that seems to be a worry of his."

"You are disapproving."

"Let me just say this: Martin Pemberton is one of those troubled souls yet to look up and see his Savior awaiting him with open arms."

"When did you see Martin?"

"He banged on the rectory door one night."

"This would have been—?"

"During those heavy rains. In April. He was the last person I would expect to see in the rectory. He didn't wait to be announced but pushed past my housekeeper. His appearance was . . . derelict, God help us all. A filthy coat worn over his shoulders, his suit muddied and torn. Half his face covered with an ugly bruise. Yet he sat himself in the chair you are sitting in and offered no explanation, but regarded me from under his brow as if he was a general of the armies and I was . . . something his soldiers had taken in battle. He said: 'I have seen something that I will describe to you, Dr. Grimshaw, and then I will ask you what I need to know, and then you will think I've lost my wits, I promise you.' That's what he said. Well, when he'd barged in, I was reading a monograph on the subject of certain Sumerian cuneiforms, recently deciphered, which give an account of the same Flood described in Genesis. . . . I needn't tell you—it was something of a wrench from the Sumerian.''

Here the doctor shot me a glance suggesting that as a newspaperman I would not let something that good go by. I obliged, saying I hadn't known he was a biblical scholar.

''Oh, heavens,'' he said with a self-deprecating smile to himself, ''not in any sense of the term. But I do maintain a correspondence with those who are. The scholarship now, particularly from Europe, as to Scripture and the life of our Lord is quite exciting. This Sumerian text is significant. If you think your readers might want to know a little about it, I'd consider it no trouble at all—''

''What had he seen?''

''Seen?''

''Martin. He told you he had seen something.''

It was another wrench from the Sumerian. The

Reverend cleared his throat and composed himself.
''Yes. You know, I have learned over the years . . .
about souls in need of pastoring . . . how they often
bristle, or present a superior attitude. This was the
case with Martin, of course. He could not bear to ask
something of me without excoriating me first. What
was it he said? 'I affiliate you with death, Reverend,
not merely because you're the family eulogist, but
because you're the priest of a death cult.' Can you
imagine? 'Your Jesus is all death and dying, though
you attribute to him everlasting life. Every communion partakes primevally of his death, and the presiding image of him, even right there dangling down
your vest, is his painful, agonized, endless death. So
I come to the right place. . . . Tell me, is it true that
the Romans themselves later banned crucifixion
some years *anno domini,* because it was so cruel as
to create legends?'

''Well, this may surprise you, but such a Chris-
tology is not unknown to me. Faith hears it all, Mr.
McIlvaine, faith is unshocked by such challenges,
true faith is surprisingly intimate with the foulest of
conceits. . . . Besides, you don't come under a roof of
God's to blaspheme unless your state of mind is tenuous. I think I was ready to concede he'd lost his wits
without having to hear the question he would put to
me.

'' 'Well,' he says after a long pause of staring at

the floor, 'so be it. I am sorry I've offended you. My mind races. I suppose I'd rather speak of anything except . . . the thing that has brought me here.'

" 'What is that, Martin?'

"He leaned forward and peered into my eyes and said in a tone of voice I could not determine to be either serious or joking: 'Reverend, will you swear my father is dead?'

" 'What?' I said. I didn't know what he meant. I was terribly alarmed. I did not like the looks of him or the sound of him.

" 'It is simple enough. We are either alive or dead, one or the other. I ask you to classify my father.' When I continued to gaze at him, not knowing what to say, he raised his hands in exasperation. 'Oh God, for some light in this brain—do you understand the English language, Doctor? Answer me! Has my father, Augustus Pemberton, died? Is this something you will swear by your God to have happened?'

" 'My dear young man, this is not seemly. I was your father's friend and I was his pastor. I gave him extreme unction and beseeched our Lord Jesus Christ in his mercy to receive him.'

" 'Yes, but is he dead? I know I did not see him dead!'

" 'This is an unusual consolation you seem to require. Perhaps you recall the obsequies . . .'

" 'They have no standing in this court. Your sworn testimony, Dr. Grimshaw!'

"I told him, feeling that I was talking to a madman, that, alas, it was so. His father was deceased. He gave a deep sigh. 'Fine. That wasn't too hard, was it? Now that you have said so, I'll tell you something has happened and you will say what you will have to say and we will think no more of the matter. And I'll be able to sleep.'

"He strode back and forth across the room and told his tale. . . . It was extraordinary. Back and forth he went, talking as much to himself as to me. Describing it all in the most vivid terms, the most vivid terms, so that it was as if I was there, with him. . . . That very morning, before the rain, he was walking down Broadway, en route to Printing House Square. Of course—to the *Telegram.* To you! He had in his pocket a book notice he had written. Is Martin a good writer, does he write as well as he speaks?"

"He may be the best I have," I said truthfully.

"Well, that is something. At least I can say of him that he lives by his wits. He has never regretted his act, insofar as it cost him the considerable inheritance that was his. He has taken responsibility."

You would think that a man who all his life had delivered sermons would have learned a thing or two about sticking to the point. Well then, as he said, and as I will tell you now . . . that morning, under a sky massing for rain, my freelance was coming to see me with his latest review in his pocket. He was headed down Broadway. Broadway, as the main route for commerce, was, as usual, chaotic. Drivers snapping their reins and teams shying with that rhythmless gait given to horses when there is no open space ahead of them. A discordant ground music of hooves clopping on cobblestone. The cries of reinsmen, the gongs of the horsecars, and the hum of their flanges on the tracks. The rattling wheels and drumming boards of innumerable carriages, stages, wagons, and drays.

At the intersection of Broadway and Prince streets, coming along in the far, or uptown, lane of traffic, was a white city stage with the customary scenic landscape painted on its doors. Stages, omnibuses, were the commonest of vehicles. But in the darkening street this one seemed to glow with a strange radiance. He stood stock-still as it went by. The passengers consisted solely of old men in black coats and top hats. Their heads nodded in unison as the vehicle stopped and started and stopped again in the impacted traffic.

Everywhere else there was the characteristic New York impatience—shouts, curses. A policeman had to come into the street to untangle the vehicles. Yet the old men sat in a state of stoic introspection, uniformly indifferent to their rate of progress, or the noise, or indeed the city through which they traveled.

I am trying here to render this account in Pemberton's immediate state of sensation. You understand this is filtered through the brain of Dr. Grimshaw and after many years in my own mind. . . .

Martin is almost knocked over in the pedestrian traffic. People pool at the crossing and then spill into the
street. He holds on to the lamppost. At this moment a
flash of lightning in the sky is reflected in the large
windows of a cast-iron storefront directly across the
avenue. There follows a clap of thunder. Horses rear,
everyone runs for shelter as the first large raindrops
fall. He hears the urgent flap of the pigeons rising in
circles over the rooftops. A newsboy cries out the
headlines. A tin cup is held under his face by a
maimed veteran of the Army of the North dressed in
the filthy remnants of a uniform.

Walking quickly, Martin crosses the street and
begins to follow the stage. He asks himself what it is
about the old men in black that draws him away from
his business. He catches another glimpse of them sitting in the darkened coach. Rain pours off the brim
of his hat. He sees as through a curtain: It is not so
much that they are old, he decides, it is more that
they're ill. They have the peaked, shrunken, sickly
look of his father in his last illness. Yes, that's what
is so familiar! They are old men, or ill enough to look
old, and eerily unmindful of the world. They might
be a funeral party, except there are no black plumes
on the coach. He has the strange impression that if
they are in mourning, it is for themselves.

The light is gone and the rain pours. It becomes
more difficult to see in the windows. He is reluctant
to run up alongside, which he could easily do, but he

hangs back because he's afraid that they would see him . . . even though he is convinced that these strange passengers do not see—that they could look out at him and stare right through him, unseeing.

Where Broadway bends at Tenth Street, in front of Grace Church, the traffic thins out, and the omnibus of old men gathers speed. Martin is now running to keep up. The horses break into a trot. He knows that at Dead Man's Curve, and Union Square with its widening lanes, the race will be lost. He dashes into the street and grabs the handles at the rear door and swings himself up the foot ladder. His hat flies off. The sky glows green. The rain pours. Union Square goes by in a blur—the equestrian statue, some trees, a cluster of people leaning into the storm. Reluctantly, fearfully, with breath held, he peers into the rear window of the stage . . . and sees in this ghostly rolling wagon of old men . . . the back of one with the familiar hunch of his father's shoulders . . . and the wizened Augustan neck with its familiar wen, the smooth white egglike structure that from Martin's infancy had always alarmed him.

A moment later he is on his knees in the street, the horses having suddenly been reined and just as abruptly whipped forward again, as if the driver up on the box had deliberately intended to shake him loose. He hears someone shouting and manages to struggle to his feet just in time to avoid a trampling. He staggers to the sidewalk, his nose bleeding, his hands lacerated, his clothes soaked and torn, and is aware of none of this as he looks northward through the rain to the vanishing white stage and whispers ''Father! Father!'' with all the destroyed love he has ever felt reanimated in an instant of total credulity.

'' 'Father! Father!' '' Dr. Grimshaw cried out in his weak tenor. He had been made quite breathless by his account.

Seven

AT least I knew now why my freelance had shown up at the *Telegram* with his copy soiled with blood. In the interest of my own newsmaking, I would not allow myself to think of his anguish. I simply held it in my mind as something that would magnify whatever information I collected, or distort it, or bend it into its spectral bands. . . . In fact this had not been the first—what shall we call it?—sighting. The first had occurred a month before, in March, during a heavy snow, and was afterward reported by Martin to his fiancée, Emily Tisdale, but in a context of the difficulties between them that would not let her believe anything was being represented as it really was.

But I'll get to that.

When Grimshaw finished his account we sat for some moments in silence while he regained his composure. Then I asked him what his reaction had been to Martin's story. "Did you say what he said you would have to say?"

"I suppose I did, yes. I felt an immense compassion, of course. . . . I tell you frankly, I have never liked Martin. I thought his attitude toward his father quite unconscionable. He'd always been contrary, contentious—always. With everyone. For him to come knocking at the door of St. James . . . had to be an act of desperation. Obviously the apparition of his father was a torment of his mind. A phantom event summoned up by his guilt. Well, so could it be his first blind groping for forgiveness. I am not an alienist but neither am I a stranger to the healing of pastoralia. There was something to be accomplished here, there was an opportunity for Christ, or else why did the young man come to me, after all?

"I began by asking if he remembered the omnibus in any detail.

" 'Only that it was one of the white stages of the Municipal Transport.'

"It was unusual that a city stage would have only one sort of passenger, I told him. Public transport is used by everyone—humanity in all its array stuffs itself aboard these coaches.

" 'You are right, of course,' he said. He laughed. 'Was it a dream, then?' He touched his skinned forehead. 'Yes, I have heard of dreams that draw blood.'

" 'You didn't dream,' I said. 'Probably the stage was chartered by a lodge or learned society. That would account for the brotherhood of old men. And the fall you took was quite real, I can see that.'

" 'I'm grateful to you!' Color was now in his cheeks, he listened as a man well entertained.

" 'And as for the old men, they are like old men everywhere,' I said. 'They fall asleep on any and all occasions, even, as I can tell you, during the most eloquent sermon.'

" 'Another point well taken!' He frowned and rubbed his temples. 'Which leaves only my father.'

" 'Your father or the image of him in the darkness through the streaks of rain . . . I can say only that as Christian doctrine has it, Resurrection is so truly exceptional that it has so far occurred only once in history.' You see, I thought a bit of levity might not be out of place. I thought he would appreciate the joke, but perverse as always, Martin rose from his chair and looked solemnly down at me. 'I do beg your pardon, Reverend, you are not the fool that most of your calling are. I had worried you might be one of those pastors who secretly attend séances. You don't, do you?'

" 'No, I can assure you.'

"He nodded. 'I am so glad. We should have a chat sometime. You don't think I saw a ghost, do you?'

" 'Not a ghost,' I said keeping my own gaze level. 'I think, for the explanation of what it was you saw, we must look into your history.' At that he became enraged. 'Into my mind, you mean? Into my poor plagued mind? Is that where we look?' He leaned over with his hands flat on my desk and put his face up close and stared directly at me—the crudest, most pugnacious gesture, like a bully, like a common street thug. 'You look, if you wish, Reverend. Let me know what you find there.' And with that he threw open the door and was gone.''

Tea was brought in. Reverend Grimshaw poured and the cup rattled in the saucer when he reached across his desk to set it in front of me. I didn't question his account. It had the accuracy of reflection of a victim. There was always the clash of cultures from a contact with Martin, as if he carried his own thunderstorms wherever he went. More cruelly, he had subjected the old priest to a kind of roughhouse. He wanted assurance that the whole thing was a delusion—''You will say what you will have to say and then I'll be able to get some sleep''—and when the assurance was duly given, he turned on him.

But I also wondered if perhaps Martin had not believed it—that the purpose of his visit was really to look in the old man's eyes and see how much of a liar he was. Grimshaw had eulogized his father. Every wall of St. James had been buttressed by Pemberton money. The old families had fled, but the once-indentured servant had remained steadfast. Martin's vision was precise—and the ground for it was the noisy, heedless everydayness of the commonest scene in New York. Augustus Pemberton was among the living. He was the old man seen twice riding a public stage through the streets of Manhattan. I did not know it at the time, I was still to hear of the other, but it was possible to understand that even if madness was the more desirable of the explanations available to my freelance . . . for, after all, what was worse than thinking he was insane was knowing that he was not . . . nothing Grimshaw said could alter the reality of the experience, and when he suggested the answer was in the imagery Martin himself had projected, the opportunity for Christ and the healing of pastoralia was lost.

It all had to do, more than Grimshaw knew, with those sandwich-board enthusiasts wandering the streets and appropriating his church stoop for their ministries. A prophet of the Millennium would have understood the vision of the white stage and laid his hands upon Martin Pemberton's head and pressed him kneeling to the New York City pavement and shouted his praise to the Lord for giving to this youth the power to see Satan and recognize evil in no matter what insidiously loving form it appeared . . . and would have been not far off the mark. But in his rectory, behind his walls, his steeple lost in the shadows of factories, Charles Grimshaw was thirsting for historical verification of the words of Scripture. He was right in thinking the Sumerian account of the Flood in *Gilgamesh* was good material for the *Telegram.* We ran filler like that all the time—everyone did: Mrs. Elwood, an English traveler, reported that she stood on the shore of the Red Sea at Kosseir at dawn and saw the sun rise over the water not in its usual form but in the shape of a shimmering column. We put it at the bottom of page one . . . as confirmation of the pillar of fire that for forty years gave light to the Israelites in the wilderness. But this was for our readership of imperfect believers. Did Grimshaw understand that looking for confirmation of the ancient claims could lead to disastrous, looming . . . error?

I had nothing against the good doctor except that he had worn away, as we all do, and his religion no longer had any authority . . . other than as organizer of his daily life and conduct and as filing system for his perceptions. At this time, in the seventies, phrenology was all the rage, and of course it was nonsense, but as a system for organizing perceptions it was about as good. There were three basic Temperaments to be deduced from the configurations of skulls, Martin with his slight figure but high brainy brow being of the Mental Temperament—Grimshaw himself a weaker example of this—the other two being the Motive Temperament, which described the long bones and homely visage and reliably logical thought of the late president—and perhaps my own dour Scotch-Irish self as well—and the Vital, which described the fleshy, life-loving appetitiveness and vulgarity of someone like Harry Wheelwright. Of course these were the pure strains, whereas most people participated in more than one, impurely, and

there was some question as to whether the race of
women wouldn't require their own special skull
readings. . . . It was absolute nonsense, of no scientific value whatsoever, but a convenience of thought,
like astrology, or the organization of time into the six
days of the week and the Sabbath. I'll give you more
filler: In 1871 archaeologists found a sacred ossuary
cave at Monte Circeo on the coast of the Tyrrhenian
Sea and uncovered the skull of a Neanderthal buried
in a circle of stones among the bones of deer, horse,
hyena, and bear . . . with the cranium severed from
the jaw and brow and used for a drinking bowl. And
so we knew at last how old God was—as old . . . as
the mortuary cult of the people of the Middle Paleo-
lithic before the last glaciation.

After Martin stormed out of the rectory, Grimshaw took up his pen and wrote a letter to the widow
Pemberton at her estate on the Hudson in Piermont,
New York, informing her of his opinion of the tenuous state of her stepson's mind, which, perhaps out
of guilt, had summoned up a haunting delusion. He
suggested that he could call on her at such time as
she visited Manhattan, or, in turn, would be only too
pleased to journey to Ravenwood . . . that was the
name of the estate . . . but in any event she should be
assured Christ's ministry was available to the Pemberton family as it always had been. This was a reasonable course of action but apparently it was the
only one he took. He had seen Martin the evening of

the same rainy day I had seen him, and in more or less the same torn, bloodied condition. And he had made no effort to see him since. So what was the nature of his faith and the degree of his concern? Sarah Pemberton had not replied to his letter, which I might have thought puzzling, but which apparently did not surprise him into renewing his efforts. Was he only worn away . . . to the level of the laity? So that the rudeness and patronizing ironies of the offensive young man were finally too much to forgive? Or was there an impacting loyalty to the father, of what protectiveness I could not imagine, but which put the image in my mind of a dog baying for his lost master?

It was dark when I left the rectory. Grimshaw saw me outside and stood with me in the churchyard. The old gravestones cast shadows in the light from the street. Around them the grass was high, untended.

"Which is Mr. Pemberton's grave?"

"Oh, he is not here. And it wouldn't have been the churchyard, it would have been the mausoleum reserved for the elders. I offered it, but he refused. He said he was not worthy."

"Augustus Pemberton said that?"

Grimshaw smiled in satisfaction, the same fearful, ingratiating smile that took him through every manner of joy and suffering that rolled day and night through all the years of his pastorate. "People who didn't know him are surprised to hear of Augustus's humility. I grant you he was not always—what can I say?—in his conduct as . . . selfless as he might have been. But there it is. No, by his own request he is buried up in Fordham, in the Woodlawn Cemetery.''

Well, that is a fashionable enough place, I thought to myself. It was at the time the most blue-blooded of our graveyards, the consecrated ground of choice. Apparently, Dr. Grimshaw was not disposed to wonder why the man who had not cut his ties with St. James in his long life did abandon her for the duration of his far longer death.

Eight

EMILY Tisdale consented to my call because she knew of me as Martin's sometime employer and thought I might have word of him, if not
from him, and could tell her where he was. Since
this, in fact, was what I hoped from her, it took me
only a moment to understand that the young woman
sitting before me, her intelligent brown eyes widened
with a receptiveness to the news I might have, but
with the head just a shade averted in anticipation that
it might be bad, knew no more than would the author
of those unopened blue vellum letters I had seen
stuck by their points in the ashes of the hearth on
Greene Street.

I called on a Sunday afternoon. The room where
we sat had a high ceiling and was furnished with
comfortable sofas and chairs, polished wide-board
floors, lovely worn rugs. It was not an ostentatious
room. Breezes lifted the curtains from the sills and
ushered through the large open window the sounds
of the occasional passing carriage and the cries of
children at their games. The homes on Lafayette
Place were harmoniously composed to accompany

one another, all Federal in style and with a small plot in front of each with a low wrought-iron fence. The pillared entrances were not up a stoop but at street level. This was a piece of the old city that had still not given way to progress, though it would in a few short years.

Miss Tisdale was petite but resolute, with a forthright, unaffected manner. Though she was not a beauty, she commanded one's attention with her high cheekbones and fair skin and the eyes slightly slanted at the corners, and a melodious voice that tended to break charmingly at the peaks of her sentences. She seemed to have no interest in the usual strategies of feminine presentation. She wore a plain dark gray dress, simply cut, with a white collar at the neck. From the collar hung a cameo brooch that rode minute distances, like a small ship at sea, as her bosom rose and fell. Her brown hair was parted in the middle and held behind the head with a clasp. She sat in a straight-backed chair with her hands folded in her lap. I found her quite fetching. Oddly enough, as a result, I felt I was intruding in Martin Pemberton's personal life to an extent that he would deem intolerable. Emily Tisdale was his, after all. Or was she? I had enlarged the circle of concern for Martin, which until that moment had included only herself . . . and so, quite readily, she made me her confidant. ''Things have not been going well between us. When I saw him last Martin said: 'I live with this burden of your waiting for me. It is always Emily waiting. Don't you understand what hell you face? Either I am mad and should be committed, or the generations of Pembertons are doomed.' All that inflamed, Wagnerian sort of thing . . . that the Pembertons were a doomed family up from some hideous underworld they were destined to return to. . . . How does a person respond?''

''He had seen his father,'' I said.

''Yes, he had seen the late Mr. Pemberton, riding in a crosstown omnibus.''

''You mean on Broadway,'' I corrected her.

''No, not Broadway. While he was walking past the holding reservoir on Forty-second Street. The snow was falling.''

''The snow? When was this?''

''In March. In that last big storm.''

At the time he confided in her, the snow had melted and the season in New York was spring, which one knew because crocuses and gladioli and foxglove appeared for sale in the flower carts at Washington Market, and the swells had begun to race their trotting horses on the track up in Harlem. The climate having moderated, people resumed the practice of paying calls, as did Martin on Emily, in her home, where he assured her she could despair of ever having his proposal of marriage because—at least insofar as she could understand his logic—Augustus Pemberton was abroad on the earth.

I'll tell you now I found this earlier incident more ominous, more truly unsettling, than the other. I don't know why, precisely. It had not the awful specificity of the wen on the old man's neck. . . . In the shadow of the retaining wall of the holding reservoir, Martin walks east on Forty-second Street, leaning headfirst into the wind, clutching his collar about him. From the gusts of snow blowing across the thoroughfare a carriage emerges, a public stage. He turns to look. The horses are at a gallop and though the driver, swathed in a fur robe, whips them to even greater speed, their passage is stately and silent. The stage sails past in a cloud of whirled-up snow. . . . And he sees in the rimed window, as if etched there, the face of his father, Augustus, who at the same moment turns an incurious gaze upon him. A moment later the entire equipage is swallowed by the storm.

Now the chill set in. Martin's boots were frozen. His Union greatcoat seemed to absorb the wet air. The falling snow smelled metallic, as if machined, and he looked into the opaquely white, flaking sky, imagining it as an . . . industrial process. That is what he told Miss Tisdale.

She sighed and sat straighter in her chair.

You know I am an old lifelong bachelor, and the truth of my breed is that we fall in love quite easily. And, of course, silently, and patiently, until it passes. I think I fell in love with Emily on this day. She put a theory into my mind . . . the idea of the unremarked development in America of an exotic Protestantism. I mean if there was voluptuousness in virtue, if there was a promise of physical paradise in a chaste and steadfast loyalty, it was here in this heartbroken girl.

I found myself resenting her treatment at the hands of my freelance. She looked at me brightly. She had enrolled, she said, in the Female Normal College up on Sixty-eighth Street with the purpose of becoming a teacher of public school children. ''My father is quite shocked. He thinks the teaching profession is only for women of the working class— quite unsuitable to the daughter of the founder of the Tisdale Iron Works! But I am so happy there. I am reading ancient history, physical geography, and Latin. I could have chosen French, I know a bit of French, but I'm inclined to Latin. Next year I take the lectures in moral philosophy given by Professor Hunter. The only bad thing—they have a weekly review in English grammar and—horrors!—arithmetic. Oh, the children will have fun with me in arithmetic.''

At that point her father came in and I was introduced. Mr. Tisdale was quite old, with a fringe of white hair, and he kept a hand cupped behind his ear in order to hear better. He was a dry, stringy old Yankee, of the sort who live forever. In the manner of the aged he promptly informed me of everything I should know about his life. He confided in a loud voice that after Emily's mother had died giving birth he had never remarried but had devoted himself to raising the child. Emily sent me a silent glance of apology. ''She is the light of my life, my lifelong consolation and pride,'' said her father, speaking as if she were not in the room. ''But since she is mortal I cannot claim perfection for her. She is already twenty-four and, if I may say so, stubborn as a mule.''

This was an allusion to a marriage proposal that Emily had turned down. ''You'd agree with me, sir,'' he said, ''if I told you the name of the family.''

Somehow his daughter excused us, gracefully but firmly, suggesting that I would want to see the garden. I followed her down a hall to the rear of the house, and into a large drawing room with broad leaded-pane doors that led to a granite terrace. We stood at the balustrade.

What she had called the garden was actually a private park that extended behind the entire block of Lafayette Place homes. A serpentine gravel path went among formal flower beds, and offered wrought-iron benches where there was tree shade. It was a lovely, peaceful place, with pedestaled sundials and birdbaths and a crumbling brick wall the ivy had long since conquered. Here and there in the wall was an arched niche with the bust of a weathered, eyeless Roman.

''Right next door, in Number Ten, is where the Pembertons used to live. When Martin's mother was alive. We ran in and out of both houses all day, we did not distinguish between them. This garden was our playground,'' Emily said.

So that was the paradisial beginning. I could look out and imagine Emily and her Martin, their young souls urged into wing, their voices from dawn to dusk in this garden as constant as the birds' . . . and think of the superior state of childhood, when love is lived without knowing it is called that. Can the love that comes later be more powerful? Is there any in maturity that will not long for it?

''I fear for my friend,'' she told me. ''What does it matter where he places the omnibus with his father . . . inside his mind or in the world . . . if his torment is the same? I would like to ask you the favor of letting me know if he writes to you or comes back for an assignment. Will you?''

''Immediately.''

''Martin has always been terribly careless of his own welfare. I don't mean that he is someone who is likely to walk in front of a train. He is not absent-minded. But ideas take hold of him. His convictions take over and almost seem to perform themselves in him . . . whereas other people merely have . . . opinions. He is heedless, arrogantly so. He's always been like that. He was not humbled by being a child. He noticed things and pointed them out. Often they were funny. He was a wonderful mimic when we were young, he imitated adults, he did Cook with her brogue and the way she dried her hands on her apron, which she picked up first from the hem . . . and he did the policeman who walked here in our street with his feet pointed outward and his hand on his nightstick as if it were a sword in his belt, and his head tilted up to keep his topi from falling over his eyes.''

She was now happy to be talking about her Martin and for a few moments was able to chat about him as if nothing were the matter—as people do in their grief.

''Martin was wicked boy! He satirized Mr. Pemberton, usually making him into an animal of one sort or another. . . . It was very funny. Of course all that stopped as he grew older and more somber . . . except when—he was by then at college—he came to me with the letter that disowned him . . . and he hadn't forgotten his impersonation after all! I thought it was a catastrophic thing that had happened, but there he was reading the letter in his father's grumbling voice and having his father's difficulty with the words that had obviously been written by a lawyer . . . having great fun repeating the hard words, his brow swollen in rage and his lower lip curled out like a bulldog's. . . .''

Well, I am giving you a conversation of that young woman of many years ago—in all of this, you must be aware, I represent matters which only I seem to have survived. But I'm fairly sure it was on this occasion I understood that my moody imperial freelance was not for any reason of his own absent from his boardinghouse and his job . . . and from his Emily . . . who was, for all the letters he'd tossed in the fireplace, the inevitable lovely associate of his sorrows, the one he would leave but return to, the one who knew him, the twinned soul. And I considered that a municipal authority, learning of these circumstances, might justifiably find Martin Pemberton to be legally missing.

Nine

I HEARD a slightly different account of Martin's experience in the shadow of the wall of the holding reservoir . . . as he reported it to Harry Wheelwright, and as Harry told me, much later, after everything was over. At first Martin was not terribly surprised by the sight of the stage. He thought of it as a hallucination brought on by the night just passed. He had reason to believe he'd conjured it up, it was early in the morning and perhaps he was not quite sober . . . having spent the night in a shanty on the West Side, with a young housemaid, whose soul knew nothing but service . . . so that . . . this is a delicate matter . . . so that as she kneeled before him and he held her head and felt the working muscles of her jaw and the rhythmic pullings of her cheeks, he realized in himself his father's imperial presence, his father's cruelty rising to a smile in the darkness like the inherited beast of himself breaking into being . . . and he felt not pleasure but the brute disposition of a man he loathed as no other.

It was only later that the doubts set in. He became convinced the coach and its passenger were as real as they appeared to be. In such ways as we all deal with our symptoms of illness, taking them lightly and seriously by turn, he was cycled in his torment, swinging from mind to world and back again—though more driven, I can imagine . . . more in the way of an electromagnetic motor in his frantic changes of mind.

I'll tell you here that I was ready to believe in every dark vision if it appeared at the Croton Holding Reservoir. Which is gone, of course. Our public library stands there now. But in those years its massive ivy-covered walls rose over a neighborhood monumental in its silence. . . . The few brownstone and marble mansions across the street along Fifth Avenue stood aloof from the noisy commerce to the south. Our Mr. Tweed lived just a block north, practicing the same silence. It was an unnatural thing, the reservoir. The bouldered retaining walls were twenty-five feet thick and rose forty-four feet in an inward-leaning slant. The design was Egyptian. The corners were relieved by trapezoidal turrets, and bisecting each long wall face were temple doors. You went in, climbed up a stair to the parapet, and came out in the sky. From this elevation the rising city seemed to fall back before something that wasn't a city, a squared expanse of black water that was in fact the geometrical absence of a city.

I grant you that it is a very personal feeling I had. New Yorkers loved their reservoir. They strolled along the parapet arm in arm and were soothed in their spirits. If they wanted a breeze in summer, here is where it would blow. Puffs rippled the water. Children launched their toy sloops. The Central Park, well to the north, was not yet finished, all mud holes and ditches and berms of shoveled earth, a park only in the eyes of its imaginers. So this was the closest we could come to pastoral.

But I am sensitive to architecture. It can inadvertently express the monstrousness of culture. As the complicit expression of the ideals of organized human life it can call forth horror. And then something happens appropriate to it, and maybe from its malign influence. . . .

Several years before Martin walked in the shadow of its wall, a boy was drowned off the cobbled bank at the west end of the reservoir. I was there on the Fifth Avenue side—I was there with the one woman I have ever seriously considered marrying. Fanny Tolliver was her name, a generous, dear woman with a glorious head of auburn hair who was much amused by me . . . but within months was to succumb to heart failure. . . . It was not clear what had happened, I heard shouts, people were running. The sun had spread over the water's surface. And then the scene clarified as we went toward it along the parapet. . . . The child was pulled feetfirst from the water by a man who . . . I have since decided . . . was bearded, and this bearded man wrapped him in his frock coat and rushed him directly past us, down the steps to the street, where, as I looked down over the ivied wall, the . . . blackbeard, in his shirt-sleeves, summoned a waiting hackney and rode off with his burden, the carriage rattling over the cobble-stones down the avenue—I thought to a hospital. But then the boy's mother appeared, coming along the walk, tearing her hair and screeching, falling, sobbing. It was her child, and as for the man, who had said he was a doctor, she didn't know who he was. . . . And Fanny sank to her knees to hold the distraught mother, and in the brilliant water of this sunlit afternoon I saw the lad's toy boat sailing like a clipper at sea, its prow falling and rising in the laplets, still on the tack he had set for it, its sail puffed in the soft June breeze as it dipped and reared among the fracted diamonds of water and light.

Who these people of the parapet were, their names, addresses, the circumstance that brought them together, or if the boy lived or died, or if the blackbeard killed as well as kidnapped, are questions I can't answer. I report, that is my profession, I report, as a loud noise testifies to a gun. I have given voice to the events of my life and times, and from my first timid type-inch of apprentice writing until the present moment I have taken the vow to do it well and truly. But that Sunday at the reservoir, the faculty was suspended, there was to be no account for the *Telegram* from me.

Remembrances take on a luminosity from their repetition in your mind year after year, and in their combinations . . . and as you work them out and understand them to a greater and greater degree . . . so that what you remember as having happened and what truly did happen are no less and no more than . . . visions. I have to warn you, in all fairness, I'm reporting what are now the visions of an old man. All together they compose a city, a great port and industrial city of the nineteenth century. I descend to this city and find the people I have come to know and for whose lives I fear. I tell you what I see and hear. The people of this city think of it as New York, but you may think otherwise. You may think it stands to your New York City today as some panoramic negative print, inverted in its lights and shadows . . . its seasons turned around . . . a companion city of the other side.

The scene of that day is indelible in my mind but sealed up in the information I've given, and memory cannot recover the moments after—what we did, what we offered that woman, or where she went. It makes it no easier for me now to confess that at the time I was assistant managing editor of my paper.

But is there any street, any neighborhood, any place in the city that won't eventually be the scene of disaster, given enough time? The city compounds disasters. It has to. History accumulates them—I grant you that. The reservoir was in fact an engineering marvel: From an upstate dam across the Croton River, the water flowed through Westchester in conduits, crossed the Harlem River on a viaduct of fifteen Roman arches, and came to its containment at Fifth Avenue and Forty-second Street. When it began to operate the danger of fires was considerably reduced—pumping stations were built and firemen now had water under pressure, and were municipal employees. So it was badly needed, our reservoir. Crucial to a modern industrial city.

But I happened to be present the day it was dedicated, a July Fourth. It had taken years for our incorruptible government to bring it to us—you need the money to flow freely before the water can—years of men in top hats poring over blueprints and raising their arms and pointing and giving instructions to the stolid engineers awaiting their pleasure . . . blastings, the ring of pickaxes on the Manhattan schist . . . dray teams groaning with loads of rubble. . . . Years of this . . . inverted temple building. . . . And now here is young McIlvaine in his first months on the job as a reporter of monumental news. His lean face is unlined and shining . . . he does not at this time in his life require spectacles. . . . It is Independence Day, 1842. The War Between the States is two decades ahead. . . . He stands on the elevated bank of a huge cubic crater. In his nostrils is the odor of wet sand, the dank air of new stone construction. Arranged along the south embankment in solemn black ranks are the shades of municipal life—the mayor, former mayors, would-be mayors, aldermen, commissioners of this and that, philosophes of the chamber of commerce, ward heelers, and fellow newspaper wretches. And after speeches spoken grandly and at inconsiderate length, oratorios of self-congratulation, the ribbon is cut, the wheels are turned, the sluice gates are opened, and the water thunders in . . . as if it were not a reservoir at all, but a baptismal font for the gigantic absolution we require as a people.

Ten

I'M not sure what obligation I'm under to give you a sense of the life around this matter, the degrees of my consciousness taken up with all my regular duties, or indeed my sense of the expanding, pulsating city pumping its energies outward furiously in every direction . . . except that, of course, all of it was indicative, all meaningful of the story I sought out, just as any chosen point on the compass can lead you to the earth's core. . . . I suppose I would be justified in reciting to you all twelve pages of our paper every day for several years of the post-war, from the shipping news to the commercial reports on the corn and cotton crops, the fortunes made or lost on the Exchange, the latest technical marvels from our inventors, the murder trials, the social scandals, the politics from Washington, and the glories of the western tribal expurgations. But this is a municipal matter, a municipal matter . . . and I should keep to the streets, whether they are paved with stones or, as they were farther north, merely laid out with string over mud lots. In any event you will see that invariably what it is we need to discover is exactly what we already know.

Somewhere in this season, in May, or early June, working men in various industries began spontaneously to leave their workplaces in support of the idea of an eight-hour workday. In fact the legislature had several years before made this the law, but the employers of our city had simply ignored it . . . and now, their patience spent, brewery workers, mechanics, carpenters, blacksmiths, bricklayers, were laying down their tools, removing their aprons, and taking to the street. Even the stolid burghers at the Steinway piano factory walked out. All over the city men were meeting in halls, making speeches, marching through the streets, throwing up picket lines, and police units were dispatched to break up these meetings, arrest these marchers, and crack the heads of these speakers, who were disturbing the peace and refusing to do an honest day's work for an honest day's pay. Our headline by the third day defined the circumstances as a general strike. I looked over my editorial floor and dared any reporter to join the fun. Instead they spread out over Manhattan and came back to file their war reports. From Elizabeth Street as far uptown as the gasworks, from the Eleventh Avenue abattoirs with their hooked cow carcasses to the Water Street docks, police and workingmen were doing battle. I stood at my open office window and imagined I could hear a kind of ground song, as if I were overlooking a prospect of woods and fields with burbling freshets and the chirrups of small perching birds.

Our publisher dictated an editorial for the front page to the effect that the infamous communistic ideas of the foreign workers' internationals had finally taken root in American soil. Other papers published similar sentiments. After a few weeks the whole thing blew over with a series of symbolic agreements that left things substantially as they were, and everyone went back to work. I mention this here to impress upon you what a realist I am . . . and what a hard historical city this was . . . going through the same kinds of affairs it goes through today, rising in some quarter to excess and subsiding again, a city of souls whose excitements have always been reportable, who have always been given to that nervous, vocal, exhausted but inexhaustible combat that defines a New Yorker, even if he has just yesterday walked off the boat. This is my caveat, in case you were beginning to think I am proposing to make of the white stage with old Pemberton riding it, conveniently, on those streets just where his son happened to be, some sort of . . . Spiritualist notion. To me, a ghost is as tired and worn-out a fancy as the Romish conceit of my friend Grimshaw. I abhor all such banalities. I am extending myself in a narrative here—it is my own mind's experience that I report, a true deposition of the events, and the statements, claims, protestations, and prayers of the souls whom I represent as seen or heard . . . so that my life is wholly woven into the intentions of the narration, with not a thread remaining for whatever other uses I might have found for it. I would not so hazard myself on behalf of some hoary convention, heaven help us all. This is not a ghost tale. In fact I'm wrong even to use the word *tale*. . . . If I had another word to connote not a composition of human origin but rather some awful Reading out of Heaven, I would use it here. . . .

But if you're entrenched in the Parlor Faith, let me remind you that by your own dicta, ghosts don't come in crowds. They are by nature solitary. Secondly, they inhabit defined places, such as attics, or dungeons, or trees. They are sited to do their haunting—they are not detached and collected and given rides about the city in public stages.

No, the world I am spreading out for you here in the flat light of reality is the newsprint world, with common, ordinary, everyday steamboat sinkings, prizefights, race results, train wrecks, and meetings of the moral reform societies going on simultaneously with this secret story invisibly in the same lines. Every day on the way to work I would buy a flower from a child named Mary who stood in front of the *Telegram* building holding a basket of bedraggled second-day blooms in the crook of her arm. The Pemberton matter came out of as common an everydayness as that . . . common as the vagrant children who flowed among us and around us, under our feet and off the edges of our consciousness. Flower Mary, we called her. She was solemn and shy in her business, a tyke with a profusion of unwashed brown curls, a ragged smock, and the drooping socks and the lace-up shoes of a boy. She could be made to smile, but when once I questioned her—as to where she lived and what her last name was—the face went blank and with the flick of a curtsy she was gone.

All of them had lost their family names, these vagrant Flower Marys, these Jacks and Billys and Rosies. They sold papers or day-old flowers, they went around with the organ grinders to play the monkey's part, or indentured themselves to the peddlers of oysters or sweet potatoes. They begged—swarming on any warm night in the streets and alleys of the bawdy districts. They knew the curtain times of the theatres and when the opera let out. . . . They did the menial work of shops and at day's end made their beds on the shop floors. They ran the errands of the underworld, and carried slops, and toted empty beer pails to the saloons, and hauled them back full to the rooms of their keepers, who might pay them with a coin or a kick as whim dictated. More than one brothel specialized in them. They often turned up in hospital wards and church hospices so stunned by the abuses to which they'd been subjected that they couldn't speak sensibly but could only cower in their rags and gaze upon the kindest nurses or ministrants of charity with abject fear.

These urchins—or street rats, as we called them—were as common and unremarkable as paving stones. When I described Martin Pemberton in his greatcoat striding down Broadway under a dark, threatening sky, I would have given a more accurate picture by including the storekeepers in their white aprons letting down their awnings, the luggage merchant bringing his stand of umbrellas to the front door, a millenarian moving slowly through the shoppers, his five-cent God-written pamphlets woven between his fingers, the unsettleable pigeons in a perpetual flutter off the sidewalk . . . and the children, the ubiquitous children, weaving through the pedestrian crowds of Broadway under no authority but their own, flashing a mop of hair or a furtive glance back, and a moment later becoming invisible, as if not air was their medium but dark river water.

Of course we had mission homes, children's aid societies, orphanages, and industrial schools, but this surplus of a bustling democracy overwhelmed them. For every lost or runaway child reported by a parent or guardian there were a hundred whose disappearance from their homes had been noted with no more than a shrug or a curse. It was the boring editorial writer who called for yet another commission to study the matter, the naïve politician who proposed to his colleagues a social policy for the young. The public had no taste for the topic, any more than the ruminant herd would meet to consider what to do when one of their number was cut out by the wolves and run down for a meal.

This was the world traveled by your ghostly white stage. It was a hard world, but are we less hard now? The awful indulgences of society change from era to era, but if they're not entirely invisible to their generations they are borne patiently enough. . . . For certain religious sensibilities such children fulfilled the ineffable aims of God. For the modern folk, Mr. Darwin was cited, and the design was Nature's. So the flower girl Mary, and the newsies and the rest of these child beggars who lived among us, were losses society could tolerate. Like Nature, our city was spendthrift and produced enough wealth for itself to take heavy losses without noticeable damage. It was all a cost of doing business while the selection of the species went relentlessly forward, and New York, like some unprecedented life form, blindly sought its perfection.

None of this was not in tune with the disappearance of my freelance Martin Pemberton. Every day I bought my bedraggled zinnia and went to work . . . and while I composed my paper, picking from the clips and cables and filed copy the world picture I would invent for my readers, and while I made my assignments and shouted out my orders, so as to have the news that I must have because everybody else

had it, but also to have the news that I must have because nobody else had it . . . the shadows of my secret story took form and dissolved and re-formed and
dissolved again as I considered its possible shapes.

I was still wary of seeking out Harry Wheelwright. I remembered the allusive fragment of his
conversation with Martin that I'd overheard at the St.
Nicholas Hotel. As a friend and confidant of Martin's he was a putative conspirator. If he knew where
Martin was he wouldn't tell me. If he did not know
he could not tell me. In either case he could mis-
chievously dissemble knowing or not knowing. Or
his predilection for irony might persuade him to confide in me only what he believed I already knew. I
didn't want to put myself at the mercy of such a fellow—he was no one to confront unarmed, as it were.

But I did find myself thinking of Sarah Pemberton . . . that she had never answered Dr. Grimshaw's
letter. I knew nothing of her relations with her stepson, but even if they were the most indifferent or cur-
sory, how could she completely ignore an alarmed
description of his mental state? Was she made in the
mold of her husband, was this an entirely and forever
combative family? But then the rudeness to a concerned pastor—a proven friend of her husband's—
had to be accounted for. If Sarah Pemberton and
Martin were completely severed from each other she
would still respond, if only to affirm that.

The answer was provided by the Reverend himself, who informed me in a note that he now had met with Mrs. Pemberton, who was staying at the home of her late husband's sister, Mrs. Thornhill, on East Thirty-eighth Street. So this was the comforting humdrum answer. Sarah Pemberton and her son, Noah, were not in residence at Ravenwood, and his letter had simply been delayed in forwarding. In any event she had taken quite seriously his observations concerning Martin's mental state . . . and had spoken with Emily Tisdale and now hoped, in his words, ''that I would call on her to discuss the matter.''

So there I was, in the midst of things, who only felt honest outside of them . . . but flattered, to tell you the truth, by my inclusion in the private discourse of family, fiancée, and pastor. I arranged to call in the early evening, after the final edition of the *Telegram* was under the arms of the homeward bound.

The Thornhill home at 60 East Thirty-eighth Street was a brownstone in a row of them, with trees lining the sidewalk. This was a preferred northern neighborhood of the wealthy . . . just a few quiet blocks from the reservoir, in fact. I don't know what I had expected of a stepmother, but Sarah Pemberton was the loveliest, most pacific of human beings, a mature beauty in her late thirties, I would say, more womanly than the piquant and honest Miss Tisdale, with a fuller, larger frame and a paradoxically placid manner, on which her trials had made no apparent inroads. She had light blue untroubled eyes. She wore her dark hair parted in the middle and tight over the temples. A wonderful curved, clear forehead, white as alabaster . . . like the housing for a soul. She was a calm, handsome woman, one of those who with the least attention to themselves maintain their good looks . . . with an effortless grace, everything about her harmonious, unforced, and her voice a low melodious alto—but all of this making, finally, an odd impression on me, given the circumstances I was about to be informed of.

"Shall I ask for coffee or tea? They grumble, but they bring it."

I assumed she meant Mrs. Thornhill's servants, whose loyalties did not, presumably, extend to her houseguests.

The atmosphere was oppressive. This was summer, you understand, not long after Independence Day—coming uptown in my hackney I'd noticed people still had the red and blue colored papers in their windowpanes with the candles shining through. The sitting room was furnished with a plush sofa, end tables inlaid with mosaic, and needlepoint chairs that were too small to sit in comfortably, and some quite bad European landscapes. The bay window was covered with a velour drapery of the darkest red. There was no concession to summer in this room.

"Mrs. Thornhill is very advanced in years," Sarah said by way of explanation. "She is sensitive to drafts and complains often of the cold.'' And then with a self-deprecating smile: ''We old widows are like that, you know.''

I asked her how long it had been since she had seen her stepson.

''A few weeks . . . perhaps a month. I'd assumed he was busy. He says he earns his pay by the word. That would keep anyone busy, wouldn't it? I thought it was you who might be keeping him occupied, Mr. McIlvaine.''

''Unfortunately not.''

''Since speaking with Dr. Grimshaw I can only hope Martin is doing what he's always done. He goes off by himself. He did that as a boy. He broods, he sulks. I can't think anything would happen to him that is not under his control.''

''He told Grimshaw and he told me . . .'' I hesitated.

''. . . his father was alive. I know. My poor Martin. You have to appreciate that with Augustus's death, everything was left unresolved between them. He died . . . without the reconciliation that would have made his dying easier for both of them. The effect on Martin has at various times since been . . . a peculiar kind of grief. It's hard to explain. This family's life has been, always, terribly intense.''

She then gave me this account of the family history.

Within a year of his first wife's death Augustus

Pemberton had proposed marriage to Sarah and she had accepted. She didn't speak, Sarah, of her own background but did give me her maiden name, van Luyden. The van Luydens were one of the old Dutch families who'd made their fortune growing tobacco when Manhattan tobacco was considered the equal of Virginia's. Over two hundred years, however, the fortune had declined. In certain circles, Sarah's marriage to Augustus Pemberton would have been widely noted . . . and deplored . . . though the union of a lovely young woman and a brash nouveau riche thirty years her senior was not without precedent in the Social Register.

For their new home, Augustus built the place in Piermont—on a promontory overlooking the Hudson some twenty miles north of Manhattan—that he had named so grandiloquently after the ravens who were common to the area. "Martin all his life had suffered from his father's imperious nature," she said. "I came to know something of it myself over the years. . . . His mother was his consolation. He felt our marriage, coming so soon after her death, was a betrayal of her memory. It is a vulnerable time of life to lose a mother. . . . I hoped as time passed to become her surrogate.

"When Ravenwood was ready, Augustus sold the house on Lafayette Place where Martin had been born and raised . . . not thinking he would do anything but come with us. This the boy refused to do.

He would lose his schoolmates and so on . . . the only life he'd ever known. Augustus relented, saying it suited him just as well. Martin was boarded at the Latin Grammar School and from that time—he was then fourteen—they lived apart. I had to get used to this . . . family of males. I am still not sure I have.

"But Martin had a quick mind and a natural boyish honor . . . that endeared him to me. I persuaded him to come up to Ravenwood for holidays. I wrote to him regularly and plied him with clothes and books. But while all this softened his judgment of me, it did nothing to improve his relations with Augustus."

Sarah Pemberton's cheeks flushed when she told of the great and final schism. Martin was by then an undergraduate at Columbia. In his junior year he wrote a thesis for a course in moral philosophy on the business practices of certain private suppliers to the Union during the war . . . showing that they engaged in profiteering, and delivered goods of substandard quality, and so on. For documentation he used Augustus's merchandising house as his prime example. My God, that awed me. It was so brilliantly . . . brazen, wasn't it? To do a reporter's job on your own family? I tried later on to get hold of that thesis. . . . I thought the school would have it on file somewhere. But they claimed not to.

At any rate, as Sarah Pemberton told it, Augustus was sent a fair copy and invited by the author to

make a statement in his defense, which, he could rest
assured, would be included in the final text. ''Of
course Martin had been outrageous but I hoped he
could be dealt with diplomatically. One look at my
husband told me that was not to be. I had never seen
Augustus so enraged. The young man was summoned to Ravenwood and was no sooner in the door
than he heard his father condemn him as a . . . callow
idiot . . . who did not know the first thing of the real
world about which he was so quick to make his
high-and-mighty judgments. Augustus had indeed
testified before a congressional committee in Washington, as Martin had written . . . not under subpoena
but, as he said, on a simple invitation which as a gentleman and patriot he'd hastened to accept. A majority of the committee had decided the allegations
against his firm were unfounded. Had this not been
the case there would have been an indictment issued
by the district attorney in New York. There was no
indictment. And Martin had managed to leave out of
his moral philosophy the fact that his father was
among the commercial contractors given a dinner at
the White House by President Lincoln in recognition
of their service to the Union.

''Martin had shocking answers to these argu-
ments. He claimed . . . that Augustus would certainly
have been indicted had he not paid out substantial
sums both to members of the congressional committee and to the district attorney's office in New York.

. . . And that the White House dinner was held long before the charges came out, and by a president who could see evil at a distance but not where it crept up behind him. At this my husband rose from his chair and approached Martin with such fury in his face— he was a stocky man, with broader shoulders than his son—that I had to step between them.

"I wish I never heard the words that flew past me, Martin shouting that trading in shoddy was the least of Augustus's sins and that had he more time he could have documented also a maritime business of outfitting . . . slave ships . . . and Augustus assuring him with a raised fist he was a miserable . . . treacherous, lying . . . *dog,* was the least of his epithets . . . and if Columbia College was going to endorse such libels in the name of education, it was no university to which he would contribute tuition, room, and board.

"You know, Mr. McIlvaine, I came from a very . . . quiet home. I was an only child. I never heard a voice raised in all the years of my late parents' lives together. I cannot tell you how stunned I was by all this . . . outright . . . warring. I knew nothing of Augustus's business dealings. To this day I don't know what was true and what was not true. But Augustus renounced his son . . . renounced and disowned him from that moment, and he assured him he would never see a penny of the legacy he could have enjoyed. And Martin said . . . 'Then I'm redeemed!'

And he stormed out of the house and walked all the way to the railroad station because Augustus forbade me to order the carriage for him.''

"And that was the end of it?"

"And that was the end of it. Except that I deceived my husband and sent sums from my own allowance so that Martin could complete his studies . . . and when he began to write for the papers he sent me his published pieces from time to time, also secretly. I was very proud of him. . . . I hoped the time would come when I could show some of the writings to my husband. . . . But Augustus fell ill, and two years ago he died . . . and the reconciliation never took place. It is such a sad terrible thing, isn't it? Because its consequences go on. The finality . . . echoes.''

I suppose I could have wondered at this point if what she had learned from her stepson . . . the shock of it . . . might have caused Sarah to act, to take some action of her own—what action I don't know. She would never have been a business confidant of her husband's, at least in part because, it was quite clear, she was not the kind of person to approve of his practices. Yet Martin's accusations notwithstanding, her life apparently had gone on as before, whatever misgivings she might have had. She had made no effort to come to a conclusive judgment . . . in the way women do who have no choice but to set their course for life and never veer from it. Or was this more like living in the state of irresolution most of us live in with regard to our moral challenges?

I found her gazing at me from her clear beautiful eyes, and the slightest of smiles lighting up her face . . . and here was my answer walking into the room, a tow-haired boy of eight or nine who was unmistakably her son and unmistakably a Pemberton. A comely, well-formed boy—I saw a bit of Martin in him, in the solemn, hurt look of the eye, but also saw the mother's poise. He did not acknowledge me but went right to her in that single-minded way children have. He held a book in his hand. He proposed to do his reading outside, on the front stoop, while it was still light.

"Noah, first . . . this is Mr. McIlvaine," she said, tilting her head in my direction. Noah turned and said his how-do-you-do. He received my greeting, standing with his hand possessively upon her shoulder . . . more like a lover than a son.

She gazed up at him, her mother's passion a kind of all-encompassing calm. "Noah is used to the broad halls and porches and wide-open spaces at Ravenwood. He needs lots of room to move about in. He can hardly wait till we settle all this." And then to him: "On the front steps, but don't wander off, please, sir."

The book the boy held was a novel of Scott's, *Quentin Durward,* a quite grown-up book for a nine-year-old. When he had left, his mother went to the window and moved the curtains to see him safely settled.

"Martin said he would come and spend some time with Noah and show him around the city. Noah adores him."

She turned back to the room and sat down. Here was the flaw in the woman, that odd calmness, that steady forbearance in the face of trouble that made her deny that anything could be wrong . . . that convinced her there was a reasonable explanation for Martin's absence . . . even after she had heard from Grimshaw that his mental state might be fragile . . . and had to understand from this visit of an . . . employer . . . the concern other people had. But Sarah's voice never faltered, nor did a tear come to her eye. What had happened—was happening—to her family couldn't have been more distressing, and the words conveyed this, but in tones so quiet, so self-possessed—and with the expression on the beautiful face never more extreme than . . . thoughtful—that I wondered if she was emotionally . . . sluggish . . . which would be a failure of intelligence, finally.

But she admitted Martin had asked her an odd question when she'd seen him last. He wanted to know the cause of his father's death. "It was a blood ailment, an anemia. . . . Augustus had begun to have these periods of weakness . . . when he could hardly lift himself from the bed. And one day he fainted. I thought Martin knew."

"This was—"

"This last time, a month ago. It seemed such an urgent matter in his mind."

"No—I meant when Mr. Pemberton fell ill."

"That would have been three years ago last April. I sent a telegram to his doctor, who came up on the train from New York. Martin wanted to know the name of the doctor. It was Dr. Mott, Thadeus Mott. He is an eminent physician of the city."

"Yes, I know Mott."

"It was Dr. Mott who made the diagnosis. He wanted my husband removed to the Presbyterian Hospital. He said it was a most serious illness. Did you know my husband, Mr. McIlvaine?"

"I knew of him."

She smiled. "Then you would know what his reaction would be. He wouldn't hear of going to the hospital. He told Dr. Mott to give him a tonic and that he'd be up and about in a few days. And so they argued until the doctor's back was to the wall Augustus always put people up against. . . . So Dr. Mott told him."

"Told him what?"

She lowered her voice. "I was not in the room, but in the gallery outside the door I could hear every word. . . . He told Augustus his disease was progressive and usually fatal . . . that in rare cases it reversed itself but he probably had no more than six months.

"Augustus called Dr. Mott a fool and assured

him he had no intention of dying at any foreseeable time in the future and then shouted for me to show him out. He was sitting there against the pillows with his arms folded and his jaw thrust out. . . . The doctor withdrew from the case.''

''So he did not see it to its end?''

''He said he wouldn't take responsibility where he couldn't prescribe the treatment. I wanted to bring in someone else, but Augustus told me the illness was nothing. I couldn't admit to him I had heard what had gone on. After a few weeks had passed and it became apparent to him that he was weakening, he decided on another consultation. He sat outside, wrapped in blankets on a chaise at the far end of the lawn . . . near the bluff, where he could look out over the river and see the gulls flying below him.''

''What doctor did you consult?''

''Not I—his secretary arranged it. Mr. Simmons, Eustace Simmons, my husband's secretary. He conferred with him every day. Augustus conducted his business out on the lawn. Simmons would sit next to him on a shooting stick with a dispatch case across his knees and receive instructions, and so forth. . . . When Martin heard me mention the name Simmons he could not keep still. He jumped up and began to pace back and forth. He became . . . almost happy . . . even giddy.

''One morning I found Augustus's things

packed. A carriage was at the front door, and I was informed by my husband that he would be taking a course of treatment at a sanitarium in Saranac Lake in the Adirondacks. Simmons was to travel with him. He would write in due course. Noah and I stood on the piazza to watch him go. His attentions to Noah were never . . . lavish . . . and were negligible during his illness. Noah loved his father . . . how can a child not love his father? They would rather blame themselves for a parent's conduct toward them. In any event that was the last time we ever saw him.''

''You told Martin this—about Saranac?''

She nodded.

''But I'm having trouble understanding—Saranac is for tuberculars. Did this doctor say Mr. Pemberton was consumptive?''

Sarah Pemberton turned her calm gaze upon me. ''That is exactly what Martin asked. But I never spoke with the doctor. I was able to learn his name, Dr. Sartorius, but that was all. I never spoke with him. I was never allowed to visit. I did receive his telegram . . . not three months had passed . . . informing me of my husband's death and expressing his condolences. The body was brought back to the city by train and Augustus was buried from St. James. He did entrust me, my husband . . . in his will . . . with fulfilling his wishes regarding the funeral arrangements.''

Sarah Pemberton lowered her eyes. But then with the slightest of smiles, as if to herself: "I'm quite aware of the impression an outsider must have from all this, Mr. McIlvaine. I understand . . . I'm told . . . there are marriages between equals . . . who live, unthinking, in simple devotion to each other."

It was quite astonishing—the effect upon me of Mrs. Pemberton's soft-spoken admission of the contempt in which she was held by the man she had given her life to. His universal contempt made no exception of her. What I had supposed was her recessive nature—was it not rather an aristocrat's training? What did I know of these things . . . the grace that enables you to ritualize your pain . . . and lay it out quietly through your sentences?

But she had such patience for everything—patience for the monstrous thieving husband . . . patience for the absent stepson . . . patience for her current, enigmatic situation, of which I was now made aware. It was so terribly oppressive in that old woman's sitting room, you see. I did not appreciate why someone with a country estate would choose to be in Manhattan at this time of year. But Sarah Pemberton was destitute. From obligations signed by her late husband that she still did not understand, the wife and legatee to the Pemberton fortune had not only lost the family home, Ravenwood, but, with

Noah, was reduced to living upon the charity of her sister-in-law. There was no end to the surprises this family had in store for me.

''Are you sure you won't have some tea, Mr. McIlvaine? They grumble, but they bring it.''

Eleven

I COULD not sleep that night after my meeting with Sarah Pemberton. I confess that as I thought about it, I found her endless capacity to suspend judgment . . . very attractive. I mean . . . the recessiveness of spirit that made her so lovely, even gallant, would appeal to any man who wanted endless reception, endless soft reception of whatever outrage he could conceive. But then there was the boy: I hadn't realized I was so moved by him—a sturdy, solemn, forbearing boy reading his book, a reader—was that it?—does the old bachelor merely have to see a child reading a book to lose his critical faculties?

Augustus had been worth millions. How was it possible? I had asked the woman. What on earth had happened?

"Every day I speak with this lawyer, or that, and ask the same question. It's become my life's work. My husband was a very secretive man. For different matters he hired different attorneys. In that way no one would know more than a part of his business. . . . We, Noah and I, are the sole heirs, accord-

ing to the will. That is not in question . . . but exactly
what happened to our legacy . . . where it went . . . is
not clear. I'm sure at least some of it is recoverable.
We'll leave here as soon as I sort it all out. We're on
the top floor and have to tiptoe about like mice.''

She believed a mistake had been made. What
else could it have been?

I would later have occasion to see Ravenwood.
Rising from a bluff over the western bank of the
Hudson, it was a large shingled mansion with many
windows and bays and a piazza running around three
sides under coupled columns . . . a sprawling house,
all its important rooms facing the river or the sky
over the river, the roof gabled and crowned with a
belvedere. The bulk was Victorian but the spirit
vaguely Italianate Queen Anne. It came with several
outbuildings and a tract of a thousand acres. Its command of the river completed the effect of defiance
that you get from much money when it combines
with little taste.

I thought at the time of the boy, Noah, growing
up there. Would he have had town children to play
with? The children of staff? His compensations were
the trails through the great woods behind his home
. . . or the broad halls and porches that his mother
mentioned, where he could hide, or spy, or listen for
his father's footsteps. The front lawn was overgrown
when I saw it. It went downward in a long gentle
reach to the bluff . . . which was more like a palisade.

And then there was a great caesura of air, a gorge of sky that implied the Hudson. And then the land resumed again with the bluffs of the eastern bank.

This . . . Ozymandias of the slave trade. He had built his Ravenwood as a monument to himself. And he had implanted his beautiful wife and son there as monuments to himself.

There was a rail line running through the village a few miles away, but also a river sloop that came right up to the landing at the foot of the bluff when the hand flag was raised at the stairhead. I was sure that was the way they had left their home. I found myself . . . imagining them opening the big oak doors with the insets of oval glass, coming down the wide porch steps, and crossing the gravel carriageway, the mother and son, their luggage preceding them down the sward to the river . . . steamer trunks and cedar chests strapped to the backs of the men who were tracking the thick grass of the sloping lawn like porters on safari in one of the boy's adventure tales. At the land's end, sheer, without warning or fence, I stood for a moment to experience what they would have felt . . . the illusion of living in the sky. It was true, I was higher than a pair of gulls beating their way south over the river.

A slanting cut led to the stairhead, and the long descent by a scaffolded stairs of wood planks and railing. . . . As for Sarah, she was leaving the house where she had learned about love from Augustus

Pemberton. As for Noah, he would of course be thrilled by the boat, not thinking he was leaving the only home he'd ever known.

The catastrophic loss of that home would finally occur as the event of a few moments' duration. I imagined them walking to the cliff's edge, climbing down the stairs to the river pier. . . . Noah would go aboard first and find them seats at the port rail, where the wind was keen. And while Sarah tied a kerchief over her hat and under her chin, and other passengers stared, he would stand beside her, his hand on her shoulder.

The captain tips his hat, the lines are cast, and the sloop slowly slides midstream into the sun and points for Manhattan.

I have traveled downriver, on Day Line side-wheelers from Poughkeepsie and Bear Mountain. . . . The wind and current together would speed them along to New York, so that it might seem to Sarah their fate was rushing toward them. In an hour or so they would see the sky over the city stained black from the smoke of chimneys and stacks and steam locomotives. Southward, the masts of the sailing ships in their berths on the river would look like a kind of stitching of heaven to earth. Then, as the packet came to the northern reaches of the island, she would see the world glare up much larger. It is a strange feeling. Your boat is . . . humbled. You are all at once in a churning traffic of ferries . . . the very water hurries and plashes like New York . . . and moving past the piers of tall masts, hearing the shouts of the stevedores, you come around at the Battery with the harbor rolling with sail and funnel, proud clippers and Indiamen and coastal steamers and lighters with iron hulls, which sometimes pass so close the sky is blocked out by their black bulk and they resound with great echoing booms in the slap of the waves.

And so Mrs. Pemberton and her son had sailed down into our city, and in my terrible insomniac visions I saw the boy swept into the life of nameless children here. I define modern civilization as the social failure to keep all children named. Does that shock you? In jungle tribes or among the nomad herders the children keep their names. Only in our great industrial downtown they don't. Only where we have newspapers to tell us the news of ourselves . . . are children not assured of keeping their names.

On the pier Noah Pemberton would realize what he had given up for a ride. He would no longer be thrilled. Not this boy, not by my New York. Swarms of cabbies surround them. Porters shoulder their trunks without being asked. And beggars with their hands out . . . and beggar pigeons. And he is going to live with his aunt Lavinia, an old woman whom he knows nothing about except that she has no children. And then he is in a carriage, with the harsh unceasing music in his ears of urgent city life and its rattling transport. The hackney goes up the West Side along Eleventh Avenue, and the lungs of the young country boy fill for the first time with the sickening air of the meat district . . . the stockyards and slaughterhouses. Perhaps he thinks he has landed not in New York but on the chest of a monstrous carcass and is inhaling the odor of its huge bloody being.

Sarah Pemberton, with the great calm by which she modulated their dire circumstances, would take her son's hand and smile . . . and tell him . . . what? That soon they would see Martin, that Martin would be part of the family now.

But I had learned something about Martin Pemberton that let me sleep, finally. He did not live only for himself. He had a mother who had seen him through college . . . and a young brother who adored him. We may stride about with our principles at the ready . . . and hammer everyone we meet with our hard, unyielding worldview. But we have our mothers and brothers . . . whom we exempt . . . for whom the unrelenting intellect relents . . . just as I know in my case it does for my sister, Maddie, for whose dear sake I go to Improvement Society dinners. And if I could not say where Martin Pemberton was, I knew what he was doing. I was sure of it. He was gone in pursuit. Every detail of what I had learned of these matters he already knew . . . though he knew far more. And what I knew, in the lightening darkness of my suspicions, was enough for me to make the inspired, though insufficiently considered, decision to deepen my involvement and put me in pursuit as well.

As the city editor at the *Telegram* I was entitled each summer to a week's leave. However, it must be not only summer but that wilting heart of it when the heat waves rise from the pavement . . . when the sanitation drays take the dead horses from the streets and the ambulances of Bellevue the dead folks from their tenements . . . and—the key thing—when anyone left alive in the baking blanched light is too enervated to make news. All these conditions were met, and I was off.

I decided first of all to tell what I knew to Edmund Donne, a captain with the Municipal Police. You may not appreciate how extraordinary it was that I, or anyone else in the city of New York, for that matter, would confide in a police official. The Municipals were an organization of licensed thieves. Occasionally they interrupted their graft-gathering for practice with nightsticks on the human skull. Police jobs were customarily bought. Every exalted rank, from sergeant up through lieutenant, captain, and on to the commissioner, paid the Tweed Ring for the privilege of public service. Even patrolmen paid if they wanted to be assigned to one of the more lucrative precincts. But it was a large organization of two thousand or so, and there were some exceptions to the rule, Donne being probably the highest-ranking. Among naturalists, when a bird is seen well beyond its normal range, it is called an accidental. Donne was an accidental. He was the only captain I knew who had not paid for his commission.

He was also atypical of his trade in being neither Irish nor German nor uneducated. In fact, he was so clearly misplaced that he was a mystery to me. He lived in the tension characteristic of the submitted life . . . like someone who has taken holy orders or serves his government in an obscure foreign station. I could think, in his presence, that my familiar tawdry New York was the exotic outpost of his colonial service . . . or perhaps a leper colony to which he'd given his life as a missionary.

Donne was exceptionally tall and thin and had, when standing, to look down at anyone he spoke with. He had a long, narrow face, gaunt cheeks, a pointed chin. And because his hair was gray at the temples and through the mustache, and his brows had thickened and taken wing, and when he was seated at his desk his long back curved into the hunch of his shoulders so that the twin ridges of his shoulder blades indented his blue tunic, you were put in mind of a rather impressive heron settled on its perch.

His was a lonely eminence. He was anywhere between forty and fifty. I knew nothing of his personal life. He had come up through the ranks, re-

maining always outside the order of connived loyalties that passes for brotherhood among policemen.
This was not from any righteousness on his part . . .
merely that he was not the sort to ask for confidences
or give them. His skills, which were considerable,
were not questioned, but in the perverse thinking of
his fellow officers, they were part of the brief against
him. He'd achieved the rank of captain slowly,
through the administrations of several commissioners, who found him useful when they needed to advertise the Municipals' worthiness of the public
trust. Since that was a periodic necessity, his employment was secure, if not comfortable. It helped
also that some of us in the press had written about
him from time to time. He never asked for this, of
course. For us, too, he simply was what he was and
went his own way.

Donne was glumly at his work when I called on
him in his office on Mulberry Street. He looked almost pleased to see me.

"Do I interrupt something?" I said.

"Yes, and I'm sure I'm grateful."

His latest humiliation was to be in charge of the
office that certified deaths in the city by age, sex,
race, nativity, and cause—zymotic, constitutional, or
sudden—and recorded them in an annual table for
the city atlas that nobody ever read.

I told him of the whole Pemberton matter—everything I knew, and also what I suspected. I had his

interest. He sat hunched over his desk and was absolutely still. There was something else about Donne—he held the whole city in his mind as if it were a village. In a village, people don't need a newspaper. Newspapers arise only when things begin to happen that people cannot see and hear for themselves. Newspapers are the expedient of the municipally dissociated. But Donne had the capacious mind of a villager. He knew the Pemberton name. He remembered the dismissed slave-trading charges against Augustus, and the wartime congressional inquiry into his quartermaster contracts. He knew who Eustace Simmons was—he called him 'Tace Simmons—and understood immediately why I thought it would be nice to find him.

But finding anyone in our city, how one went about finding someone in those days, was something of an art, as all reporters knew—especially if it was someone who didn't have a professional or commercial life. You understand—there were no phones then. No phonebooks. No street-by-street names and addresses. There were listings of city officials, listings of doctors in the medical society rosters, lawyers and engineers could be found in their firms, and socialites at their well-known residences. But if you wanted to talk to someone you had to go where he was to be found, and if you didn't know where that was, there were no general directories to tell you.

" 'Tace Simmons once worked for the port

wardens," Donne told me. "There is a saloon on
Water Street that they like. Perhaps someone will
know something. Perhaps 'Tace comes around for
old times' sake."

He didn't tell me what he thought, or if he believed my reasoning was well founded. He just went
to work. I had to defer, of course, to his way of doing
things, which was tiresomely . . . methodical. "First
things first," he said, and asked me to describe Martin Pemberton in all the particulars—his age, height,
eye color, and so forth. Then he turned his long back
to me and began to file through the stacks of loose
pages on the table behind him.

The Mulberry Street headquarters is a raucous
place. People flow in and out and speak only in
raised voices, and with all the shouting and protesting and laughing and cursing drifting into Donne's
office, I was made aware of the necessarily practical
view of mankind that is produced in a police building. It's much like a newspaper office.

But for all the distractions, Donne might have
been a scholar working in the silence of a library. A
gas lamp hung from the center of the ceiling. It was
lit now in the midmorning because the long, narrow
windows gave almost no light. The walls were a pale
tan color. Against the walls, glass-covered book-
cases were bowed with the weight of law books,
manuals of municipal regulations, and volumes of
papers in their folders. The floor was covered with a

threadbare Belgian carpet. Donne's desk was a scarred and battered walnut. Behind the wooden chair where I sat a gated balustrade cut the room in two. I could see nothing that might have given a personal character to this office.

After a length of time he was able to tell me there was no Caucasian male body of Martin Pemberton's description that had not been identified and claimed.

He was a very thorough fellow, Edmund Donne. We had next to take ourselves by hackney to the Dead House on First Avenue and Twenty-sixth Street and go through the holding rooms to look at the new arrivals. I walked the rows of zinc tables, where the livid bodies lay face upward under constant showers of cold water, until I was able to assure myself that my freelance was not among them.

"This rules out nothing," Donne advised me, with his policeman's logic. "But it rules out something."

The character of this odd, misplaced policeman, misplaced for life, is an important piece of my story. The way enlightenment comes . . . is in bits and pieces of humdrum reality, each adding its mosaic bit of glitter to the eventual vision. It is almost mysterious to me now that I sought him out, this carefully stepping creature bowed by his own height. I had other recourses in a city of almost a million souls . . . and at the beginning of our cooperative inquiry, I admit, I was prepared to go on to them . . . except that he was so engaged by the problem I had brought as to take possession of it. I saw immediately that his interest had nothing to do with his lack of serious duties. In fact he had all sorts of investigative pursuits of his own that he had not abandoned since leaving his previous command of the woeful, understaffed Bureau for the Recovery of Lost Persons. There was something else, something else . . . a look of recognition in the eye, as if he might have been waiting for this . . . waiting for me to arrive . . . with what he was expecting.

So now we are in his office, after two or three nights of a so-far-unproductive search for a sign of Eustace Simmons on the waterfront—walking from one tavern to another, along the East River under the looming prows of the packets and clippers that lie at berth with their bowsprits in the chalky night casting shadows on the cobblestone . . . some hidden language in the sound of creaking mast and groaning hawser . . . the riverfront stink of fish and ordure suggesting to me a crawl through the city's nether parts. So, as I say, we are in his office midway through my glorious summer holiday . . . and I have thought for the first time to tell Donne about Martin's allusive conversation with Harry Wheelwright at the St. Nicholas Hotel.

But now a sergeant enters, pushing before him through the gate another diversion—a muscular fel-

low in a dirty sweater and baggy trousers, white
haired and with a face well pounded, the nose and
cheekbones flattened, and the ears curled up on
themselves like blossoms. He stood before the desk
in his considerable redolence, twisting the cap in his
hands and smiling at nothing in particular as he
waited to be acknowledged.

Donne had been reading some sort of document—whether to do with my subject or not, I had
no idea. He glanced at me, then he arranged the papers neatly on his desk, and only then did he look up
at the man before him.

''Well, look at this. It's Knucks has come
calling.''

''Yes, Captain,'' said this Knucks with a defer-
ential nod.

''So we're restored to the good opinion of
crime,'' Donne said to the sergeant, who laughed in
response. ''And how is your health?'' Donne said to
the man, as if they were club members together.

''Oh, I'm doin' poorly, thanking you, Captain,'' said the old tough, taking the question as an
invitation to seat himself on the edge of the chair
next to mine. He grinned, showing his gapped and
blackened teeth, and his face lit up appealingly, like
a boy's, with the perverse charm that is given sometimes to the brainlessly amoral. ''This leg o' mine,''
he said, stretching out the offending limb, and rub-
bing it vigorously. ''It aches terrible and sometimes

won't be trod upon. It ain't never healed right from the war.''

''And what war was that?'' said Donne.

''Why, Yer Honor, the War Betwix the States.''

''I never heard you had gone for a soldier, Knucks. And where did you see your action?''

''It was on the Fifth Avenue—I took a ball by the steps of the nigger orphanage there.''

''I see. And were you one of the gallants putting a torch to the place?''

''I was, Captain, and 'twas one of your own rifles who nicked me in that skirmish when I was fighting for my honor against the illegal cons'ription.''

''I understand now, Knucks.''

''Yessir. And withal I p'r'aps have said the wrong thing, given what I am to divulge, with your permission. But I'm an older and wiser sod now, and whilst childrens, black or white, are no affection of mine, I have more sympathy for every soul of God since''—he generously turned to include me in the conversation—''all of us is God's dear souls, ain't that so? And so there have come to be things I see that I cannot countenance.''

''There is hope for us all, Mr. McIlvaine,'' said Donne. ''In the old days Knucks here made his living by breaking bones, twisting necks, and tearing off the ears of people. Prison was a normal condition of his life.''

"True enough, Captain," the fellow said with a grin.

"These days," Donne said, regarding the wretch but addressing me, "he makes his living no longer with his muscles but by his faculties of observation and deceit."

"Right as ever, Captain. Take this matter. I don't know when I have been so alarmed to speak of something. But, sir, it is at some risk to meself that I have come here, and for all of that I am sorely in need of an oyster or two and a glass of Steinhardt's German," he said, looking at the floor. "It's the least for putting my life in danger."

Donne said, "What is it you have to tell me."

"It's most horrible, sir. Even I know that. I aver an' detest there is a man going about these nights offerin' to buy up loose children."

"Buy them?"

"Exactly so. They must be sound and not older than ten nor younger than five. And it don't matter if boys or girls but they must not be dark skin."

"He approached you?"

"Not me. I heard him at the Buffalo Tavern. He was talking to the barkeep, Tommy, with the red beard."

"What did he say?"

"Just that. He would pay a fat sum."

"Whom else did he speak with?"

"Well, I knew you would want me to, so I followed him to two or three places, and watched him tell the same tale, and God help me, there he goes then right up to my own abode and enters in there and after a while I sneaks a look in the window, for you know my landlord Pig Meachum keeps the ground front for hisself, and there is the man at his table and Pig is nodding and taking puffs on his pipe while he listens.''

''When was this?''

''Not two nights ago.''

Donne leaned forward and folded his hands on his desk. ''He was not known to you?''

''No, sir.''

''What did he look like?''

''Why nothing special, Captain. A man like the rest of us.''

''What was he wearing, Knucks?''

''Ah, now that was true, a straw with his linen suit. But he was no swell, of that I'm sure. He was not skittish, he looked like he could take care uv hisself.''

Donne said: ''I want you to find him and befriend him. Offer your services. . . . You're not without reputation. You will see what he's up to and give me the tip.''

''Ah, Yer Honor.'' The informer twisted his cap one way, then another. Suddenly added to the rankness of his unwashed person was the acrid smell of fear. "I don't fancy that. I would rather not be party to that, if you please."

"But you shall."

"I have done a citizen's duty. I am an old gimper, and the lowest street life takes its licks at me knowing I am not the Knucks I was. I must live by the wits alone these day, and the wits tell me a man mustn't show himself too inquirous about such dark matters as these."

"Here," Donne said, removing a half-dollar from his vest pocket. He snapped it down on the desk. "No harm will come to you. You are in the employ of the Municipal Police of the City of New York."

When the sergeant had ushered the man out Donne stood, though it was more like an unfolding. He stretched his arms and then took himself to the window in his stately wading-bird glide. Putting one hand over the other behind his back, he looked out as if there were a prospect worth seeing.

" 'Such dark matters as these,' " he said in Knucks's intonation. "Such dark matters as these," he said, as if by pronouncing them he was investigating the words themselves . . . and then he quietly drifted into his own thought.

I myself was thinking that what I had heard was in the continuum of original sin . . . not pleasant to contemplate but not disconnected from anything else either. I was anxious for us to get back to the matter at hand. Then Donne asked me the question that flashed across my brain and spanned the poles of our dark universe: "Who do you suppose would want to buy them, Mr. McIlvaine, when they are in the streets for the taking?" I know you will think this is the overwrought fabulation of an old man, but the means of human knowledge are far from understood, and I am telling you here, it was this question that afforded me my first glimpse of Dr. Sartorius . . . or sense of the presence in our city of Dr. Sartorius . . . though it may have been nothing more than a moment's belated awareness of the shadow cast by his name as it was uttered by Sarah Pemberton.

Twelve

O̶R else, as I had brought in the protagonist for my quest, he brought with him, like his shadow, his opposite.

Taking Edmund Donne into my confidence would put the whole matter of my freelance's disappearance into another realm, making it the concern of a particular class of people in our society. For think, now, of the community we made—the press, the police, the clergy . . . the family . . . and the childhood lover waiting to bear his children. All of us against . . . everything else. Yet I wasn't quite aware of this. In fact I found myself thinking just the opposite, that confiding in Donne reduced my chances of understanding the truth of the situation, that the introduction of a municipal officer into things compressed my thought into the small space of . . . law enforcement. He wanted us to speak immediately with Martin's friend Harry Wheelwright. Of course that was the logical next step. But I felt peculiar leading him there. I felt as if I was giving up . . . my diction . . . for his. As astute as Donne was, he was a policeman, wasn't he? With a policeman's simple tools of thought? In a way it was like having Dr. Grimshaw as a partner—I mean with that sort of theological rope around my neck. How perverse of me . . . that having solicited Donne's help, I would then deplore it.

You didn't need an appointment to see Harry Wheelwright, he kept an open house . . . I suppose to make it convenient as possible for collectors to stop by. He occupied the top floor of a commercial ironfront on West Fourteenth Street, the equivalent of one large room, and with a bank of windows characteristic of the ironfronts. The windows, which faced north, were covered with a sort of crystallized grime. The light that came through was diffused, a flat white light that fell evenly over everything . . . injudiciously. A big bed, loosely covered, was on one wall. An armoire next to it . . . a sink and icebox half hidden by a folding screen . . . a lithography or etching press of some sort . . . odd pieces of furniture, whether to be lived in or used for props, it was hard to tell. And all of it on a splintered wood floor that appeared never to have been swept.

When we arrived Harry was at work with a live model, an unfortunate skinny young man who was seated on a packing crate, shirtless, but with the dark blue uniform trousers and boots of the Union army. Galluses hung from his bare shoulders, and an enlisted man's cap sat upon his head. The poor wretch had one arm cut off above the elbow, the reddened skin of the stump sewn together like the end of a sausage, and he was smiling at me, with his broken and stained teeth, enjoying the shock I suppose my face registered at the sight.

But when I introduced Harry to Donne, who was in mufti, so that I gave his rank with the Municipal Police, the model stood up with an expression on his face of absolute horror and struggled to put on his shirt. "Wait—keep the pose, stay where you are!" the artist shouted, going toward him. There was a flurry of remonstrations, curses . . . and the one-armed man was fleeing down the stairs.

Harry looked at us balefully with his bloodshot bulging blue eyes.

"We're here about Pemberton," I said.

"I see." He tossed his paintbrush across the room. "How like Martin to ruin a day's work." He went behind the screen and I heard the clink of glass and bottle.

The place was a pigsty, but on the walls were exhibited the artist's meticulous habits of observation—oil paintings and sketches in oils—of his society. His subjects, along with the maimed and disfigured veterans painted in unflinching detail, were the more academic portraits or fashionable New York scenes designed for the market. So it was really quite visible, the same conflicted mind I saw in Martin Pemberton—the critique, and the necessity of earning a living, side by side. And there were sketches I had never seen before, drawings on paper tacked up there unceremoniously . . . of the squatters' shanties on the West Side . . . people scavenging the garbage scow at the dock off Beach Street . . . the vagrant children of the Five Points warming themselves over a steam grate . . . the mob at the Exchange . . . the traffic of Broadway with its drays and stages and two-in-hands all pressing forward under a net of telegraph wires with the sun lighting up the store-window awnings. . . . In squares and rectangles, sketched and painted and etched and pulled . . . the sensibility given to his era . . . flung out and spattered into the civilization I recognized as the one I lived in.

But the piece that struck me most was a large unframed portrait half hidden by another in a stack of canvases leaning against the wall. A young woman. He had posed her in the broken-down armchair that still stood in the middle of the room. She wore a plain dark gray dress, simply cut, with a white collar . . . a young woman seated without coyness, in full presentation of the honest self, but also, from the way he laid the light upon her face, and in her eyes, he'd gotten her genuine virtue, the loyalty of her spirit . . . and even more difficult, what I had noticed about her when I had met her, the erotic moral being. And he had also caught in her expression the first signs of an unrewarded schoolmarm life that I had myself seen in our interview, as if a darker mood were bearing down upon her from the background of solemn umber. The whole painting was done in grays and blacks and browns.

"Emily Tisdale," I said.

"Yes, good for you, McIlvaine, that is indeed Miss Tisdale." I explained to Donne . . . this was the young woman whom everyone, including herself, had presumed to be engaged to Martin Pemberton. Behind me I heard the artist's robust laugh.

Now I knew it was not in itself remarkable that someone who would know Martin would know Emily, but I was struck here as if by an extraordinary coincidence. Perhaps it was an effect of the art—it was of such intimacy, this portrait—but I felt that I had stumbled upon the inner workings of this generation . . . who were all so different from my own . . . each in his own character, to be sure, but with this common quality of creating gaps in my understanding of what was happening to them, of what fate they were seeking for themselves . . . as if I had lost some of my hearing and could not always get the sense of their words, though the tones were clear enough.

The artist had come up behind us. He had set out some chipped and dirty tumblers and a bottle of brandy. It was not yet noon. There was a slight whistle to his respiration. He was really stout, Harry, with large pudgy hands, and he reeked of tobacco and his unwashed smock. "It's good, isn't it?" he said. "Notice I didn't pose her leaning forward with chin up, ankles crossed, and hands in her lap, which another painter would have done. Emily's grace is her own . . . it is not trained. I let her seat herself in the chair and that's the pose she took . . . the feet flat on the floor before her, with her skirt draping the thighs, you see, and her arms at rest on the arms of the chair . . . and looking straight at you with those clear brown Siberian eyes.''

"Why Siberian?" said Donne.

"The cheekbones are high, and see here? the way they seem to lift the eyes at the outer corners? Don't tell old man Tisdale, but somewhere in his line of pious Protestants was a wild woman of the steppes. Yet I'm constrained from acting upon it . . . by the simpleminded friendship that some women assume . . . and install between you like a chastity belt.''

Harry was a boor. It has been my experience that artists are invariably boors. That is the paradox . . . a mysterious God lets them paint what they will never understand. Like all those Florentines and Genoans and Venetians . . . who were scoundrels and sybarites, but whom this God trusted to give us the angels and saints and Jesus Christ himself through their dumb hands.

"And not constrained by your friendship with Martin Pemberton?" Donne said as we continued to look at the painting.

"Oh, that too, of course. If you insist. I mean I

have acted toward him as a friend, though by now I would rather not be his friend. And I am Emily's friend, though I would rather be more than her friend. And she is Martin's lost friend. . . . Yes, I think that more accurately describes it.''

''Why is she lost?'' said Donne.

''Because she stubbornly insists on it,'' Harry said, triumphant, as if he had just given the answer to a riddle. He offered us chairs and poured us each a drink, though we had not asked for one.

I had told Donne what I thought he should know about Harry Wheelwright. That the best of him would be on the wall. That he was totally untrustworthy . . . that he lied for sport . . . that we would not get the truth from him even if he knew what it was. Donne sat in the same upholstered old chair Emily had posed in. His knees rose up before him and he placed his elbows on the chair arms and pressed the fingertips of his hands together and asked a question or two, in a tone of voice that didn't exactly demand an answer but was irresistibly confident that he would receive one. I'm not sure that was all there was to it, but he got Harry talking.

''I don't know where in God's name Pemberton may be, or what he is up to, nor do I want to. You can believe me—I have no more curiosity in this matter,'' Harry said. ''I'm through with that damned family.''

''Well, he hasn't been to his job in some weeks.

He's arrears in his rent. What do you think can have happened?''

''Nothing worth worrying about. Not to Martin Pemberton. You know when harm has come to someone that there was a . . . susceptibility there. But that can't be so with my imperial friend. It is not in his nature to be . . . deprived . . . of his full measure of what life, even the life of ideas, has to offer.''

''You last saw him—when, did you say?''

''Here, Martin came up here. When Emily was sitting, in fact. Came barging right in. It was June but he was still wearing his damned coat over his shoulders . . . and pacing back and forth with that locked-knee gait of his. It broke her concentration. Her eyes followed him, her head moved. . . . Women love Martin, why I can't imagine. . . . After he got himself disowned I used to take him home for dinner. . . . We roomed together at Columbia, you know. He was exactly the same then. I think he was born striding about, pale and thinking metaphysical thoughts. Contemptuous of his fellow students . . . hating his professors . . . in every way superbly, brilliantly insufferable.''

''You were good friends?''

''Well, I found him amusing. But, you know, I never cared to see him without a shirt . . . with that white and concave chest of his that I thought an ideal vessel for consumption. But when I brought him home, my mother and two sisters were delighted with him. They fed him and listened to his ideas. They adored him. Perhaps because he is far too serious to ingratiate himself with women or solicit their good opinion. Yes, that must be it. Women trust a man who seems not to notice them as women.''

But why had Martin interrupted the sitting?

''I don't know—to interrupt it, I suppose. To inflict his mood on us. He upset her. They argued.''

''About what?''

''Who knows? Even if you're sitting right there listening, you can never tell what lovers are arguing about. They don't know themselves. But the subject appeared to be fidelity. Not infidelity, mind you. Martin was attacking Emily for her faithfulness. 'You see?' he shouts as she sits in my chair there, weeping. 'Every time we meet I try your patience and abuse your nature. It doesn't seem to matter. You wait for the next time! Don't you understand what hell you face? If I give myself to you in my present state, with nothing answered, nothing understood? You will ache with longing for your unhappiness of waiting, you will long to be back in that damned garden of our childhood . . . with its stupid child fantasies of life.' And so on, endlessly, like that.''

''So Emily knew of Martin's . . . visions?''

''Oh, yes. He generously shared them with everyone.''

''What did he mean, 'with nothing answered,

with nothing understood'? Did he use those exact words?'' Donne had almost whispered this last question, and with a concern that somehow had the effect of illuminating Harry's youth. I realized again how young they all were. It is harder to see someone's youthfulness who is so portly, and double-chinned, but Harry was not yet thirty. He sighed. He poured himself another inch of brandy and held the bottle aloft. ''This is very civilized—you sure you won't have another?'' And then he looked at each of us in turn. ''This doesn't all have to be unpleasant, does it? I think Martin meant he had seen Augustus Pemberton . . . and then missed seeing him.''

''What do you mean?''

''I can't say anything more. He made me swear to it.'' Harry settled his bulk onto a wooden chair. We were silent while he composed himself to break his oath. He stared at the floor and a low moan escaped from him. He said: ''When I write my memoirs I myself will be the subject of them. I do not intend to go down as a mere chronicler of the Pemberton family. I absolutely will not. My paintings will hang in museums. My own fate is another story, not this one. Not this one.''

Thirteen

S O now we come to it. I knew we would
come to it. I knew we would,'' Harry said.

"Well then, we were sitting one night in a saloon on East Houston Street where the ladies who
come in without escorts are not necessarily professional but merely restless . . . or foolish—yes, Harry
Hill's, that saloon of impeccable manners. A violin
and a harmonium played for the dancing. This was
this past June, toward the end of the month, because I
remember the papers had proclaimed the summer
solstice. Papers make much of what nobody thinks
twice about, you have to admit that, Mr. McIlvaine.
. . . Martin on this particular night conceived the notion of going up to the Woodlawn Cemetery and seeing his father. He wanted me to go along, then and
there . . . to go to the cemetery and open the coffin
and look upon the glories within. It was past midnight, I was quite drunk, and I remember thinking it
was not an idea that particularly interested me, dig-
ging up Augustus Pemberton. I had met him once or
twice in his life and would not on my own have
thought to renew the acquaintance. But Martin said

he wanted to make sure the old man was all right.
. . . There was a stout woman at our table and she was
laughing uproariously. I pointed out to her that Augustus Pemberton, being dead, was surely all right
. . . that in fact his state of being might be described
as a kind of perfection. Before I understood what was
happening, Martin had grabbed my arm and we were
climbing into a hack and galloping up to the Central
Railroad Terminal, where we managed to catch the
last train of the night—or was it the first train of the
morning? But we had an entire car to ourselves, and
we rode to the village of Woodlawn. It is there the
old man is buried, at the cemetery in Woodlawn.
You know it, all the wealth and money likes to be
buried there, it is a fine and fashionable graveyard.
. . . We got off at this dark station and didn't have any
idea of how to get to the place or what we would do
once there. I was cold. I was shivering. There is no
question about that, I don't see why the weather has
to kowtow to your calendar. We had nothing left to
drink. I urged Martin to reconsider. The waiting
room was unattended but a coal stove was still warm
from the night before and I thought we could sit beside it and wait for the train going back to the city. I
knew it had to come eventually. Or perhaps I argued
that we should wait for daylight to desecrate his father's grave so that at least we would be able to see
what we were doing. I understood why he was possessed by this peculiar idea, he had told me of these

odd sightings all spring, and I knew it was nonsense but could not make up my mind whether it would be better for him to actually see his papa's corpse or not to, so I was irresolute. Martin was as drunk as I, but it was a drunkenness of hard, concerted intention, as if drink had not dulled his wits but brought them to a sharper focus. The fact is that when my dear Martin sets his mind on something you cannot argue with him. He has a powerful presence and a way of considering you that, even as he needs you and your help, makes you feel foolish or inconsequential in one way or another . . . as someone lacking resolve or moral vision or even simple courage. So we had this drunken dispute and I, who had secretly to concede myself to be without any one of these qualities—I of course gave in and was persuaded, and dragged my sodden and surly self after him as he went looking for the family mausoleum.

"I remember it was a walk uphill that left me short of breath. The village street was an unpaved lane with a few houses and a general store and a clapboard church. There was light from a half-moon. We passed an alley where there was a livery stable and we heard the snort and shudder of a horse, at which point Martin described his sightings once again, as if I hadn't already heard about them, and asked me why he always saw the white omnibus when the weather was bad. I couldn't begin to think of an answer. Only when we were beyond the village and going along a

high retaining wall did the full meaning dawn on me
. . . finally . . . that my friend had every intention of
exhuming his own father. Good God! These are
modern times! Our city is lit in gaslight, we have
transcontinental railroads, I can send a message by
cable under the ocean. . . . We don't dig up bodies
anymore!

"I think I was sobering rapidly . . . which one
experiences as the appreciation of consequences. We
went in by the main gate, and eventually Martin
found in the hills of the Woodlawn necropolis a
modest marker, considering, a single marble angel
on a tall thin pedestal, and a footstone telling the
name and dates and protesting the goodness of the
departed in that trite way people go about speaking
to posterity. I had expected something equal to the
man, a monumental vault, fenced about to separate
Augustus from the surrounding folk and richly
carved to advertise his life's splendor. Martin too
was taken aback by the modesty of things, so much
so that he thought this might be a different Augustus
Pemberton and looked about for the actual one. But
we knelt again in the moonlight before the stone and
Martin said these were his father's dates and that it
would be too terrible a joke if there had been two Augustus Pembertons living in the world at the same
time. And so we knelt there in drunken puzzlement,
not being able to understand why modesty and econ-
omy would be the choice in death of such a man.

"And somehow or other, as I sat there with my teeth chattering, I could now see the shadowiest outlines of the surrounding trees, and then as I peered through the dark, of the hillsides and the stones upon them, and then I understood it was not darkness I was looking into but the milkiest mists of the minutes before dawn. Everything was wet, the air painted the skin of my face with its wet mist, and as I stood and brushed the wet dirt that clung to my trousers, I saw Martin coming down the lane out of this dripping gray light with two fellows behind him, one with a shovel on his shoulder, the other with a pick. Apparently I had fallen asleep against a stone. . . . He had gone searching and found these habitués of the graveyard, as if they were known always to be on call to disinter loved ones for anyone who requested it. To this moment I do not know where he found them or what he told them. But I know I paid for them since I was the one with money that night.

"So they removed their jackets but not their caps, and spit upon their hands and rubbed them and went to work. Martin and I stood side by side, a bit uphill on a knoll, and watched them, the pick first loosening the sod, then the shoveler piling it off to the side, and so, picking and shoveling, and making a gradual sort of descent into the hole they dug around themselves. I noticed as they worked that the sky was getting lighter and whiter, and the mist was lightening into a visible fog, for which I thanked God, for I was of course anxious that we not be discovered, prisons being what they are these days.

"I tried in my mind to rationalize this awful thing we were doing. I tried to believe this act was not entirely bizarre, and given Martin's lifelong struggle as Augustus's son, that it made a kind of peculiar sense . . . as if by seeing the old man's remains Martin would be relieved of his sick . . . visions . . . and find some peace for himself, if that was ever possible.

"And then there was a different sound, of the shovel hitting the box, and I felt Martin's hand, like a claw, in my shoulder. Now that the moment was here, he could not move. I enjoyed that. You know, I have no fear of looking at dead things. I have drawn dead things all my life—dead insects, dead fish, dead dogs. Cadavers in anatomy class. I told him to wait where he was and I went down to the rim of the pit. The men had constructed earthen ledges on which they could crouch, and from these ledges they scraped the top of the coffin clean, and with great effort they were able to pry up the lid with a small sledgehammer and an iron wedge they had known enough to bring with them. I wondered if there was a craftsman's guild for such things. . . . The lid came off and was hoisted up and slid aside. On my friend's behalf I summoned up a steadfast heart. I knelt and looked. A figure lay there in some disarray on its padded white silk couch. And I tell you now, Captain Donne, I tell you this with impunity because the greater crime was not committed by us. It was a very shrunken corpse . . . in odd clothing . . . with a tiny leathered face with its eyes closed and lips pursed . . . as if it was trying to understand something or recall something it had forgotten. . . . The light I had for my examination was not actual daylight, you understand. I had to see through it, as if through a milky suspension. The air was wet, the ground was wet, and even as I looked, the silken folds of the shroud cloth darkened from the atmosphere. I looked on stupidly, wondering at the arms . . . one of which lay upon the chest, the other dropped to the side . . . with their small hands extended from a cuffless sleeve. There was no cravat or collar or frock coat but a short jacket and white shirt with a red bow tie. The trousers came to the ankles. The feet were not booted, but wore patent-leather shoes. I tried to reconcile these odd data with what I remembered of Augustus Pemberton. I heard Martin's whisper, 'For God's sake, Harry . . .' It seems to me now that an eternity passed before I realized I was looking at the corpse of a child. It was a dead boy in that coffin.

"The diggers hoisted themselves out of the grave. My stovepipe fell across my face and into the box and it landed upright on the chest. It looked as if the boy was holding a hat over his heart . . . perhaps at a passing parade. I laughed, I thought it was funny. 'Here, Martin,' I called, 'come say hello to our young friend.'

''I was not as sober as I thought. Who knows now what he would have preferred to see there through the white fog in Woodlawn Cemetery. Once he was bent on discovery the result would be terrible, no matter what it was. He came down the knoll and got to his knees and peered in . . . and I heard a moan . . . an awful basso sound . . . not in his voice at all but brought up from the lungs of a shaggy ancestry . . . a million years old. My bones resonated. I never want to hear such a sound again.

''Martin made me swear I would never tell anyone, which I was only too glad to do. The gravediggers closed the coffin and reburied it. I wanted to get out of there but Martin insisted that we stay until the job was done. I remember he tamped down the grass where it didn't lie to his satisfaction.

''I saw him only a few times afterward . . . and now I don't see him. He stopped coming around. I should run into him now and then—we have the same haunts, after all—but I don't see him. I don't know where in hell he is . . . and I don't want to know. It is dangerous being around him. Any curiosity on my part . . . what has happened to the body of his father, what the child is doing there in his stead . . . if I allowed myself to think about this . . . lurid . . . family struggle . . . Well, they deserve each other

with their awful battles that they carry on past death.
. . . I refuse to think about it. . . . It is a kind of deep
moral damage that can be contracted by too close association, like the cholera. And to think who paid for
that glorious evening! As to a man's strength of character, I assure you Martin Pemberton has not been as
good or great a friend as Harry Wheelwright, and
never was and never can be. . . . Certainly he would
not comport himself with the same grace and forti-
tude if, God forbid, the situation was reversed and it
was a Wheelwright who escaped from the grave.

"But I do feel contaminated. . . . It has only gotten worse. . . . The image of that dead boy sits in my
brain. I would paint it if I could.

"I will never tell of these things in my memoirs.
When I write my memoirs I will be the subject of the
narrative. I do not intend to go down as a passionate
devotee and self-appointed secretary of the Pemberton family . . . that lived for a while . . . in the brilliant
heart-quaking civilization of New York. My own
fate will be another story . . . not this one."

Fourteen

$\overline{\overline{}}$

T HE tale as Harry told it was so clearly the kind that sold newspapers that Donne assumed my blood was up. When we left the artist's studio, he suggested lunch in a nearby beer garden. He knew about my trade—that the reporter is a predator . . . and the story is something he brings back in his jaws and drops at his publisher's feet. And since animals have no discretion and cannot act against their natures, he wanted to impress upon me the need for restraint. I wasn't offended. After all, I had made Donne my partner in the enterprise. In a good partnership each is supposed to save the other from his worst instincts. I couldn't imagine what his would be but I trusted I'd know when they cropped up. At the same time I wanted to make sure we understood each other.

"How will the Municipals dig up a body without the whole city knowing about it?" I asked him.

"I can't order an exhumation unless I have the permission of the deceased's family."

"That would be Sarah Pemberton."

"Yes," he said. "And I can't apply to Mrs.

Pemberton solely on the basis of Mr. Wheelwright's claims.''

''I believe him . . . liar that he is.''

''I believe him as well,'' Donne said. ''But I would want to go to a widow with something more.''

''What more?''

''That is the point. There are things that have to be found out, you see, corroborative things. This is the way it happens—you want evidence of what you already know. According to Wheelwright, the child was in a full-sized coffin, which suggests . . . a deception was intended. But we can't rely on what he thought he saw. He was drunk and the light was bad. We still have to make sure a mistake was not made by the cemetery. I need to see their calendar of interments from that year. That there was not some misidentification . . . and that two bodies brought for burial on the same day were not placed in the wrong graves.''

''That's hardly likely.''

''Systematically, step by step, Mr. McIlvaine. In a disciplined manner . . . beginning with the hardly likely. I need to see the death certificate for Mr. Pemberton. It will have a doctor's signature. I would like the chance to speak with the doctor. . . . Also, in the Hall of Records, we want to go through the registries of deeds and contracts . . . to see what transactions were undertaken by Mr. Pemberton in the year, say, preceding his listed date of death . . . and so on.''

"Can you do these things without attracting the dogs?"

"I think so."

We were talking hunched over a table, talking softly, conspirators ourselves. "Christ, you know what the newspaper business is. I want your assurance . . . I brought you into this . . . in the assumption you'd protect my interests."

"I understand," he said with a nod.

"This is an exclusive," I told him. "This is mine—there wouldn't be a story if I hadn't found it."

"Exactly so."

"And if the moment approaches when you can't keep it exclusively mine . . . you give me fair warning."

"Agreed," he said.

My blood was up, but so was Donne's. He'd gotten a new light in those mournful eyes, there was a blotch of color on those ascetic cheekbones. The fact of the matter was that I concurred with his plan of investigation and may have protested as I did because it was something he expected of me. I was saying what he thought a journalist would say. In Edmund Donne's thoughtful company you found yourself wanting to be what he expected you to be. Isn't that what happened to Harry Wheelwright? Donne had expected him to tell what he knew and so he had.

At this point I believed that, someday, I would have to apologize to Wheelwright. I understood about the arrogance of this generation of young men . . . that they kept to themselves, as a separate community of the Sane, with neighbors usually their own age to be recognized by sight walking on the same street. But Martin's behavior had struck to the heart of that pretense; he'd put them under the same suspicion as the rest of mankind.

So I felt sympathy for the artist. And gratitude, though that I would never express. His story was overwhelming. But truly, if you think about it, the precise way to lose my exclusive was to run it prematurely . . . in imitation of Martin Pemberton's own heedlessness. As a member of the journalistic profession Martin knew he could have applied the same careful methods Donne was now advocating. Instead, he'd leapt over all of them and—desperately, awesomely—had dug up a grave at night. But if I followed, I would end up standing in that grave . . . and every reporter in town would be in there with me. . . .

No, Martin had sworn his friend to secrecy, and the secret would remain intact with us, with Donne and me. I wanted my freelance and my story . . . the one I secretly coveted . . . the writing of which might transcend reporting. Harry's confession was, among other things, the rendering of an inspired pursuit. To me it was—to use Donne's word—corroborative. It was evidence of what I already knew. My freelance was alive . . . but had simply disappeared now into that region where the fact of people's existence, or nonexistence, was . . . inconclusive. He was there . . . together with his father . . . and with his father's factotum 'Tace Simmons, and perhaps as well with the doctor who was supposed to have treated Augustus in his last illness, that shadow doctor, Sartorius.

I was now certain I knew as much as Martin Pemberton knew when he disappeared. It seemed to me that I could continue my own pursuit in keeping with the magnitude of his. Certainly I had not given Donne any assurances that I wouldn't. When I resumed work at the *Telegram*—this must have been not more than a day or two after seeing Wheelwright in his studio—I immediately sent off a wire to our political reporter in Albany and asked him, in a quiet moment—perhaps when the esteemed legislators of New York State, exhausted from the effort of passing Mr. Tweed's bills, had recessed for some recreative poker—to take a trip up to Saranac Lake . . . for a possible series we were thinking of doing on the achievements of modern American medicine. I wanted the names of the sanitaria, their physicians, the kinds of medicine they practiced, and so on.

He mailed his notes a few days later: There were two small sanitaria for consumptives. Tuberculosis was the sole disease treated. The leading doctor of the better institution was a Dr. Edward Trudeau,

himself a consumptive, who had discovered the salutary effects of the Adirondacks' mountain air when
he had come up there one winter. The list of names
of the attending physicians did not include a Dr.
Sartorius.

In no way was I surprised, having reasoned that
whatever Augustus Pemberton told his wife would
be a lie. But the name Sartorius was unusual . . . and
if it was fabricated, it was not by Pemberton or his
business manager, neither of whom had the wits to
fabricate so . . . specifically.

There were always freelances sitting about on
the bench outside my office hoping for assignments.
I sent one of them over to the New York Medical Society Library on Nassau Street to check the name
Sartorius in the registry of New York physicians. It
was not listed.

I had staked out my claim to a story, in effect
negotiating with the police for my rights in it . . . but,
after all, how phantom it was . . . no more than a hope
for words on a page . . . insubstantial words . . . phantom names . . . its truth and actuality no more than
degrees of phantomness in the mind of another
phantom.

Yet I will tell you now about the seven columns
of the newspaper. In those days we ran stories
straight down, side by side, a head, subheads, and
story. If you had a major story you ran it to the bottom of column one and took as much of the next col-

umn as you needed. It was a vertical paper, no heads shooting across the page, no double-width columns, and few illustrations. . . . It was a paper of seven columns of words, each column supporting its weight of life, holding up, word by word, another version of its brazen . . . terrors. The first papers were commercial sheets, mercantile advices, with cotton prices and ship sailings—sheets you could serve on a dinner plate. Now we ran off eight pages of seven columns, and only if you stretched your arms wide could you hold the paper taut to its full width. And we had readers of the city accustomed to this . . . who scanned our columns the instant they got them, hot from the hands of the newsboy . . . as if our stories were projections of the multiple souls of a man . . . and no meaning was possible from any one column without the sense of all of them in . . . simultaneous descent . . . our life of brazen terrors spending itself across seven word-packed columns of simultaneous descent . . . offered from children's hands for a penny or two.

So in this news story, now, my, this . . . yesterday's news . . . I warn you, the sense is not in the linear column but in all of them together. Of course I would not find any Dr. Sartorius in the registry of doctors . . . any more than I had found Eustace Simmons in the waterfront saloons . . . or Martin Pemberton up the stairs in his room in Greene Street. Linear thinking would not find them. But then one morning, looking through the police blotter for items

I would print, I read that the body of a Clarence "Knucks" Geary, age unknown, had been found floating in the river off the pier at South Street—unless I was mistaken, the same hoodlum I had seen in Donne's office—and I was diverted for the second time, by this brainlessly amoral charmer, from what I had rather been thinking about.

I suppose it was that same afternoon that I stood with Donne in the Dead House on First Avenue, a regular venue of his, and fast becoming one of mine, and looked down at the body of that poor sod Knucks: The boyish blue eyes were opaque. Circles of coagulated blood outlined the nostrils of his flattened boxer's nose. His lips were curled back over his teeth, as if he had attempted a smile at the moment of death. Donne held the head up by the hair under the spray of water. The neck had been broken.

"You see its girth?" Donne said. "And look at his chest, these shoulders. He's built like a bull. Even catching him unaware . . . You know the strength someone would need to break a neck like this?"

I had not expected Edmund Donne to be so terribly upset. But he was—he was distraught, though this was only measurable as a more grim . . . impassivity. He laid the head back down with what I thought was undue respect, an inappropriate gentleness. What odd affections grow up in this city . . . like the weeds that spring from cracks in the pavement. Knucks's death was the only matter he would talk about. I waited for the moment when he would return to our mutual concern, but it didn't come. I was disappointed to see Donne's . . . vulnerability. He could only think of the thug, for whose death he felt responsible. And whatever else was on his mind, he went about immediately trying to find the possible meaning or justice from the thing . . . as if this pathetic hoodlum had been the most important personage in the city.

For my part I was stymied by not having gotten any further on my own—after Harry's revelations I thought the truth would tumble out. I found myself irritated by how easily Donne had been diverted from our search. I didn't appreciate that he was like a walking newspaper who could carry the stories simultaneously in their parallel descents. He said, without giving me the reason, that he needed to speak to all the newsboys he could find. I remember how startled I was. Shocked into an impassivity of my own, I took him and his subaltern sergeant to Spruce Street, to Buttercake Dick's, where the newsboys went for their supper at the end of a night's work.

Dick's was the newsboys' Atheneum, a cellar hole, down three steps. It was fitted out with plank tables and benches. Up front was the counter where a boy bought his mug of coffee and one of Dick's blackened scones, split, and stuffed with a gob of butter. Earlier it had started to rain in the city. The cellar with its low ceiling stank of kerosene and rancid butter and the wet clothes of thirty or forty unwashed boys.

Donne and I sat just inside the door . . . the sergeant went to the middle of the room and spoke. The boys had fallen silent, like schoolchildren in the presence of the principal. They stopped eating as they listened to a matter whose seriousness did not have to be proven to them.

They had known Knucks Geary, just as they knew every other adult who muscled in on them. Apparently, one of Knucks's schemes in his declining years involved working for the newspaper carriers, or jobbers. I hadn't known this, Donne hadn't told me . . . though it particularly implicated my profession. Knucks threw the baled papers off the horse cart at a boy's corner, or stood dispensing copies at the trucking platform of the press buildings. He was the middleman's middleman. The carriers paid a dollar seventy-five a hundred and charged the boys two dollars. Knucks added a surcharge for Knucks. So this professed moralist of the plight of street children had, during certain hours of the working day, been stealing from them.

"Rot in 'ell," one of the boys said. "I'm glad he got hisself croaked."

"Now, now," the sergeant called out.

" 'E beat you, Philly?"

"I'll say . . . Knucks bastard."

"Me too, Sergeant. If'n you doan pay off, 'e goes'n slams yer."

There was a general agreement, the boys all talking at once.

The sergeant shouted for order. "Never mind that. Worse for you if the sharp who killed him takes his place. Now we're talking about yesterday's paper. Speak up if you saw Knucks Geary and what time that was."

I was not comfortable here, at the most shameful point of the newspaper business. New Yorkers got rousing good fun out of their newsboys, but looking at them in this yellow light, as yellow as the butter in the scones, I saw only undersized beings on whose faces were etched the lines and shadows of serfdom. God knows where they slept nights.

Slowly, reluctantly, they began to testify. A boy would look at his mates and get some sort of confirming glance and then he would rise and speak his piece. "I got me papers four o'clock by the Stewart's Dry Goods same as always." Or "He dropped me mine by Broad Street at the Stock'xchange." As more of them spoke up I was able to see in my mind a street map of Knucks's last journey: Starting from Printing House Square, he went downtown along Broadway, over to Wall Street, and then east to the river, Fulton and South streets.

A small, weakish boy rose and said he saw Knucks hop off the rear of the carrier's dray in front of the Black Horse Tavern. It was dark by then, the streetlamp was lit.

The boy sat. The sergeant looked around. No one else spoke. The room was silent. Though the questions had come from the sergeant, it was Donne's intelligence behind them. Donne rose from his chair. ''Thank you, lads,'' he said. ''You will all have another coffee and cake on the Municipals.'' And he laid two dollars on the counter. Then we were off to the Black Horse.

I prided myself on my knowledge of the city's saloons but I did not know this one. Donne led us right there. It was on Water Street. There was little about the city he didn't know . . . perhaps because he was so estranged from its normal life. He'd cultivated his skills in the face of bitter lifelong employment . . . perhaps that accounted for it . . . the knowledge that comes with estrangement. God help me, I could not spend ten minutes trekking after him without feeling myself estranged too, as if this roaring, teeming city thrumming with the steam pistons and cog wheels and rotating belts of a million industrial purposes was an exotic and totally inexplicable culture.

The Black Horse was an old clapboard house from the Dutch days, with a gable and shuttered windows. When they'd made a tavern out of it, an entrance door had been cut athwart the corner and introduced with a stone step so as to be visible from both Water and South streets. The sergeant waited outside while Donne and I went in.

It was a quiet, dark, dead place, with the harsh excoriating smell of whiskey rising like a vapor from the creaking floorboards. A few of the regulars sat drinking. We sat at a table and I took the opportunity to have a dram or two. Donne left his shot untouched in front of him. He was oblivious of the glances the barkeep and the patrons sent his way. He was lost in thought. He did not seem to be looking for anything, he made no attempt to ask any questions. I respected his silence, granting it a specific purpose which, as it turned out, he did not have. He was merely waiting, as policemen do . . . for what, he didn't know, except, as he would tell me much later, he would know it when he saw it.

And then a child came in the door, a girl of six or seven, with a basket of wilted flowers . . . a scrawny little thing. She bowed her head in shyness or abject fear, as if she could only come toward us by pretending not to mean anything by it. Her face was smeared with dirt, she had the slack lower lip of the slow-witted, her lightish hair was lank, her smock torn, and her overlarge shoes were clearly from the trash heap. She came right up to us and in the tiniest of voices asked Donne if he would buy a flower. All at once the barkeep was shouting and coming round from the bar. ''Here you, Rosie, I toldjer doan come in here! I toldjer doan let me catch you in here. Did-

din you cause enough trouble! I'll teach you to listen—'' Or words to that effect. The child made no
attempt to run, but cringed, raising one shoulder and
tucking her head behind it, and screwing her eyes
tight in anticipation of a blow. Donne of course held
up his hand to stay the man. He spoke softly to the
child. He asked her to sit down and gently and with
great deliberation withdrew from the basket three of
the least-fresh flowers. I don't know what they
were—they were the flowers of penury, the drooping
faded flowers of the land of orphans. ''I would like
to buy these, Rosie, if you please,'' he said. He
placed some coins in the small palm.

And then Donne looked up at the hapless barkeep, who was standing behind the child, red in the
face, and clutching fitfully at his apron. ''And what
trouble did she cause, bartender? What sort of trouble can a child bring to the Black Horse?''

Donne called the sergeant in and they took the
barkeep into a back room for their interrogation. A
few minutes later the sergeant left the Black Horse.
Donne had asked the little girl to stay with me. She
was sitting across the table and keeping her eyes
averted and swinging her foot. I chafed at being kept
out of things. Apparently, Donne could confide in
me one moment and exclude me the next. We could
be associates in one enterprise, and police and press
in another. I was aware at this point of no more than
. . . shadows, my own misgivings, a certain unsettled

feeling of . . . ominousness. But I was angry too that Donne could become so obsessive, or feel so guilty, about the death of a worthless thug. This is a shame-faced admission of sorts for the city editor of the *Telegram.* I heard a horse and carriage stop outside. I was not prepared to see the sergeant come in escort-ing, of all people, Harry Wheelwright. The artist was glum, surly, barely civil. "You again, McIlvaine!" he said. "I suppose I've you to thank for the cap-tain's interest in art." His evening clothes were askew. But as a confessed desecrator of graves he perhaps felt a certain obligation to the man he'd con-fessed to. Or was it that when you come clean, you're committed, inescapably, to redemption?

Donne had had the inspired idea of having Wheelwright draw a pencil sketch, from the bar-keep's description, of the man who'd fought Knucks Geary. It was remarkable to see. Harry asking the precise questions, by way of clarification, only a trained artist would ask . . . and then adding more details from the little girl. . . . As we all stood looking over his shoulder, he drew and erased and redrew for their recognition, and composed from the combined words, what we would not know until much later was an astonishingly accurate portrait . . . of the driver of the white omnibus . . . with its complement of old men in black . . . that Martin Pemberton had twice seen riding through the streets of Manhattan.

So we were on my freelance's case after all.

Not, I emphasize, that we consciously knew it at the time. We did not look at the sketch and know it was Dr. Sartorius's driver and all-around handyman, Wrangel. We were looking at a sketch of the stolid, shaven-headed killer of Knucks Geary. But I was unaccountably . . . elated. It had been a good night's work. Donne was actually smiling. He bought a round of drinks, and tea for the child, and congratulated Harry, who smiled sheepishly for his earlier bad humor and bought a round in turn, and placed his top hat on the head of the little flower girl . . . there in the Black Horse Tavern.

Fifteen

I'M fairly sure . . . I make the claim . . . Donne was the inventor of description-based portraiture for police purposes. Of course the idea of publishing these so-called composite portraits in newspapers came later . . . and was not Donne's. He stubbornly insisted on police work as a profession, if not a calling, and would not think of advertising for the public's help to apprehend a criminal—in effect deputizing the population of New York. You should remember that in this time we all held constantly in our minds images of the ragged western edges of civilization. Out there, where Mr. Greeley of the *Tribune* was urging all young men to go, the law was anyone's to devise, ad hoc, as circumstances required. In New York, by contrast, it should be demonstrated to be something like a civil religion . . . at least, as I interpret the priestly mind of Edmund Donne.

So the use of that sketch would be for his use alone, or his trusted sergeant, or one or another of the very few colleagues in the Municipals he could rely on, as they patiently made their way into every depraved precinct of the city's depths to find the strongman to match it.

But I realize now I may be giving you a false idea of Dr. Sartorius . . . whom you know so far only as a name. I'm concerned that you should not have your first impression of him as a tactician . . . who had made a mistake. Sartorius mentioned his requirements and left it up to others to fulfill them . . . on the model, I suppose, of God giving free will to the human race. It was a measure of the degree of loyalty this doctor inspired that everyone in his employ was free to create what was needed to serve him. The driver of the omnibus and all-around handyman of the place . . . or the cooks, the nurses . . . the members of the board . . . and his hospital—if you want to call it that—administrator, Eustace Simmons, formerly in the employ of Martin's father as slave-trade expediter . . . all of them lived and worked with the relish of free people.

I withhold here the circumstances of our first sight of Sartorius. I want to keep to the chronology of things but at the same time to make their pattern sensible, which means disrupting the chronology. After all, there is a difference between living in some kind of day-to-day crawl through chaos, where there is no hierarchy to your thoughts, but a raucous equality of them, and knowing in advance the whole conclusive order . . . which makes narration . . . suspect. I want you roughly in the same suspension we were in, as family and friends and counselors of the family, who understood this as a Pemberton matter, when in fact it was far more than that.

The first actual details we had of this doctor, more than the sound of his name, came from the practitioner it was said he had replaced—Dr. Mott, Thadeus Mott. What happened is that Sarah Pemberton, acting upon Captain Donne's request, wrote to Dr. Mott and asked him if he would provide her with his records of her late husband's medical history. Another example of Donne's love of documentation. . . . I don't know how much she confided of her lamentable circumstances, but Dr. Mott, a gentleman of the old school, replied with a fair copy by mail . . . and so we had a look at Augustus Pemberton's insides.

Until the last year of life he had suffered only from the normal variety of ailments of a man his age, including a moderate hearing loss, gout, prostatitis, and occasional mild pulmonary insufficiency. Then, a few months before he took to his bed at Ravenwood, he visited Dr. Mott's office in Manhattan with a complaint of fainting spells and loss of vigor. The preliminary diagnosis was anemia. Dr. Mott wanted to put him in the hospital for observation. Augustus refused. So this was somewhat different from what Sarah Pemberton had understood. Her husband knew he was ill prior to his collapse at Ravenwood. What was not different was the old man's reaction, on both occasions, to Mott's diagnosis. Mott's final words were that on the date he visited Ravenwood, he found Pemberton in the terminal stages of a virulent anemia, for which medical practice had only palliative treatment. I use the word *virulent,* but it was a more specific term . . . some form of irreversible anemia that led to death, usually in under six months.

Now it turned out that the disparity between Mott's account and Sarah Pemberton's recollections was of no significance. The old man had simply hidden something else from his wife. But it did lead Donne to call upon the doctor for the purpose of clarification. I went along . . . and when Donne introduced Sartorius's name into the conversation Dr. Mott said: "I am not surprised that he would take on a terminal case . . . probably with all sorts of arrogant expectations."

My heart skipped a beat. I glanced at Donne, who showed no emotion, but said, mildly, "Are you saying, Doctor, this Sartorius is a quack?"

"Oh no, not at all. He's an excellent physician."

I said: "His name isn't in the registry of the New York Medical Association."

"There is no rule that a doctor must be a member. The majority find it . . . meaningful . . . collegial . . . to join. It's a worthy organization. Another credential, without question, but also good for medicine as a whole. We have conferences, symposia, we share our knowledge. But Sartorius had no regard for any of that.''

''Where is his practice?''

''I've no idea. I haven't seen or heard from him in many years . . . though if he were still in Manhattan I think I would know.''

Dr. Mott was a distinguished member of his profession. He was a handsome man, still trim despite his age—I would say he was close to seventy at this time—with dark gray hair and mustaches, and a Phi Beta Kappa key drooping across his vest. He wore a pince-nez, through which he regarded each of us in turn with the same thoughtful gaze he must have turned on his patients. We had called on him in his home on Washington Place.

Donne asked him when he had known Sartorius.

''He served on the Sanitary Commission of the Metropolitan Board of Health, of which I was chairman. This would have been in 1866. . . . The commission anticipated a major cholera epidemic that summer. We cleaned up the slums, we changed the manner of garbage collection and put through measures to discourage contaminations of the public water supply. We prevented a major outbreak . . . like the one of 1849. I'm not sure I understand why this is a police matter,'' he said.

Donne cleared his throat. ''Mrs. Pemberton is burdened with some estate problems . . . in which the municipal government figures. We're documenting what we can, by way of a legal resolution.''

''I see.'' He turned to me. ''And does the press usually sit in on such matters, Mr. McIlvaine?''

''I'm here as Mrs. Pemberton's friend and adviser,'' I said. ''It's entirely personal.''

For a moment I felt measured in the doctor's scales. I modeled my impassivity on Donne's and held my breath. Then Dr. Mott leaned back in his chair. ''We still don't know the cause of cholera, although clearly the poison spreads through the diarrheal and vomitous discharges of infected persons. But the question of contagion . . . Well, there are two theories—a theory of zymotic infection, that is, that the disease spreads through an atmospheric miasma of poisonous matter . . . or a theory that a microscopic animal organism, called a germ, lives inside the body fluids. Dr. Sartorius was an exponent of the germ theory, on the grounds that only something animate can reproduce itself without end, which it would be required to do to generate an epidemic illness. The choleric poison seems certainly to have this capacity. . . . Since those days, his point of view would seem to be gaining authority, especially from the fermentation experiments of Mr. Pasteur, in France, and new rumors of the isolation by Dr. Koch in Germany of a cholera vibrio. But in all his ideas, Dr. Sartorius exhibited . . . well, a terrible intolerance for opposing points of view. He was rude in our meetings. He was generally scornful of the medical community, often mocking us as a cupping-and-leeching fraternity, even though the heroic procedures are no longer seriously maintained by most of us. . . . I don't customarily talk about a colleague in this way. . . . But I am not questioning his competence. He was arrogant, cold, and, needless to say, quite unpopular with his brother physicians. Yet we would never put social quarantine on a man so brilliant, no matter how unfeeling as a person, in hopes of making a decent Christian of him. He withdrew from us, not we from him. I have to think with pity of his patients . . . assuming he still practices. He was the kind of doctor who didn't care what he treated, a man or a cow, and hadn't a trace of the gift for the soothing word, the comforting assurance, that patients need from us as much as our medications. I say all this in confidence, of course. If you do find him, he'll probably refuse to see you.''

I remember, after that, walking down Broadway with Donne in the late afternoon heat. The air seemed suspended, unmoving, with a specific attar projected by each shop, store, restaurant, or saloon. Thus we walked through invisible realms of coffee, baked goods, leather, cosmetics, roasting beef, and beer . . . at which point, on no scientific authority whatsoever, I was willing to endorse the miasma theory of zymotic infection. We were both peculiarly elated. I found myself amused by the stick-legged glide of Donne's walk. His shadow was longer than anyone else's. It was the late afternoon, visible columns of sun crossing Broadway at the intersections. The cross streets, lacking traffic, were corridors of sun. . . . I could see the air, in cinders, sifting through the filigree of fire escapes and telegraph wires. Ladies, laden with their packages, were pouring out of the stores, the doormen of the hotels were blowing their whistles for the hackney cabs, the city was beginning its turn toward evening. We walked among all manner of men . . . striding, shuffling, limping, begging, ogling the ladies, telling stories, listening to stories, clasping their hands in moments of overwhelming piety. A legless Negro on his wheeled board pushed rudely through legs. . . . A man dressed as Uncle Sam gave candy to children. . . . A long-haired millenarian moved slowly among the shoppers, the gospel of the day printed in chalk on his sandwich board. . . . The horsecars humming, the stages clopping along . . . In my elation over this new knowledge of this arrogant doctor, this cold scientist impatient with the ordinary men of his profession, I looked at the world around me with affection, I was filled with an uncharacteristic love for my city, I thought of it as my city, and lamented my missing freelance, that his Broadway was not this one, but a concourse for a white omnibus of ghosts.

I suppose this was the thrill of pursuit, though I couldn't have known it. It is a kind of cold, selfish feeling. . . . You hold in abeyance all thoughts of suffering. The name Sartorius is Latin, of course, but it comes out of Germany. I learned that upstairs, on the compositors' floor at the *Telegram*. The compositors knew everything. They were older than the reporters, and remembered the early days, when they collected the news as well as set it in type, and so had nothing but scorn for the new profession of journalism. They drove me mad by freely editing what we sent up, but when I wanted to know something, it was to the compositors I went. And so I was instructed that as the bourgeois class arose in the German Middle Ages, tradespeople who wanted to elevate themselves socially took the Latin forms of their names. The miller became Molitor, the pastor became Pastorius, and the tailor became Sartorius.

I reasoned then that our Latinated German doctor could have come over in the great immigrations after the failed democratic revolutions of 1848. His medical education was European, which could explain, at least in part, his wish not to associate with American-trained doctors. And if he was a 'forty-eighter he might have joined the Union army, as so many of them did.

You know Washington. . . . By the time the U.S. Army Medical Corps replied to our inquiries their information was of course of no practical use. . . . But it does allow me to begin here to trace the arc of a vaulting soul. When Dr. Wrede Sartorius took his examination for the medical corps in 1861 he posted first among the candidates. He was commissioned first lieutenant and assistant surgeon and attached to the Eleventh Infantry Regiment in the Second Division of the Army of the Potomac under General Hooker. These were the people who fought at Chancellorsville, Gettysburg, the Wilderness, Spottsylvania, and Cold Harbor.

His army service was spectacular. Commendation after commendation. He operated in field hospitals under enemy fire. His innovations in surgical procedure were incorporated into the manual of the Army Medical Corps. I don't remember all the details, but he became famous throughout the army. He could amputate a leg in nine seconds, an arm in six, and it sounds ghastly now but his skill and speed—especially when anesthetics weren't available—earned him the gratitude of hundreds of soldiers. He apparently invented procedures—excisions, exsections, of the wrist, the ankle, the shoulder—that are still followed today. His skill in treating head wounds brought him into demand as a consultant to other surgeons. Some of his ideas that were resisted by his superiors were later adopted as evidence bore him out. . . . All sorts of things . . . In those days they used collodion dressings. He said no—the wounds should be exposed to open air, even rain. He used creosote solution and later carbolic acid for asepsis . . . before anybody else. He designed a new kind of hypodermic syringe. He insisted, for postoperative therapies, on fresh food and daily replacement of hay pallets . . . which sounds obvious now, but he had to buck the whole medical bureaucracy to get these things. When he resigned his commission in 1865 he was a full colonel and surgeon. He was brilliant and masterful and brave. It's important to understand this. . . . Among other things we are speaking of the noble lineaments of the grotesque. I am not interested in sentimentalizing Dr. Wrede Sartorius's career as a personal tragedy.

Sixteen

E ARLY that September, Edmund Donne, with the report of the official exhumation in his breast pocket, invited Sarah Pemberton for a stroll around the holding reservoir. It happened to have been a lovely warm day . . . one of those autumn days in New York that are what the summer should have been. . . . There is a sort of stillness to such days, as there is on water between tides, and the light of the sun angles in to make every edifice—every stone and brick and window—intensely, meaningfully vivid. Donne had prepared carefully for the occasion but the weather was his good luck. It was just past four in the afternoon. Noah Pemberton, a new student in public school, had been brought home by his mother at three. . . . Donne arrived at Thirty-eighth Street with a beautiful model boat of polished mahogany and presented it to the boy. It was rigged as a sloop with linen sails and a swinging boom, brass capstans, and a spoked helm that really worked the rudder—a considerable boat that must have set him back a fair sum. Noah held it in both his arms as they all walked to the reservoir.

Donne had asked us to arrive at the house by five in order to be there before they returned—Dr. Grimshaw, Emily Tisdale, and myself—for this inverted . . . wake. He had a few days before on an earlier visit, in uniform, spoken to the servants. In the absence of Lavinia Thornhill—who'd gone abroad—they might have been emboldened to represent her interests as they saw fit . . . except that they were made to understand Mrs. Pemberton and her son were now under the protection of the Municipal Police, which in a manner of speaking was true.

The fact is . . . that in the course of the two or three conferences Donne had had with Sarah Pemberton, as well as a more or less daily correspondence . . . they had become alerted to each other with that peculiar sort of attention characteristic of matched pairs, whether of birds or grazing animals or people. For my part, I long ago became content to live alone with my feelings and judgments . . . but I recognize that life shifts as desires are contained and released . . . and that situations do not remain stable. I am not sure I was entirely aware of what had developed between them before this day I speak of . . . but when they returned from the reservoir and we three were there waiting . . . and there was a tea in the English style ready to be served . . . it was as clear to me as if I had read a headline in the paper.

Many years later, over dinner, Noah Pemberton suggested to me that he thought his mother and Captain Donne had known each other earlier in their lives . . . that perhaps Donne was even his father's rival for her hand in marriage—the unequal rival, if that was so, since he had no fortune. This was on the basis of a remark or two Noah had overheard of their conversation that day at the reservoir: '' 'Now both of them are missing, Mrs. Pemberton . . . and time has moved backward to turn you into the impoverished girl you were, and the fellow with his head in the stars is again blessed to be sitting by your side,' '' or embarrassing words to that effect. But I am not convinced. By his own description, Noah's state of mind that day was . . . beleaguered. Also, Donne's impassivity when I first came to him with the news of the Pemberton family's ordeal would have verged on the inhuman.

In any event, at the reservoir he showed the boy how to watch the puffs on the water to get the sense of the wind, and to set the sail and rudder according to the tack he wanted for her. ''Then,'' Noah told me, ''I got down on my belly and launched her with a gentle push. Oh, what an excitement that was! I'd often watched children sail their boats in the reservoir. Now I had my own and it was better than any of them. I ran along the embankment, following her, running around the great square to meet her where I thought she would make her landing. I saw she sailed swiftly before the wind and discovered that didn't please me as much as a tack into the wind or crosswise to it. I experimented, back and forth, and finally achieved the perfection of a slow but resolute sail that showed her mettle . . . how she could take water over her bow and still keep coming. I lay on my side in the sun on the embankment with my head propped in my hand and waited for her on her slow sure passage across this . . . ocean . . . of floating light . . . is how it seemed.

"Now you know through all of this . . . change of our circumstances," Noah said, "my child's innocence had acted as something of a governor on all my fears and hurts. What I understood without being able to express it in so many words was that we had dropped down in class. We were living on the charity of my aunt, an elderly woman with a wig, who had no taste for children. At school, though I was better dressed than most of my classmates, I stood in the same lines and was pushed and shoved about with a . . . breezy evenhandedness. I realized soon enough that in a class of forty children I would not be recognized by my teacher for the charm of my mind. . . . I'd been instructed at Ravenwood by tutors whose constant praise and sheer pedagogical delight in my achievements were tributes to my father's wealth. But to tell the truth I was not cowed by public school and in fact was . . . livened by it. . . . I developed a keenness for the boisterous ways of public school children . . . though I didn't confide this to my mother. She took me there each morning, to Primary

School Number Sixteen . . . and met me at the entrance every afternoon to see me home. She worried about the harm that might come to me from being with the other children. She distrusted the city and everything about it.

"At any rate, as I watched my marvelous ship of the ocean, my mother and Captain Donne sat talking on the bench behind me. I had half heard bits and pieces of their conversation as they strolled after me and I ran back and forth to meet them and report what my ship was doing. Now, in my happy drowse, I heard more of it. I received it without thinking. . . . I believe it was the strangest, most frightening conversation I had ever heard. Only gradually did its meaning come through. I thought the sky was growing dark, though it was still quite blue. It was as if my child's joy was . . . draining out of the universe. I imagined the voices were from my ship, that it was my ship talking as it sailed toward me with a cargo of adult secrets and sickening mysteries. . . . I was learning that my father had impoverished us in a willful act. It had been deliberate. We were poor and without a home because he wanted it that way. And all his money he had put somewhere else—nobody knew where. The police captain had found this out. He had chosen to bring us this most awful news out in the sun, by the reservoir. Someone, a colonel, or a coroner, I was not sure who, had written a report. And that had the worst news of all. What was it? Was

my brother, Martin, dead? I could hardly breathe.
Were we all going to die? Had somebody killed my
father and my brother—who was now coming after
me?

"I sat up and looked back at my mother. She
was holding a sheet of paper on her lap and reading
from it, all bent over as if she had trouble seeing. Her
hand went up to comb her hair back away from her
eyes. I heard her gasp. She raised her head and gazed
at me. . . . My calm and beautiful mother had turned
ashen. The captain took her hand. 'Both men are
missing now, Sarah . . . and time has moved backward to turn you into the impoverished girl you were
. . . and the tall fellow with his head in the stars is
again blessed to be sitting by your side.' I looked for
my ship in the dazzle of watered light. I hoped it
had gone down. I was angry at the captain for bringing me a boat to play with as if I were a stupid
child. . . ."

My recollection is that when they returned,
Noah went immediately upstairs with his boat. In
Mrs. Thornhill's absence, Sarah felt free to draw
open the sitting-room curtains and raise the windows
and let some of the balm of the evening in. The tea
was served and we sat there like mourners . . . con-
triving to speak the comforting words of continuing
daily life to each other . . . though the bereaved had
just heard that her husband was among the living.

Donne had previously informed Emily Tisdale

and Dr. Grimshaw of the essentials: That Augustus Pemberton's death had apparently been feigned . . . for what purpose was not known. That he had been ill, seriously ill, but had made preparations that indicated the self-concern of someone . . . continuing. That Martin had in fact seen him and was believed to have sought a confrontation with him . . . and had disappeared—where or how nobody yet knew.

Donne's idea was that in the face of such revelations Sarah Pemberton would need the support and comfort of friends of the family . . . such despair, such despair, the family itself, its idea, its name, blasted from her. Yet she sat with her back straight and chin lifted, its implications of an . . . indolence erased by the pose, and with her hands folded upon her lap . . . her handsome face drained of all color, but otherwise undistorted by the contemplation of this . . . news. Of course, she had been toppling into it by degrees. She'd had an inkling when she'd agreed to the exhumation. She kept losing her husband . . . as he died, as he lived. Her impoverishment had been confirmed as a deliberate act. Her pale blue eyes glimmered but her beautiful full mouth did not tremble. She was a woman in the profound humiliation of an entirely fooled life. But she had the composure of a queen who's been informed that one of her armies has been defeated.

And what Edmund Donne hadn't considered . . . or relied on, in his diffidence . . . was his own importance to her as another kind of news in her mind. He could not stop looking at her. And while she spoke to all of us in her calm alto, it was clear from her glances . . . or in some of the hesitations of their conversation with each other . . . Well, what shall we call this common thing?—that aliveness to another person that comes unbidden, unsought, and is composed of the idea of a future? For if you think about it, we live mostly by habit . . . waiting . . . sustained by temporary pleasures . . . or curiosity . . . or diffuse hopeless energies . . . including malice . . . but not by that sustaining idea of a future that only comes humming in the secret aliveness that everyone can see except the two . . . idiotic . . . starers. So there was news of Sarah's future alongside the columns of her devastation.

I'm not suggesting this was a practical measure for her, relying on Donne . . . and on what he could do for her. If what Noah told me years later . . . if he was right, and they were reanimating their feelings for each other, hers would be bathed in mortification . . . atonement . . . a perception of her life with Augustus Pemberton as sweet justice for the wrong choice . . . for the love not heeded. If this was so, I think I would have seen it. On the other hand, there should have been an unbreachable difference in class between the wife of Augustus Pemberton—a van Luyden—and a policeman from the street. And there certainly was not. If the situation was as Noah de-

scribed it, could Donne have been destined for something other than a career as a municipal worker? Was
she the cause of his devotion to an unsuitable life? I
don't know . . . I don't know.

But it was, of course, the others who needed
comforting. In the midst of the small talk Emily Tisdale said to Donne, ''You still don't know where
Martin is—why aren't you looking for him?'' Before
he could reply she was on her feet, pacing back and
forth the way Martin paced when he thought aloud
. . . balling her hands into tiny fists and roving the
sitting room. ''They fought. He was disowned. It
was sad, it was unfortunate, but it happened. Why
wasn't that the end of it! Still, they go on! Who can
live—who is allowed to live—when these . . . unnatural things go on? Martin has such honor in him,''
she cried out in that appealing cracked voice.
''There's no telling what he could have done if not
for this awful pit . . . he's been trying to climb out of
all his life. Yes, it's like a pit he's fallen into. Where
is he, what has happened to him?''

Donne said: ''It's reasonable to assume he
would have sought out Eustace Simmons, Mr. Pemberton's . . . business associate.''

''Yes, well then, let us seek him out, this business associate.''

''Having been found once, Simmons cannot
easily be found again.''

''What is to be done! They are all . . . somewhere . . . aren't they? Living or dead? Find him! I don't care—God, please, let it be one or the other. . . . I can understand one or the other. I am ready to marry Martin or grieve for him. I am ready to go into mourning. Why can't they let me do . . . even that . . . this monstrous, monstrous family?''

By way of agreement, Sarah Pemberton said to the girl, ''And yet, it's so peculiar . . . I can't think even now that I'm not one of them,'' at which point Emily threw herself down beside her on the sofa and wept. Sarah held the girl to her bosom and looked over to Donne. ''We'll find Martin, won't we, Captain? I will not think I've offended my God so that he's designed in me some . . . declivity of soul . . . some pocket flaw in which calamities collect and collect.''

All this time the Reverend Grimshaw had said nothing. With a frown on his face and his arms folded, he'd sat staring at the floor. I didn't know what he'd been doing since I'd first seen him—counseling Sarah? . . . consoling Miss Tisdale?—but I felt at this moment the superiority of my own role insofar as I had brought Donne in and got the issues clarified . . . at least as far as this. I suppose it was an uncommon experience for a newspaperman, to feel for a moment more righteous than a minister.

But he spoke up now . . . fretfully, clearly disconcerted. ''This is beyond any Christian understanding. I admit I'm unable to understand it from my faith . . . which is a test of faith itself. As you know, Mrs. Pemberton, I had the greatest respect for your husband. He was my friend. A vestryman of St. James. I'm not claiming he lived a blameless life . . . but he loved you and he loved the son you gave him. I heard this from his own lips.''

The minister turned to Donne. ''Augustus was . . . rough-hewn . . . not always aware of the impact of his words . . . on gentler sensibilities. There's no question of that. I'm even willing to grant you a lack of clear moral criteria in the conduct of business . . . a tendency to keep his Christian soul here''— Grimshaw indicated a place in the air above his head—''and his business methods there,'' he said, indicating the floor. ''Let us grant that . . . he was like most men of his interests—investors, founders of business, captains of industry—complicated . . . contradictory . . . and capable of the full range of human feeling, from the noblest to the most repre-hensible. But this . . . conspiracy you suggest! That he has pretended to die merely to abandon his family and leave them destitute? . . . destitute . . . though for some reason or cause you cannot account for . . . I simply cannot reconcile this . . . paganism—I don't know what else to call it—with what I knew of Augustus Pemberton, for all his . . . Christian . . . imperfections.''

I wanted to leap in at this, but Donne raised his hand. He was seated, ridiculously, in one of Mrs.

Thornhill's needlepoint side chairs, his body folded up behind his vaulting knees. "We're not ascribing the motive to Mr. Pemberton . . . that he contrived his death to abandon his family."

"Then what is it you're doing, sir! What is the purpose of your . . . speculation?"

"It is hardly speculation, Reverend. In the Hall of Records a contract is registered showing that a year or so before Mr. Pemberton's final illness he mortgaged Ravenwood to a partnership of dealers in properties in the amount of a hundred and sixty-five thousand dollars. . . . We find also that he sold his seat on the Exchange and his interest in a Brazilian maritime firm, among his other interests. We have to conclude that after he knew he was seriously ill, Mr. Pemberton sought to liquidate his assets."

"Who are you to conclude anything, sir!" And to Sarah he said, "Why do I hear of such things from . . . policemen? Why has Mrs. Augustus Pemberton tainted herself with such associations. . . . The police and"—glancing at me—"the press, God help us all. My dear woman, is the loss of your home so bitter that you would not consider any recourse but the desecration of your husband's grave?"

"His grave," Donne said, "was not desecrated, since he was not in it. We desecrated someone else's grave."

Donne had said this matter-of-factly—he would do nothing else in the situation—but Grimshaw heard otherwise. ''So in your view as a functionary of the esteemed and brilliant church of the Municipals, Martin Pemberton is our prophet . . . and the shade of Augustus rides a city omnibus on Broadway!''

''Perhaps, Reverend, you would like to consider the circumstances all together, as I have,'' said Donne. ''Neither father nor son where they should be . . . one dead but not in his grave or certified dead in the public records . . . the other, a presumed lunatic, off chasing his phantom . . . the surviving family, heirs to a fortune that no longer exists . . . And tell me your interpretation.''

Emily had sat up at this and the two women, side by side, were reasonably composed as they waited—as we all waited—for Dr. Grimshaw's reply. In this moment I understood, as they must have, that Donne's researchers had provided an answer of a kind . . . that where, before, all had been chaos and bewilderment and hurt, now it was clear that something understandable . . . an act . . . had been committed . . . a deliberate act or series of acts . . . by which we could recompose the world, comfortingly, in categories of good and evil. And I felt the first stirrings of some communal perception . . . that the missing son and fiancé might be embarked on something heroic.

Grimshaw's small neat face was entirely, uniformly flushed under his thatch of silver hair. I imag-

ined I could see the little vessels of blood rushing up
to the skin like parishioners filling the pews. He
looked at each of us in turn. He was in this instant of
his anguish unnecessarily physical in my awareness.
I didn't like to see that occupational cross hiking itself up his vest with each sharp shallow breath. His
mouth was slightly open. He removed his spectacles
and massaged them with a handkerchief, and it was
as if he had taken all his clothes off. I would have
liked to suppose his bright blue eyes were an unalter-
able theological composition. He had believed himself the ceremonial authority on life and death. How
must it have felt . . . to be as much a victim as Sarah
and her son? To understand the depth of humiliation
. . . as if you had never understood Christ before?

He reset his glasses and returned his handkerchief to his pocket. In his light voice he said, ''I am
ordained to seek out suffering . . . and to embrace it
. . . to take on the burden and sink to my knees under
it. I will console and pray and absolve and celebrate
as a priest of Christ's church, where suffering comes
round as regularly as day and night. But this . . . this
tolls inside me as something cataclysmic. I am not
prepared. . . . I am not prepared. I feel the need to
pray to begin to understand, and to call upon God
. . . to let me hear the soft summons of Jesus Christ
somewhere from this . . . from this . . . this family of
Godless Pembertons''—here he raised his eyes to
Sarah—''that is so magnetically awry as to threaten

to destroy all of us who have circled about them . . . including the ministry.''

Of course he was wrong, the Reverend, in thinking this was only a Pemberton family matter. We were all wrong insofar as we thought these misfortunes were circumscribed in one . . . Godless family. I would not have extended myself now, at my advanced age, if this were just the odd newspaper tale I had for you . . . of aberrant family behavior. I ask you to believe—I will prove—that my freelance, finally, was only a reporter bringing the news, like the messenger in Elizabethan dramas . . . the carrier of essential information, all eyes upon him, delivering the dire news . . . but for all his gallant duty, only the messenger.

Our little gathering had turned out not quite as Donne intended. As a result he decided to make practical use of the occasion, and to hear once again Martin's descriptions of the white omnibus going by in the snowstorm on Forty-second Street . . . and north on Broadway in the rain. He had heard it all thirdhand . . . my version, which reported what Martin had told Emily and Charles Grimshaw. Now he questioned the Reverend and the girl directly. And so once more the stage rode by in snow, in rain, in all our minds, and by the time we'd adjourned, I was thinking not of Augustus Pemberton but of the other old men in that dark cabin with him.

This was something that Donne had been thinking and wondering about for some time. But to me it came as a revelation.

I will say here by way of addendum that from this day of his despair, Charles Grimshaw's rectorship of St. James took a turn for the better. I'm not sure it was the shock to his faith of his vestryman's empty grave . . . or if all those millenarian prophets parading past his empty church—Shakers and Adventists, Mormons and Millerites—had anything to do with it . . . but the pastor who cherished historical confirmations of biblical events stepped up to the pulpit the next Sunday and delivered a blazing sermon that was reported in several newspapers. I myself reported it for the *Telegram,* not that I intended to, having gone to St. James that morning in the luxurious state of mind we call suspicion. I had been wondering if Grimshaw knew more than he had let on of our haunting concern and I had wanted to have a leisurely look at him.

Quaint as it may seem, sermons in those days were considered newsworthy. The Monday papers were filled with them . . . substantial excerpts or even whole texts of representative sermons delivered from pulpits around town. The clergy were considered dignitaries of the city, and religious diction was assumed to be applicable to the public issues of the day. We had reformer churchmen like Reverend Parkhurst who were out to unseat the Tweed government, and well-known theatricians like the Reverend

Henry Ward Beecher, brother of Harriet Beecher Stowe, the author of *Uncle Tom's Cabin.* My own Charles Grimshaw was not so eminent, but what he said was picked up that day by a few of us . . . and brought some new faces to the following week's services . . . and thus began a run, as it were, of increasingly well-attended Sundays, the major attraction of which was the novelty of a pastor's conversion to his own Episcopal certitudes.

"From all sides are we assailed, my friends, from all sides . . . by natural scientists whose science is unnatural, by religious scholars whose scholarship is blasphemous—so that these learned, oh-so-learned, men close around us like a circle of pagan dancers around a missionary being prepared for the pot."

His voice still lacked resonance, but fire flashed from his pince-nez. I thought he rose a bit higher over his lectern, that perhaps he had made himself a platform of hymnals to stand on.

"For what do they tell us: that mankind, whom God gave dominion over the birds and beasts and the fish of the sea, is really only descended from them, so that the first ape stood up on the hind legs of a mammoth, and when he shed his hair, there stood Abraham and Isaac and, God forgive them, Jesus himself.

"Or, according to those scholars who look for corroborations of the Word of God in foreign tales

. . . or who analyze his style . . . that Moses is not the author of the Pentateuch . . . but several writers after, who added on, added on, each with his own version of the Word . . . until hundreds of years later, all was amended and revised by the ultimate author, R, the Redactor! No, my friends, not the Revelator, not the Revealer of all truth and being, not the Resurrected God of every breath that has ever been breathed . . . not the Reigning Creator of the Infinite Realm . . . but a mere redactor, a wretched bookworm who, with his dictionaries and etymologies, took upon himself the establishment of our religion. . . .

"My dear friends, it is so astonishing—we should all laugh heartily if these self-important . . . pagans did not get respectable hearings in our academies and divinity schools.

"But take heart . . . for even within their impious professions are scientists and scholars who, undaunted, claim the faith . . . and find in the latest scientific evidence only more of the glory of God. So this is our good news, this morning: In the first instance . . . that the story of God's creation of the universe in seven days, as is written in Genesis, is not disproven by the geologist's tabulation of rocks thousands of years in formation or the zoologist's dating of the ancient fossils in those rocks . . . because the Hebrew word for *day* does not define any particular length of time, and the creative days of God could have been separated by aeons of his thought . . . infinite thought from verse to verse. Thus, not in human chronology, but God's, came the burgeoning of his designs. . . . For can anyone imagine that everything we study, from the depths of the oceans to the constellated stars, in its chemical composition, in its taxonomy, and in its . . . evolution . . . is the happenstance of chaotic event? That it is not God plying his pen who draws us, in our dominion over all living creatures, out of the slime of the earth? So this is what our true natural science says, and to that we may say . . . Amen.

''And in the second instance, of our scholars of the Bible in the divinity schools, who are become literary stylists, and place their own false idol, their infamous Redactor, their anti-Christ, in his place . . . We may watch them, as their claims split into further claims, finding tales, discarding other tales, and burrowing their way back through the Greek, Aramaic, Sumerian, and Hebrew dialects . . . in their endless search for . . . authentication . . . and there will be a hundred of them tomorrow, and a thousand the day after, all babbling away in their learned tongues . . . that we will thunderously silence in our hymns of praise to the only Author of the only Book . . . and will pray for, unto our Lord, whom we entreat to have mercy upon us all . . . in the name of His only-begotten Son, Jesus Christ, who died for our sins. And to that we say . . . Amen.''

Seventeen

THOUGH sermons were respectfully published in the newspapers, though churches were numerous and spires were everywhere on the skyline, not Christ's but Tweed's image inhered in the shifting formation of clouds, or in the light of each season . . . as the presiding image of our sense of ourselves . . . the face of our time. It was the struggle, or ordeal, of some of us—not enough of us, apparently—to cast off that terrible collective self-regard of which he was the apotheosis. I could imagine him in private moments of physical gratification of all his appetites sitting up on Forty-third Street in his millionaire's mansion . . . a total triumphant success in all his thieving enterprises . . . and still affirm his essentially disembodied nature. I felt him as an awful presence riding lightly about our head and shoulders . . . or lodged in the roots of the jaw, behind the throat, as something vague but tenacious installed in us . . . the deity of our rampant extortions.

Not to try your patience, let me assure you that finally all the columns will be joined to be read across the page . . . like cuneiform carved across the

stele. I had summoned a freelance off the bench outside my office and assigned him to go through the
basement morgue and look for any stories about men
of wealth who had died penniless. Donne was doing
his own research. We hoped in our pursuit of the
truth to identify Augustus Pemberton's companion
riders . . . the lineaments of the . . . lodge, or brotherhood, the mortuary fellowship . . . of the white stage.
But as to their motives we had no more idea than
Martin had when they rode by him in the snow. God
knew where they were. I knew only that they would
not be found in their graves.

But even as our search for Martin Pemberton
continued . . . Well, I should remind you we were not
mathematicians working with pure numerical
thought. . . . We had jobs, duties. . . . We met our
responsibilities . . . which always appeared to us as
. . . diverse. And at least one of us was trying to live
with his affections.

A man named James O'Brien walked into my
office one day. His title was sheriff of New York
County. This was a lucrative office because the sheriff kept all the fees he collected. He'd been appointed, of course, by Boss Tweed. O'Brien was one
of the Ring . . . typically unlettered, crude, cunning,
with that kind of brute intelligence of the politician
. . . but with the additional righteousness conveyed
by his office, which allowed him a generally punitive
impulse in all his dealings. I knew that O'Brien had

done a couple of things to challenge Tweed's power in the Democratic party, and had failed . . . so when he arrived unannounced and sat down in front of me and wiped his bald head and lit his cigar, I closed my door to all the noise and distraction in the city room and sat behind my desk and asked what I could do for him.

Just at this time Tweed was beginning to chafe from the attacks on him by *Harper's Weekly* and its political cartoonist, Nast. Most of his constituents couldn't read and so he didn't care what was written about him. But a caricature of him as a fat money-bagger with his foot on the neck of Liberty had a kind of . . . illumination to it. *Harper's* also owned a book publishing company. . . . Their textbooks had suddenly been banned from the city schools. Tweed may have been irritated but he was more or less invulnerable because all the criticism was deduction or surmise. Nobody had any hard evidence. He controlled the whole of government, including the legal system, and he had the loyalty if not love of the *hoi polloi*. He sent foreigners just off the boat into his courtrooms and his judges instantly naturalized them into voting citizens. He had seventy-five percent of the opposition county Republicans on his payroll. His bribes were legion and nothing like evidence had ever been produced against him. He said one day to some reformers, "Well, what are you going to do about it?"

And now here was the moody, truculent Sheriff O'Brien, sitting in front of me. I was put in mind of the great Anglo-Saxon poem *Beowulf,* written to instruct young sachems. One of the most important of its primeval lessons is that, if you would hold power, you must share the booty. Tweed's was an ancient, savage politics, so who would know that lesson better? Yet here was this O'Brien, inexplicably scanted in Tweed's patronage . . . and he held in his lap a bundle wrapped in brown paper and tied with twine, which he claimed held the records, a copied-out set of ledgers, that showed the true extortionate dealings of the Ring—all of it duly recorded in neat columns . . . the incredible amounts stolen, and under what pretexts, and how they were divided. Migod.

"Why are you doing this?" I said to O'Brien.

"The son of a bitch welshed on me. Three hundred thousand simoleons. He won't pay it."

"For what?"

"My fair share. I warned him."

He was a righteous blackmailer, O'Brien. I had to wonder: Tweed had many ambitious, overreaching men to deal with—why had this one become a problem? The colossal success of his fraud, the completeness of it, the systematization of it, as big and smooth-working in its machinery as the Corliss steam engine, had impressed him into believing . . . not in his invulnerability—more than that. He must have begun to receive from his most private self-reflections . . . intimations of immortality. I can think of no other explanation for what he'd done—waving O'Brien off, giving him no satisfaction at all. That is just what you cannot do to a co-conspirator.

Sheriff O'Brien regaled me with unassuageable bitterness. He said he was looking for a newspaper that would publish the story the numbers told. I told him to leave his bundle with me. I told him I would study what he had, and if it was the truth, the *Telegram* would run it. You would not think from my matter-of-fact demeanor that I knew what I had just been given.

That night I sat at my desk reading the ledgers of the most brazen and colossal cabal in the history of the Republic. I will never forget that night. Can you imagine what it meant to a newspaper wretch to have it in black and white under his reading lamp? After all, what do we live for? Not wealth, certainly, not philosophical enlightenment . . . not for art, or love, and not in any hope of salvation, certainly. . . . We live for proof, sir, we live for the document in our hand. . . . The glory we seek is the glory of the Revelator. And here it was, all recorded in neat columns. I think I wept for joy—I felt as privileged as a scholar holding in his hands fragments of Mosaic scrolls, or a parchment of Homeric verse, or a Shakespeare folio.

Well, not to prolong the pain . . . You know, one reason I kept so many freelances out on the bench and had so few reporters on staff is that Tweed almost always got to the staffers. I had a man in Albany, covering the state legislature, who wrote favorably one day about a bill designed to make the monopoly of gas companies report their true earnings and reduce their prices . . . and the next day wrote about this bill as if it had been devised by European communists. Regulation of the gas companies had wide support in both houses, but in the same twenty-four-hour period in which my man changed his views, the Tweed people, who had paid him off, and most every other reporter up there, paid off the legislators. So I am not saying our press stood clean and shining apart from the ordinary life of the city. Tweed committed advertising to our pages—unnecessary, and very profitable, city advertising. I knew that, I knew all of it. . . . But I thought . . . I thought . . . this story was so monumental . . . the truth so overwhelming in its demands . . . and the condition of the city so precarious . . . that journalistic honor would prevail. But on instructions of our publisher, the editor in chief would not let me run the biggest story since the War of Secession. Let me compose myself a moment. . . . To this day the memory buffets my poor soul.

Not just the *Telegram*—paper after paper looked at the evidence and refused to print it. The eminent *Sun* under the eminent Richard Henry Dana carried the mayor's messages to the people . . . as

advertising. . . . They had a contract for city legal notices in eight-point type at a dollar a line. Either the
publishers needed Tweed, or they counted themselves his friends. Others were afraid of what he
would do to them—there were all sorts of reasons.

What would save American journalism from in-
famy would be the death of a member of the *Times*
board who was a partner in Tweed's printing firm.
This left the surviving director, George Jones, and
Louis Jennings, the editor, free to run the material.

As for me, I am a lifelong bachelor. I had no
wife and children to worry about. I thought about it a
day or so. . . . I had not been able to move my publisher, Mr. Landry. . . . I had gone rushing up to his
sanctum to protest . . . to appeal. He listened quietly
enough to my ranting and raving. Tweed's effect on
the city had been like a vampire's arterial suck. I saw
him in every seeping mound of garbage . . . in the
sewers emptying into the streets . . . in the moving
shadows at night of the rats in their furtive numbers
. . . in the plodding city wagons of people dead of the
diseases of filth. . . . I emptied my desk and left the
best job I'd ever had . . . took my hat and coat off
the rack and walked out of my city room.

But that is not to speak of here. After the accounts were published in the *Times* . . . that fall there
was a public rally at the Cooper Union on Astor
Place and a citizens' committee was formed that
brought a taxpayers' suit, and the Ring began to

crack. Connolly, the ring's comptroller, said he would cooperate, and a grand jury was formed to bring indictments.

All hell seemed to be breaking loose. The collapse of a system, even a system that subjugates them, unsettles folks, and there was an agitation all through the city, like a storm blowing this way and that, tearing up the store awnings, turning people around in the street, spooking the horses. Three banks that had Tweed on their boards went under. Dozens of small newspapers that had lived on his largesse ceased to publish. Businesses of all kinds closed their doors. Strangers were getting into fistfights, something like a deep bass hum was coming up through our feet, like the roaring down from the mountains of a flash flood, as if despite ourselves, we were going to have to face up to the truth, all of us who made up this town of calamitous life.

I would not say Donne was not diverted by the imminent doom of the Ring. But neither was he distracted. This was all anybody in the city could talk of, and he had to have been personally gratified—he had lived in a kind of professional slavery to this culture, and now it was crumbling. Yet he was not given to triumphing—that was not his nature, he did not make of all this an occasion to think of himself. What I did see in his face was an intensity, almost like feverishness, as he went through these same revealing account books, which I entrusted to him before I reluctantly turned them back. I remember thinking how odd it was of him when he said afterward, at dinner, that what he found meaningful was not the usually inflated sums warranted to this or that transaction, but the occasional entries that seemed legitimate in their accounting. The Ring's books recorded not only the transactions in which the city was the ostensible buyer of goods or services, but also those in which it was the seller, and in these cases very often of legal entitlements or charters it had no legal right to sell. How out of character, he said, to find an entry where a piece of legal paper was signed without apparent compensation.

"Like what?" I asked him.

"There is a newly founded orphanage, the Home for Little Wanderers, with an address up on Ninety-third Street by the river. Yet the ledger reveals that no money passed hands to expedite a charter."

I thought this was rather a peculiar observation in the context of a great scandal . . . and my own misfortune. But you see, Donne was taller than most men and so he had a better view of the lay of the land. In a day or two he'd found the charter document and certificate of incorporation in the Hall of Records. The Home for Little Wanderers was a nondenominational orphanage that was to be scientifically managed according to the latest child-raising principles. Mr. Tweed and the mayor and Comptroller Connolly were members of the board of trustees. Eustace Simmons was listed as director. Wrede Sartorius, M.D., was the attending physician.

Eighteen

A̲T this time, the city north of Seventy-second Street was no longer country, but not yet city either. The houses were few and far between. Whole blocks had been scraped clear and laid out with surveyor string, but nothing was on them. You would see two or three of the usual row houses with their granite stoops, and, after a gap, two more sharing a side wall, but none of them occupied. Here was a street set with paving stones that stopped at the edge of a pasture, there was a scaffolded half-risen apartment house through whose unframed windows you saw the sky . . . or a Beaux Arts mansion going up alongside a cluster of shanties with a pig and goats rooting about. And everywhere were great piles of brick, or stacks of lumber under tents of flapping canvas. Steam cranes stood in fields of grass and shrub. Somehow there were never any workers to be seen . . . as if, with a mind of its own, the city was building itself.

From Park Avenue and Ninety-third the unpaved road ran downhill in a gentle slope to the river. In the fields on either side pumpkins were scattered and trees were beginning to turn. The sounds of the city were distant, almost imperceptible. Donne and his men were encamped beneath a stand of yellowing weeping willow halfway between First and Second avenues. Their tunics were unbuttoned, they had canteens of water and lunchboxes, and their ac-cumulated refuse was held in a cardboard carton at the foot of the tree. They could not be seen from the riverside. The road went past them downhill, and where it leveled off was the stone mansion Home for Little Wanderers.

A police kiosk stood on the sidewalk by the front gate. Donne said, ''We have kiosks at the dip-lomatic missions. We have them in front of Mr. Van-derbilt's place . . . and at Tammany Hall. . . . These must be very important children.''

All together, out of the whole force of Munici-pals, Donne had managed to commandeer twelve or thirteen men who were loyal to him. Another contin-gent stood watch from a shed on Ninety-fourth, a block north of the mansion on First Avenue . . . and a third a block south.

But I didn't understand what they were doing—which was . . . apart from using their binoculars . . . nothing. I had joined them on the second day of their watch. Here and there in the field around us birds were scooting about in their dustbaths or hopping from brush to tree. High up over the river an undu-lant arrow of geese pointed south. I wondered if I had come all this distance to join a covey of birdwatchers. I suppose I must have said something to that effect.

"Whom shall we arrest?" Donne said.

"Everyone . . . whoever you find."

"So I'm to enter without a warrant?"

"Would any of their judges give you one?"

"What will the charge be?"

"What does it matter . . . as long as we can see what's going on in there that needs a police guard to keep people away."

"That is the way they would do it," Donne said quietly.

He handed me the binoculars. I saw the mansion shimmering in the magnification. It was a Romanesque structure of red stone trimmed in granite and with the turrets and small windows of an armory. The bottom half was obscured by a brick wall. A cast-iron gate gave on to a courtyard. It looked its part—a very substantial building, lending substance to those who lived there. It was an outpost of our advancing civilization . . . like all our other institutions out at the edges—poorhouses, asylums for fallen women, homes for the deaf and dumb.

Behind the Home for Little Wanderers the river surged powerfully southward toward the harbor, the color of silver. Perhaps I was only feeling the despair of the unemployed, but at this moment I . . . the deni-

zen of alleys, dead ends, and saloons three steps
down . . . the reporter who disdained the great national story of the West to make stories out of paving
stones pounded with horse droppings, and the street
birds picking out their meals there . . . a fellow whose
music was the cries of ragpickers, the din of the
organ grinders . . . who could watch the cat with
curved paw lift the lid of a garbage pail and feel that
was as much nature as he needed . . . I fervently
wished there were no buildings of any kind on this
island. I envisioned the first Dutch sailors giving up
on the place as a mosquito-infested swamp, and re-
turning in their longboats to their ships. . . .

It must have been about four that afternoon
when Donne told everyone to look sharp. I lifted my
glasses: The yard gate was open. Coming into the
street was a two-horse team harnessed to a white omnibus of the Municipal Transport Company. One of
Donne's men had run quickly to unhitch their own
team, which was off the road, behind the trees. Then
we were racing downhill in the police wagon and
Donne was leaning out the window and shouting,
''Don't stop them, don't stop them!'' I did not understand what was happening, but when we reached the
level avenue and caught up to the white stage there
was a battle going on. Donne's men at the corner of
First Avenue and Ninety-fourth Street had inter-
cepted the stage and were holding the rearing, snort-

ing horses by their bridles . . . and the man up on the box was laying out his whip over them . . . horses and police . . . whatever he could reach.

How can we recall sudden and violent action? I remember the sound those horses made in their fear and pain—it was such a human sound, brought up from their chests, as they turned to go forward and then were backed into the whip. We had now all joined the fray. One of Donne's men had fallen to the ground and was rolling desperately to get away from the hooves. A policeman climbing up to unseat the driver received a kick from his boot heel and fell to the street on his back. You have to understand, our police in those days did not routinely carry pistols or rifles, which were issued only for emergencies . . . riots and so on. They did carry nightsticks, which are considerable weapons, and these were being raised now against the driver's legs. But he was enormously strong, a man in a black suit and boots and a soft felt hat. The hat flew off to reveal a shaved head. Dust rose from the feet of horses and men. It was a beautiful warm sunny afternoon that seemed quickly to be filling with haze. I can recall the painted scene on the side of the stage, a Hudson River view with the Catskill Mountains beyond. Above the scene, in the windows, faces appeared and disappeared, faces that made no impression on me except that I noted the mouths were open and I seemed, after a delay, to relate them to the screams I heard coming from the inside. The police had stopped the stage and this melee had resulted. How odd. I have seen much street violence in my life. . . . I am not shocked by it, I'm made distant, reflective, and it always appears to me, finally, to be . . . inexplicable. So it was now. I can't even remember what I was doing in the midst of all of it. I can tell you what I saw but not what I did. Perhaps I did nothing, though I would like to be- lieve that in some way I was being helpful. I knew of course that this was the stage that Martin Pemberton had seen in the snow, and on Broadway in the rain, but it was such a solid piece of coachwork, all nicked and scratched and scraped with the heavy usage of route driving . . . an ordinary city stage, one of the dreary omnibuses of New York.

Donne was used to confrontation in a different way, and took a very efficient, practical approach to it. With an agility that surprised me, he got that lanky frame up the rear ladder and onto the coach roof, and as the driver realized he was there and turned to look up at him, he brought a stick smartly down on the bald skull. I don't know if I can convey the particular sound of a nightstick on a skull. I've heard it innu- merable times. It can resemble a rock falling into a pool of water . . . a soft sound . . . not pleasant. . . . Other times it has a cheerful, hard, woodpecking quality . . . cheerful because of the tonal simulation of emptiness inside the skull. At such moments you're relieved of wondering about the effects of the blow on the encased brain . . . which is always of course quite terrible, no matter what it sounds like. Here the sound was simple, blunt . . . definitive. The driver fell from his perch and landed at my feet in a great oomph of dust. He was a huge man, very strong. The blow had neither killed him nor rendered him unconscious. He pushed himself to his knees and held his head in his hands, but without making a sound . . . and before Donne was able to come down and order them to stop, the men had surrounded him and given him additional whacks about the shoulders and arms for the temerity of his reaction to them . . . though the issue had clearly been decided by that one blow.

Later, I would ask Donne why, coming down the hill, he had shouted after his men not to stop the white stage, but to let it go on. ''I don't know,'' he said, very noncommittal. ''I suppose I wanted to see where it would go.'' As it turned out, that would have been very useful. But then you have to understand . . . though I didn't realize this till much later, till it was too late to confirm . . . this was the reaction of someone who had known the white stage was sequestered behind that brick wall and would eventually be used . . . who had known enough to have the confidence to let the stage go on . . . because he understood who was riding in the coach and who the driver was . . . before he lifted the man's chin, as he did now as I stood there . . . and we looked at the

same oyster eyes and bouldered head that Harry
Wheelwright had drawn from the descriptions of
Knucks Geary's killer.

This is the question that I will never be able to
resolve to my satisfaction . . . the conjunctions of
which Edmund Donne was capable. What information did he depend on? I can never know. But at this
moment the shock to my system was stunning.

The policemen had found the rear door of the
carriage padlocked. They knelt beside the groaning
driver and took the key from his vest pocket . . . and
they went and opened the door upon six bawling and
terrified children. The horses had been quieted but
now the children were pushing out the door, trying to
get away. One of them did get through and began to
run down the street. "Get that boy," Donne shouted,
and the bewildered policeman who had come out of
the kiosk tried to intercept him. But the lad cut into
the field. No adult can run uphill after a street rat of
eight or ten and expect to overtake him. I remember
thinking . . . moments later . . . seeing his diminishing
figure on its way back to the city . . . dashing up
through the fields of pumpkins . . . toward Park Avenue . . . the boy was healthy to run that well. I suppose someone in a carriage could have caught him.
But there was great confusion now. Though the
neighborhood was sparsely populated, people were
coming up First Avenue to see what all the police
were doing there . . . and down from Second Ave-

nue . . . farm families came out on their porches to see . . . this confrontation of black and white wagons in the dust of the street, and the milling men in blue uniforms.

For obvious reasons Donne wanted to get the children and the stage back into the grounds of the orphanage. The gate had been bolted by someone inside. A policeman scaled the wall and shortly thereafter we were all pouring into the courtyard. I felt part of an invading force . . . and indeed we were treated as such by the staff and children . . . who were running through the rooms in every direction . . . screaming, sobbing, trying to get away, or hiding in closets. What must they have thought! Donne ordered his men to herd everyone into the dining room on the ground floor. I went with him back through the center hall . . . back past the pantries and the kitchen to a rear door that led out to a flagstone terrace bordered with a fence of cast iron. Here there was a drop of ten or twelve feet to the ground. A jetty of large and jagged boulders went right to the water's edge. In the river a man in a dinghy was rowing away frantically against the swift current. By the looks of it, he was making for Blackwell's Island, but the East River channel is so narrow in places that it forces the flow into rolling downriver waves . . . and this is what he was struggling with. As we watched he gave up, using the oars only to keep his boat from spinning. At that point he began rapidly to move south,

with the river. He shipped one of the oars and waved
. . . an indolent, mocking gesture. He wore a black
derby. Donne watched him, his hands grasping the
fence.

I wondered aloud if it might be the doctor, Sartorius, sailing away. Donne said nothing. We went
back in and . . . over the course of several minutes, as
order was gradually restored among the children
. . . it became apparent from the answers hesitantly,
timidly, or angrily supplied by members of the staff
to Donne's questions that Sartorius was barely
known to these people . . . whereas, on the other
hand, they referred continually to Mr. Simmons,
looking around uneasily to see where he was. So now
I knew who was in the boat.

Donne ordered names taken. There were two
teachers, a housekeeper, a nurse, the cook, four general attendants, a kitchen helper . . . all women . . . for
the thirty children boarded here.

We searched the establishment. Outside, off the
courtyard, was a carriage house and stable and a
smaller outbuilding, all in the same architectural
style. The ground floor of the main building was fitted out for classrooms, dining room, a playroom with
a new upright piano, and a modest library. All the
furniture was new primary school oak. The readers
and instruction books were in good condition.

We mounted a wide stairway of polished black
walnut whose steps were fitted with rubber pads . . .

to find two large dormitory wings, a boys' and a girls' . . . everything neat and fresh and clean . . . several baths . . . and smaller rooms for the adult staff on this floor and the top floor. On the top floor was also a dispensary with locked glass cabinets equipped with the usual implements, bandages, prescription bottles, and so on.

I had seen the insides of many orphanages . . . mission homes . . . houses for the poor . . . vocational institutes. They usually gave clear indication of the impoverished, hand-me-down nature of charity itself. This place shone like a preparatory school in New England . . . except that given the architecture—the Romanesque character—most of the windows were small and deeply alcoved, and the rooms, being for the most part wainscotted in walnut, were dark and gloomy.

The kitchen contained two cookstoves, a bank of washing tubs, kettles and long-handled pots hanging from a ceiling frame . . . a wooden icebox and open shelves of tins and boxes and jars . . . and in a corner, a bin of hard coal. It was a kitchen large and well-equipped enough to feed an army.

If a commission had come to inspect here . . . officials of the aid societies . . . and looked at the conditions under which these children were kept, they could not have been anything but impressed. The orphans were all dressed in simple, clean clothes and new shoes. They were scrubbed and groomed.

The staff, under questioning, seemed to be capable and honest servants of the establishment. It was all very puzzling.

The most disconsolate feeling came over me, something more of what I had felt up on the hill, looking at this place through the binoculars. . . . It was not fear or dread . . . but a desolate bleakness . . . diffuse, unattached, not yet precise as despair. In an office beside the kitchen, Donne found the house account books. The ledgers recorded routine house-keeping matters—payments to suppliers, payrolls. He asked the housekeeper, a large middle-aged woman with a great knot of hair coiled atop her head, if she kept the books. ''No,'' she said, ''that is done by Mr. Simmons.''

When Donne opened the key box on the wall he found several sets of keys on rings, and the house-keeper obliged him by specifying what each key opened. But one set she knew nothing about.

There was a locked closet door behind Sim-mons's desk. One after another Donne tried the keys from this set on the door. Finally the knob turned. The closet held oak filing cabinets, each with its own lock. But on one side a few items of clothes hung from a bar. He was pushing these aside to see what was behind them when I saw a coat hanging there . . . an old Union army issue. . . . I said, keeping my voice as calm as I could, ''Martin Pemberton wore a coat like this.''

If it was pursuit I was sworn to, I wanted no part of it now. With a police torch Donne led us down a flight of stairs from the kitchen to the basement, the one area left for our inspection. The basement walls were stone, but it was sectioned into storage areas with wooden walls and locked doors, like hatches in the hold of a ship. The keys he held worked for these doors. We passed through two of the areas . . . the air close, suffused with coal ash. In the third we came upon what looked like a coal bin fitted out with bars. . . . It was a cell, a windowless cell. The air was foul. Donne bent over and held up the lamp. And there, on a pallet, something moved . . . scraggly-bearded, weak-eyed and blinking, lifting a skeletal arm against the light . . . a poor soul, nothing but rags and bones . . . whom I had . . . difficulty recognizing.

Ever since this day I have dreamt sometimes . . . I, a street rat in my soul, dream even now . . . that if it were possible to lift this littered, paved Manhattan from the earth . . . and all its torn and dripping pipes and conduits and tunnels and tracks and cables—all of it, like a scab from new skin underneath—how seedlings would sprout, and freshets bubble up, and brush and grasses would grow over the rolling hills . . . entanglements of vines, and fields of wild blueberry and blackberry. . . . There would be oak trees for shade against the heat, and white birches and weeping willows . . . and in winter, snow would lie everlastingly white until it ran off as pure and glistening as spring water. A season or two of this and the mute, protesting culture buried for so many industrial years under the tenements and factories . . . would rise again . . . of the lean, religious Indians of the bounteous earth, who lived without money or lasting architecture, flat and close to the ground—hunting, trapping, fishing, growing their corn and praying . . . always praying in solemn thanksgiving for their clear and short life in this quiet universe. Such love I have for those savage polytheists of my mind . . . those friends of light and leaf . . . those free men and women . . . such envy for the inadequate stories they told each other, their taxonomies, cosmologies . . . their lovely dreams of the world they stood on and who was holding it up. . . .

Nineteen

HE had all the answers to our questions
. . . but wasn't able to deliver them. He did not speak,
or act sensibly. He was mute and uncomprehending.
Sarah Pemberton had him admitted to the Presbyterian Hospital on Seventy-first Street and Fourth Avenue under the care of Dr. Mott, the same doctor who
had diagnosed Augustus's illness . . . and there each
day we came to stand watch. The diagnosis was that
Martin was suffering from starvation and dehydra-
tion and the attendant breakdowns of function. The
women, who had been so joyous at the news he'd
been found . . . that he was alive . . . were all the more
horrified to see him in this state . . . unresponsive as
death. He lay on his back gazing at the ceiling . . .
terribly pale but with red blotches on the skin . . . the
aquiline features stressed to unnatural prominence
. . . the light hair and beard matted and long. The
form he made under the bedcovers was shockingly
. . . small. But it was the lack of thought in the eyes,
and the absence of that Pemberton personality, that
were so devastating. This was not my Martin.

Over a period of days, as he was able to take

nourishment, he began to look better, but the profound . . . remoteness continued. He was not comatose, according to Dr. Mott, who had determined that he responded to sound and turned his head toward light. It was as if he were engaged in some philosophic meditation that rendered the other demands of consciousness insignificant. I remember sitting by his bedside . . . and wondering what a philosophical meditation was, exactly. What its content would be—some depth of thought that allowed you to hear God, perhaps, or his music. You know . . . there are severe limits to a newspaperman's metaphysics. I understand our breed, and not just from myself. We start out young, full of beans, with a dislike of routine, order, and repetition—all the virtues of American commercial life—and a boyish, irresponsible love of the new, of the ever-changing . . . challenge. My first job in the business was to ride the pilot boats out to Sandy Hook, and try to get the European news from the transatlantic ships before anybody else. After a while we had our own boats, our news boats. . . . But as I say, all this means we are souls much too . . . in life. . . . Our life and times are all and everything. We're totally occupied with social and political urgencies. . . . And death . . . death is no more than an obituary. Anyone's death, including our own, is yesterday's news.

But now here he was, my freelance, neither dead nor alive, in much the same philosophical place as his father . . . which gave me considerable misgiving in my newspaperman's soul . . . testing my belief in the magnificent mess of life, that it did not after all go out to the edges of . . . whatever was possible. I realized now that I had been depending on Martin, as perhaps we all were . . . following his signs . . . for some months now working out the routes he had designated as a guide, some distance ahead. I felt . . . such loss. . . . I felt abandoned. I could easily have gone into a corner and thrown a shawl over my head and sunk to my knees . . . in bitter despair of this living death.

I had the consolation, every day, of seeing Miss Emily Tisdale seated on the other side of his bed, as he lay between us. She had left her classes. She confided in me, spoke to me over his open-eyed dream sleep, words she would not dare to speak to him. "When Martin disappeared and was gone, when it was possible that I would never see him again," she said, "I wanted to fill my mind with my schoolwork, with facts and ideas and declensions, with the very sound of words and the appearances of them in their lines . . . to evict him . . . to have him dispossessed. God help me. I longed to be rid of him in my mind, his qualities . . . how he looked at me, the voice . . . the stern judgments. But in every small accomplishment in my classes at the Normal College . . . I found I still hoped for his approval. He inhabits me . . . and there's nothing I can do about it. This I suppose is love,'' she said, glancing a moment at his face. Her hands were folded on her lap. ''But it's an awful and decidedly unpleasant fate . . . altogether unnecessary, isn't it, Mr. McIlvaine?'' she said with a laugh, though her dark brown eyes were shimmering with tears. I agreed with this honest, beautiful, plain girl that it was unnecessary.

''Yes . . . an invention of God's that needs improvement,'' she said. ''You know, it's not right to do that to children . . . because that's when it happens, it comes on one as a child, when there is such tender skin, such clear . . . reception of the light from another child's eyes . . . and when the world's arrangements, the accidents of adult business, seem to children so . . . destined for their own sake.''

''Yes.''

''So we are chained. I have always been chained to Martin. Through all his tempests . . . his struggles . . . here or not here . . . it's all equally disastrous to me . . . and if he dies . . . I'll be the same shackled girl . . . whether made love to by a man or a ghost . . . what is the difference?''

And so we sat our watch. There was an anteroom where we stayed most of the time, only peeking in now and then, as if Martin were asleep and shouldn't be disturbed, although the doctor had said the sounds of life might do him good.

The Reverend Grimshaw each day prayed for a

few minutes by Martin's bed. Emily's father, Amos Tisdale, came once or twice, shaking his head less in sadness or worry than regret for the continuing deplorable situation. Sarah Pemberton brought her calm conviction with her that, Martin having been found, he would in time be well. She sat by his side, knitting. I felt, watching her white hands, that if they stopped moving . . . she would lose her mind. Once Noah came with her . . . but the boy didn't want to go into the room where Martin lay. He stood by the window and looked stolidly at the street. But all of us were suspended in this strange, lurid business. It had stopped life.

The driver, Wrangel, was being held in the Tombs for the murder of Knucks Geary. He would not answer any questions, he simply refused to speak . . . like a western Indian, with his arms crossed. Donne, with Grimshaw's help, had arranged for the Little Wanderer children to be transferred to the Orphans' Home and Asylum of the Protestant Episcopal Church at Lexington Avenue and Forty-ninth Street. Three attending physicians and a dentist examined them and judged that they were all healthy and well nourished. Emily Tisdale had gone over there to see them, and from her experience as a student teacher at the Normal College she thought them uncharacteristically quiet children, with wary, fearful eyes. The ones who had been taken from the padlocked stage had been placed in quarters separate from the rest and questioned by a nurse attached to the Municipal Police, with Donne in attendance. The children were not forthcoming. They were on average six to eight years old. They thought they had been going for a ride to the country . . . that was what they had been told. How long had they been at the Home? They didn't know. Had anyone ever beaten them or mistreated them? No. Had Mr. Wrangel, the handyman? No. Had Mr. Simmons, the director? No. How had they come to the Home? They didn't know.

Over a period of days Donne questioned each member of the staff. Martin's incarceration in the basement was a shock to them. They were all newly employed—the orphanage had been operating for just a few months. All had been hired by Mr. Simmons after answering classified advertisements in the newspaper. One of the teachers, a Miss Gillicuddy, who was retired from the public school system, had created the curriculum and the teaching plan. It was her enlightened view that children, simply because they were from the street, should not be presumed to be capable only of vocational training. . . . Donne was satisfied the staff were not party to a conspiracy.

"You mean," I said, "they knew nothing of what was going on?"

"What was going on?" he said.

"That these were children kidnapped from the streets?"

"Not all of them, apparently. Some were referred by the children's aid societies."

"But there was some purpose to all this!"

"Yes."

"Where did the teachers and the monitors think the children were going on their ride that afternoon?"

"The children went off with Wrangel periodically, by turns. Simmons said it was for their medical examinations."

"Then why was the stage padlocked?"

"For the children's safety."

"Where is Sartorius? Where does he practice?"

"Nobody can tell us."

"The children—"

"The children give me blank stares."

Now this was all . . . late September, I suppose. Perhaps a bit later. The first stories exposing the malfeasance of the Tweed Ring were coming out in the *Times*. The city was in an uproar. The events up at Ninety-third Street had not, thank God, caught the eye of the press. Martin Pemberton had been carried up from his basement prison and taken away in an ambulance after darkness had set in. Donne had closed down the orphanage and had it sealed by the city marshal on the basis of what he certified only as "irregularities." Irregularities found in the running of an orphanage were not news in our city even in the quietest of seasons. A brief item about the closing appeared only in the *Sun*. Martin was not mentioned.

I wondered how long it would be before questions about the Home for Little Wanderers began to drift up on the whispers of the staff members who had lost their jobs . . . the people who had seen the scuffle in the street in front of the Home . . . the authorities from the Episcopal orphanage who had taken over the maintenance of the children . . . and the nurses at the hospital, who could not reconcile Martin Pemberton's state of near-starvation with the numbers of people—family, friends, pastor, and even a police official—who were so concerned about his recovery. How had they allowed him to come to this in the first place?

As a jobless editor I was still jealous of my exclusive. Sitting there in the hospital room, I experienced additionally the feelings of a private person who shudders in contemplation of the prospect . . . of serious matters of his own intimate knowledge . . . subjected to the low standards and deplorable practices of the newspaper profession. I reasoned that I had a month, maybe six weeks, before the whispers would ignite . . . until the smoke of this fire would be seen down on Printing House Square. That would be the length of time it took for people to grow weary of the Tweed Ring scandals. Until then the rule would prevail that the press, like the public, has room in its brain for only one story at a time.

So this is how things stood in this infernal city

in the autumn of 1871. Private motives and intentions began to stir in and about our misfortune . . . as worms in a grave. Harry Wheelwright in his great girth came to visit, late one afternoon. His eyes were already blasted and his speech slurred . . . but he found the gallantry to escort Miss Tisdale home. Am I too harsh? It would not seem inappropriate for Martin's friends to band together for mutual comfort. But I didn't trust the fellow. He'd seen too much of Emily in that portrait . . . his observation was . . . tumescent. He'd painted his lust.

I simmered in my bachelor state, a bachelor too long, and too old, to do anything but simmer. Perhaps my jealousy was a function of idleness. I had worked since the age of fourteen. I didn't know what it meant not to work. And I had always worked for newspapers. Yet there I sat, stupidly jealous on behalf of my supine and oblivious friend, imprisoned in my own meditations, paralleled in idleness. . . . I could not bring myself to look for a job. I would not go to the usual haunts at night . . . making myself visible for pity or gossip. I was now totally involved in this matter, as a life work.

One day the freelance I had asked to delve into the morgue for predicaments similar to Sarah Pemberton's appeared at my door with the results of his researches. It did not matter to him that I was no longer city editor—he'd done the work and wanted his wage. I paid him out of my own pocket and was glad to do it. He'd come up with a half dozen obituaries, printed since 1869, of men who were thought to be financially sound but left a pauper's estate.

I'll tell you their names: Evander Prine, Thomas Henry Carleton, Oliver Vanderweigh, Elijah Ripley, Fernando Brown, and Horace W. Wells.

Of course quick rises and falls of fortune were not unusual in New York. People lived beyond their means. Barouche-and-fours and town houses took some keeping up. In the last ten years tax levies had risen over five hundred percent. The markets were volatile, we were on a paper standard, so there was a speculative market in gold. . . . When Jay Gould and Jim Fisk conspired to corner the gold, brokerages failed . . . people on the Street lost everything. . . . No, it was nothing to see swells around town with silk hats and diamond shirt studs who were gone the following day.

But here I was looking at men centrally situated in the quiet of long-term success. And nobody related to them seemed to know where their money had gone. Carleton and Vanderweigh were bankers, Ripley ran a transatlantic cargo business using leased steamships, Brown had built locomotives, and Horace W. Wells was a dealer in city real estate whom Tweed himself had appointed deputy commissioner of streets and sewers. Their collective worth when alive was somewhere, I would say, in the neighborhood of thirty million nineteenth-century dollars.

Two of them were bachelors who had simply vanished, and their holdings with them. All of them, married or single, were of an advanced age. The family of one, Evander Prine, had been found living in hardship on Forty-sixth Street, west of Longacre Square, a neighborhood of whorehouses. They had come to the attention of one of my feature writers because they had put up Mr. Prine's sixty-three-foot racing yacht for sale . . . their only remaining asset . . . and had had no takers. And so there were Mrs. Prine and her children, living in a boardinghouse for prostitutes, whose husband had in fact been an associate of Gould's and would have been expected to leave his family in, at the least, comfortable circumstances.

Perhaps in a society less raucous, less contentious, its heart not pounding the earth like a giant steam hammer, the oddly congruent fates of these men might have been noticed. But their anguished heirs had all sunk away in time . . . just as the dead do, under the flat weight of days and years and later editions . . . leaving Donne and me to unearth a major conspiracy. Because when I showed Donne my names, he showed me those same names . . . along with Augustus Pemberton's . . . written down on a piece of paper he'd found folded in Eustace Simmons's ledger . . . at the Home for Little Wanderers.

So we had more of the detail. Yet we could go no further. Everything ran headlong into Martin

Pemberton's silence. Donne sat by the bedside and listened as if Martin had paused in the middle of a sentence and the conclusion would be spoken momentarily.

About a week or ten days after Martin's rescue Donne was suspended from duty pending an internal investigation by the Municipals: He had had no legal basis for stopping the white stage in the street . . . and he had entered the premises of the Home without a warrant. They couldn't do anything more . . . public than that. No city judge issued an order to unseal the Home and return the children. No lawyer came to the Tombs to see Wrangel . . . or to file for a preliminary hearing. The fact was that Martin's rescue—his incarceration in the basement—was a problem for them. Donne also had Eustace Simmons's records. He could be ordered to turn them over to a court . . . but Simmons would know he knew there were discrepancies—in the handling of funds, first of all, but, more important, in that not all the children who had been admitted to the Home . . . could be accounted for. And the division of responsibility among the staff, the teachers and dormitory monitors, was such that only Simmons would have known that anything was out of the ordinary.

If the Tweed government had not been in the process of collapsing . . . and its major figures had not been so distracted, and fearful . . . they would, with all of their power, have dealt with this crisis brutally and summarily. As it was, their agent, Simmons, had no recourse but to flee. In his office desk he had left a cash box with seventeen thousand dollars. Suspended or not, Donne had the loyalty of his men. He'd put them on a round-the-clock watch. Night and day a man sat in the darkness of the Home for Little Wanderers. Donne could only hope the sum was large enough to draw Simmons back.

"Large enough! Migod," I said, "that is more than double your and my salaries per annum together!"

"It's all relative, isn't it? It may have been his petty cash. You see how he took to the water. He's run slavers. He thinks of the ocean as a passage. Simmons may be on his way to Portugal." Then Donne looked at me and smiled. "What salaries?" he said.

We were all in these oddly reduced circumstances. . . . What an odd collegiality we had . . . in our disfranchisement . . . sitting in that hospital anteroom hour after hour—a defrocked policeman . . . an impoverished widow and her child . . . a student at the Normal College for grade school teachers . . . and an unemployed newspaperman. As if our lives were suspended . . . until the resolution of this awful matter. Only Donne and I knew the extent of it. The others had merely to endure their bewilderment and grief.

Twenty

$\mathbf{M}$EN had turned their fortunes over to Sartorius . . . betrayed their families. Politicians conspired in his behalf. The opportunistic Simmons had moved from Augustus Pemberton's employ to his. He'd converted these men of the world, these . . . realists, into acolytes. He was a holy man, he commanded belief. In fact he was a major intellect—one of those brilliantly assured intellects to whom the world seems to exist for the sake of their engagement with it. I wanted to think we had disrupted his strange enterprise . . . that we might not exact redress in behalf of Sarah Pemberton and the other survivors of the . . . mortuary fellowship . . . but for the moment, at least, it could not function as it had. But how much more of it was there . . . that we knew nothing about? He had resources. . . .

I don't know if I can portray the effect of an overriding mentality. . . . This man I had never seen seemed to characterize the room where Martin lay. He took the shape of everything—the painted iron bed, the wooden chairs, the white plaster walls, and the chair rail. That we were here was willed by him.

The calm, meditative face staring up from the pillow had been given its expression by him.

It was sheer misery not to have my paper . . . to read it every day and see that it was no longer mine. It did what I would not have done, it said what I would not have said. This too was Sartorius. He was my disempowerment.

I had not seen him, at this point, you understand, but I hold his image in my mind and I will assign it to him here, out of the chronology of things . . . to suggest the force of him . . . as if we were able to derive him from the disaster he had brought about.

A commanding figure, not tall, but military in his bearing . . . slender stature and with the stillness of consummate self-confidence . . . wearing the customary frock coat, slightly puffed at the shoulder seams, and the vest with fabric-covered buttons, and the wide loosely tied cravat with stickpin. The overall impression is of neatness, self-containment. Thick black hair cut short. His cheeks and upper lip and chin are clean-shaven, but burnsides frame his jaw and continue under the chin and curl around the throat like a woolen scarf tucked in under the collar. Black, implacable eyes, surprisingly opaque, with a kind of desolation in them . . . a harsh impersonality, reminding me of Sherman, William Tecumseh Sherman. Good rounded forehead, slightly domed, thin, straight nose, thin-lipped, abstemious mouth. I'll animate him with an action: He holds a watch on a fob, glances at it, and slips it back into his vest pocket.

When Martin was finally well enough to leave the hospital, all our spirits rose. He was weak, and needed support as he walked, but he'd begun to recognize his surroundings . . . and he responded with a nod or a soft, barely uttered word to our questions. It was very gradual, and natural, his return to consciousness, by degrees, with the first responsive light in his eyes as they turned to Emily as she sat by him. But he still didn't speak. Donne attempted, gently, to ask some crucial questions, but Martin could not or would not answer.

It was decided that he would convalesce at the Tisdales'. This was Emily's proposal, to which her father, a good if wary Christian, consented, and Sarah Pemberton agreed. Sarah could not really offer a home that wasn't hers. Martin's own place was long since let to someone else, and the dark rooms where I lived then, three stories up on Bleecker Street, were clearly as unconducive to recuperation as Harry Wheelwright's studio would be.

Those first warm, honeyed afternoons of October, Martin Pemberton sat outside on a chaise with a plaid blanket over his legs. From the terrace at Lafayette Place, he could look out over the private park of his childhood. I had never seen Emily so happy. She went back and forth and fussed and brought tea and whatever else she could find to heal his spirit, or to signify her prayerful desire for her love to heal him. The leaves were beginning to fall, one by one, boating down on the breeze, and mooring themselves against the stone balustrade. I came to see Martin almost every day, as did Edmund Donne. One day we were discussing Sartorius. Just for the sake of argument, I considered the possibility that he might have fled, like Eustace Simmons. That perhaps they had bought themselves a ship and taken themselves and their charges to—where was it Donne had suggested? Portugal?

''No,'' Donne said. ''He's here. He wouldn't run. He doesn't have Simmons's criminal soul.''

''He doesn't? What does he have then?''

I had been aware of Martin's alertness to the conversation. In the moment before he spoke it occurred to me that he was in agreement with Donne . . . from the glance he gave him, or perhaps the set of the facial muscles in the instant before the mouth utters agreement.

''The doctor is not an immoralist,'' Martin said. We looked at him. He was gazing at a small bird who had hopped up on the tea caddy. ''He never attempted to justify himself to me. Or to lie. Or indicated in any way that he felt . . . culpable.''

It was an amazing moment. . . . Pemberton was in total possession of himself, as if, all this time, he had been waiting for a subject of conversation that interested him. I decided immediately that I mustn't make anything of it . . . thinking he might be—what?—frightened back into his catatonia. In the next moment Sarah Pemberton had come out on the terrace with Noah, after calling for him at his school, and Martin recognized them both and held out his arms for the boy. . . . We were all so astounded. Sarah Pemberton gasped. She called out for Emily to come quickly. She was overcome. . . . She stood where Martin couldn't see her and wept and turned to Donne and put her hands over her face while he held her to him. Martin meanwhile was asking Noah about his classes. . . .

And so that was the day we began to hear of it . . . everything, from the first sight of the white stage. What was it like? I think I was put in mind of a war hero. Yes, we listened to Martin as if he were a hero returned from the front. We were not inclined to be critical. These were his war stories, told for our wonderment. But I have to admit my euphoria didn't last. I began soon enough to suspect that Martin's recovery was not complete. When he referred to Sartorius he spoke of him without the slightest anger or bitterness. Overall, he spoke from some sort of peaceful resolution, or becalming . . . of the intensity in all his feeling. I was unable to tell how much of this to attribute to his physical ordeal. But his nature was

changed . . . the characteristic impatience . . . the suffered worldview . . . all of it softened, or chastened.
He was tacitly . . . grateful. To all of us. He was ap-
preciative! God forgive me—I could only think this
spelled ruin for him as a writer.

Twenty-one

"I KNEW the way to my father was through
Eustace Simmons,'' Martin told us. "Simmons came
out of the . . . maritime life. I went along West Street,
around the Battery, to South Street. . . . I went into
every sailors' bar, every saloon, every dance hall in
the Port of New York . . . with no luck. Then I
thought, my father being . . . absent, Simmons would
represent his interests around town. The situation
elevated him to the higher class of thieves.

"One night I had the assignment from the *Tatler* to go to the Astor House, where Boss Tweed and
his friends were giving a testimonial dinner to a
Tammany Club ward leader. They all wore the em-
blematic tiger in their lapels, the gold head of a tiger
relieved in blue enamel . . . the eyes set with rubies.
A very young girl danced on a table in a belted di-
aphanous gown . . . and at her feet, following her
every move with the discrimination of a . . . connois-
seur, was Eustace Simmons. I hadn't seen him in
many years but I knew him immediately. A cadaver-
ous man, dressed well but with the effect somehow
of dishevelment . . . he was slouched back in his

chair. The dimmed light brought out the ruin of his face—he is pitted and pocked, the skin under the eyes is black, the head of wiry hair graying and combed across from ear to ear, and the whole aspect of him, somehow . . . dirty-looking.

"A few minutes later, I sat down in the chair next to his and could see he recognized me. Someone was making a speech. There was laughter and applause. I said in Simmons's ear that I wanted to see my father. He gave no indication that he heard me . . . but after a pause to light his cigar, he rose from the table and sauntered out of the dining room. I followed, as he trusted I would.

"It was peculiar and it shocked me at first, but I respected him for not attempting to deny my father was alive. He has a quick mind, Simmons, and I think he knew within moments of my appearance what he would do.

"He got his hat and left the Astor House with me right behind him. His carriage was around the corner. In the light of the streetlamp I caught a glimpse of the driver. I can't adequately . . . express what I felt at the sight of him . . . the same driver of the white stage with my father and the other old men. I didn't want to get into the hansom. Simmons shouted 'Wrangel!' and the driver leapt down and locked a powerful arm across my throat so that I couldn't breathe . . . though I could smell the onions

on his breath . . . while Simmons caught me behind
the ear with what I suppose was a sap. I saw a sudden
bright light. I don't know what happened then or how
much time passed. I was aware of motion, then of the
motion conferred to a carriage by a team of horses
. . . then of painful daylight . . . then of two or three
small faces staring at me. I was looking at children. It
was day. . . . I tried to rouse myself. . . . I was not tied
but I could not move. I think, on top of everything,
they must have drugged me. I couldn't seem to get to
my feet. I toppled over and a child screamed. Then I
was on my back, looking at the battened ceiling . . .
of what, in the moment before I passed out entirely
. . . I realized was a public omnibus of the Municipal
Transport Company.

''Let me say here that the driver, Wrangel, is of
less consequence in all of this than you think. He is
strong, fearsome to look at, with those colorless
pupils . . . and I could barely speak or swallow after
he'd put his armlock on me . . . but his appearance
ought not be held against him. He's like a good
horse. That's all he is, a loyal stolid soul who asks no
questions. He's a Prussian. They're brought up to be
that way, the Germans, with their strict parents and
titled officers . . . who teach them obedience, obedience above all. Wrangel reveres Dr. Sartorius. He
served under him in the medical corps. His most trea-
sured possession is their field hospital unit citation,

signed by President Lincoln. He showed it to me one day. He thinks when Simmons tells him to do something, it is what Sartorius wants.

"The doctor himself I find difficult to represent to you. He doesn't expend his energies on the formation of a . . . social self. He is quiet, almost ascetic in his habits, courteous, unprepossessing. He has no vanity that can be appealed to or flattered or insulted. You will wonder, as I did, how someone so careless, someone so uninterested in putting himself forward, or seeking advantage, could . . . marshal . . . the immense resources needed for his work. But he doesn't—he simply allows things to happen around him. He takes what is to hand, he accepts what his . . . devotees press on him. It's as if . . . there's an alignment of historical energies magnetized on him which . . . for all I know, is probably all . . . that makes him visible.

"I wasn't brought to him for another day or so after I recovered consciousness. I had no idea, and have no idea today, where this was. . . . There was always . . . only indoor light. I never saw a window. Up close, and third in a sequence after Simmons and Wrangel, Sartorius appeared to me in his modest demeanor as a mere medical attendant to Augustus Pemberton, a retainer, one of those doctors whose practices are limited to one or two wealthy patients.

"In this view I felt I had every right to my anger. I was Augustus's son, after all, with the contemptuous attitude of the line. I was loud and righteous. I demanded to know if I had been manhandled under standing orders from my father. 'How like him to put others between us!' I said. 'Is he still afraid to face me? Is he still afraid to answer to me?' Sartorius was calm. He asked, as if simply to satisfy his own curiosity, how I had learned my father was alive.

"'I have seen him, sir. Do not patronize me. I have seen everything. I have seen the grave in Woodlawn where a child is interred in his place.'

"He wasn't cowed—on the contrary. He leaned forward and peered at me. I told him how I had gone to Woodlawn and dug up the coffin. I then felt it necessary to tell him why I had come to that . . . desperate measure, beginning with my sight of the white stage, in the snow, going past the reservoir. I didn't quite understand how the conversation had turned so that I was . . . confiding in this man. Yet I was . . . and with relief.

"He said: 'The possibility always exists of exciting notice, of course, though . . . I think you are an exception to most people . . . in acting upon your illusions.' This was said in a tone of approval. 'What is your profession, Mr. Pemberton?'

"You understand at no point, then or afterward, did Sartorius attempt to deny anything, or to equivocate. He never tried to justify himself to me. My appearance had aroused his interest, not his concern. At moments during our interview I felt myself a specimen that had swum into his field of vision. He's a scientist. He does not think of defending his actions. He is not weakened with a conscience. . . . Once I inquired of his religion. He was raised a Lutheran, but Christianity he regards as no more than a poetic conceit. He doesn't even bother to criticize it, or mock it or disavow it.

" 'If you want to see your father, of course you may,' Sartorius said to me. 'I doubt you will get satisfaction. This is something for which you cannot have prepared yourself. The perceptions of a merely moral intelligence, even of filial love or hatred, won't suffice. I suppose it is no business of mine. But what will you say to this . . . papa . . . you thought was a dead man?'

"Of course that was the question I had never permitted myself to ask. He must have read the desperation on my face. What indeed could I do? Embrace my father? Celebrate his resurrection? Cry with joy that he was alive? Or did I just want to tell him . . . that I *knew*! That I knew . . . And salute him for having found a depth of human deceit and betrayal beyond my conceiving.

"What was my purpose? Everything and nothing. I didn't know if I'd get down on my knees and beg him to provide for his wife and son . . . or fall on him and tear his throat out for having given me this life of endless contemplation of his hideous . . . being.

"I said to the doctor by way of a rational answer: 'I thought my father was merely a scoundrel and a thief and a murderer.' He seemed to understand. He rose and told me to follow him.

"I stumbled along in a daze. I became aware of the atmosphere of his laboratories, without seeing anything in particular going on there—two or three rooms with doors open between them, and a faintly chemical smell in the air. All the light came from gas jets. . . . There were glass cabinets for instruments . . . stone-top cabinets inset with iron sinks . . . boxy machines on wheels with cables and gears and tubing. I remember a square wooden chair with leather straps at the armrests and an iron head brace. . . . The walls were draped in some brownish napped material, velour or velvet. To me all this was the menacing furniture of science.

"He has a wonderful library, Sartorius. After we came to our understanding, he allowed me to use it. I spent many consoling hours occupying myself with learning more of what he knew . . . by reading what he was reading. It was a foolish idea, no more than a kind of homage, really.

"He is fluent in several languages. . . . The scientific journals and papers lay in piles on the floor where he threw them. I made it a task of my own to keep them in order. Books, monographs from France, from London, from Germany, arrived in packing boxes. He knows everything going on in the sciences, in medicine, but he reads impatiently, looking always for something he doesn't know, something to surprise him . . . a line of inquiry, a critique. His library is not a collector's. He doesn't read for pleasure. He has no particular respect for books in themselves, their bindings, and so on, and he didn't handle them carefully. He read the philosophers, the historians, the natural scientists, and even the novelists, without differentiating their disciplines in his mind. Looking, always looking, for what he would recognize as true and useful to him. Something to get him past whatever it was that confounded him, past the point in his work where his own mind had been . . . stopped.

"I think sometimes he was looking really for a companionable soul. He certainly didn't surround himself with intellectual equals. He lived in solitude. When he entertained, as far as I could tell, it was at the strong urging of Eustace Simmons. The guests were usually politicians.

"He led me to an elevator, which rode us upward in a brass cage. He drove the thing but made no fuss about it. The floor above consisted of rooms and suites where the clientele resided—the electors, the fellowship, the funeral society of old men. There were living quarters for them and treatment rooms with leather-top tables, and there were rooms for the women who attended them. Later, after we worked out the terms of my captivity, I had the freedom of the place and came to understand and distinguish all of this. My first impression was only of a corridor of deeply shadowed rooms, all of which happened to be empty. The decor was simple, like that of a monastery or a mission.

"It was when I was elevated to the rooftop and saw, in all its humid green glory, Dr. Sartorius's—what?—facility for biologized wealth?—that I knew this is where I would find my father. I was so stunned I wonder if since then I have been under the sort of spell laid upon those who look on the forbidden.

"Here was the site of the experiment, the heart of the researches, the conservatory Sartorius had designed himself. It was in the nature of an indoor park, with gravel paths and plantings and cast-iron benches. It was all set inside a vaulted roof of glass and steel which cast a greenish light over everything. The conservatory was laid out to effect a forbearing harmony and peacefulness. At the center was a kind of courtyard paved in brownstone, and terraced up from that in single steps were smaller squares with filigreed chairs and tables. Enormous clay urns sprouted profusions of fronds and leaves that I knew on sight were not native. A kind of tepid steam or diffusion of watered air hissed out of ports or valves inset in the floor, so that the atmosphere was cloyingly humid. I could feel through the floor vibrations of the dynamo that was responsible. The centerpiece of the brownstone square was a sunken stone bath, a bathing pool with water, ocher in color and overhung with a sulfurous mist. An old man, terribly withered, was bathing, with a pair of women attending him. I have not mentioned the statuary, here and there, pedestaled or large enough to stand alone, but consistent in erotic subject, with heroic copulations, nudes of both genders in states of passion, and so on, yet all notably graceless and unidealized, as we are—the sorts of pieces an artist would not show in public but only to his friends.

''The effect of all of this . . . was of a Roman bath, had Rome been industrialized. The greenish light from the conservatory roof seemed to descend, it sifted down, it had motion, it seemed to pulse. Gradually I became aware that I was hearing music. First I felt it as the pulse of the air . . . but when I realized it was music, it broke over me, swelling and filling this vaulted place. . . . It was as if I had stepped into another universe, a Creation, like . . . an obverse Eden. Its source was an orchestrion standing like a church organ against a far wall—an enormous music box behind glass that sprung from tines of its slowly turning disc the sounds of a concert band.

''I had a premonition of the pitiful truth as I looked for Augustus Pemberton among the quiet and coddled old men of this place . . . these idlers and their companions, silently listening like people in the park, in their black frock coats and with their hats upon the tables.

"I found my father in a kind of grassy alcove, sitting on a bench . . . slumped in this misted pleasure-grove in a kind of vacuous despondency or infinitely trusting patience, which I would soon learn was steadfast . . . as it was with the other gentlemen in residence around him . . . despite the vitalistic therapies applied to them, inside and out.

"My primitive father . . . bluntly, powerfully selfish . . . stupid, intransigent, with his crude appetites and gross taste and stylish cunning . . . whom I tried to speak with and wept in front of and prayed to have restored in all his force . . . rather than as this shrunken soul lifting his eyes to look at me, without recognition, at the urging of Dr. Sartorius: 'Augustus? Do you know who this is? Will you say hello to your son?' "

Twenty-two

MARTIN lapsed into silence. None of us said anything. I felt the breeze . . . looked out over the Tisdales' autumn garden . . . listened to the ordinary sounds of the street . . . with, I suppose, gratitude. Martin closed his eyes and after a few moments it became apparent that he had fallen asleep. Emily adjusted his lap robe, and we left him there and went inside.

It was unfortunate that the ladies had heard his account. Sarah Pemberton, quite pale, asked Emily if she could rest a moment somewhere. She was accommodated, and later, when Emily went to see to her, Sarah confessed she had developed an intense headache, in her silent forbearing way containing the effect of her knowledge as a private matter . . . but the pain was so severe, Emily had to send for a doctor. He prescribed something for the pain that didn't entirely work, and that night, at Emily's insistence, Sarah Pemberton stayed over, and Noah as well . . . and Emily Tisdale found herself running a small sanitarium.

Donne and I decided to leave. He gave an anxious look up the stairs, but there was nothing we could do but get in the way. Seeing us to the door, Emily said: "I am terrified. Who are these . . . malignities of human life in our city? I want to pray but my throat closes up. Can our lives ever be the same? What is to be done, do you know, Captain? Is there something for us to do that will . . . restore the proportions of things? I cannot think of one. Will you think of one? Will you do that, please?"

Donne and I walked over to Pfaff's saloon on Broadway. The raucous good humor there seemed to me callow. We sat in a corner and had several whiskeys. I was thinking of the . . . desperate impertinence of this league of old gentlemen . . . so unsatisfied with the ways of their God as to take their immortal souls into their own hands. . . . How pathetic, not to trust their Christian theology, but to ensure things for themselves. How brazen and how pathetic.

Donne thought of things in a more practical manner. "It is a kind of new science, I suppose . . . part of the knowledge of modern times. But it seems to require enormous sums . . . to go forward. It is a complex enterprise. Expensive to run. They bought that mansion and fitted it out as an orphanage. They had the protection of the Municipals . . . the endorsement of the city fathers. There is another establishment . . . where this conservatory is . . . another entire establishment with a staff. All of this has been funded by the—what would you call them?—patients?''

''Yes, at best . . . to the tune of thirty millions.''

''Is that a reasonable estimate?''

''Twenty-five, then . . . at least that.''

''Well, it must be banked somewhere . . . under someone's name. It can't be all gone.''

''No.''

''It would be one of Mr. Tweed's banks. I have been talking to the federal district attorney. I'm trying to get him to issue subpoenas. But he needs something specific.''

''Why would the Ring not steal it for themselves?''

''They will if they have to,'' he said. ''I imagine they hope for something more.''

''What more?'' I said, and the moment I did I realized what he meant. The Ring, with their vaulting ambition, would carry ambition to its ultimate form. They were nothing if not absurd—ridiculous, simpleminded, stupid, self-aggrandizing. And murderous. All the qualities of men who prevail in our Republic.

''While Sartorius is free, the money is sacrosanct,'' Donne said. ''That's why if we hope to recover anything for Sarah—for Mrs. Pemberton and her son—we must find the accounts and impound them more or less at the same time we . . . impound him. It will take months for the Ring to be put on trial. Until then they are not without hope of preserving their last . . . best secret.''

I was comforted by Donne's analysis of this strange cabal . . . as if it were a legal, practical concern, a problem to be solved, a matter of fact . . . whereas my mind was beset by this thing. . . . The images from the conservatory . . . loomed in me. I could not sleep, I was haunted . . . not by ghosts, but by Science. I felt afflicted with intolerable reality. All my fears were compounded into a fear of the night. I was without my profession, my reason for being . . . my cockiness. Somehow, deprived of the means to report it, our life and times, I imagined myself at its mercy. Life seemed to be an inevitable disease of knowledge . . . a plague that infected all who came in contact with it.

The most terrible thing was that the only hope in dealing with it was in acquiring more of it, more of this dead spirit of knowledge. I imagined, to give myself courage, that it all might be initiatory, a kind of spiritual test in a world ruled by God after all . . . and that at its worst, at the moment of its greatest, most unendurable terror, it would end . . . in a kind of light and peace . . . that we could stagger about in, like happy drunks, until we died. But as a lapsed Scotch Presbyterian, I couldn't really believe that. What I did was pretend to have the same practical, matter-of-fact attitude as Donne. We convened each day at the Tisdales' and put our minds to hearing as much from Martin as we could. We had first of all, of course, to know where that conservatory was. And there were other questions. Martin seemed to have been seduced by the doctor's intellect . . . to the point of working for him. But we had found him dying in the cellar of the orphanage. What had happened? Donne was reluctant to put him under hard questioning—he didn't seem strong enough for it. The best course, if the most exacting, was patience.

We sat with him over several days . . . alone, the two of us. We did not think it advisable for the women to hear any more of it. Martin told us that in a very short time he had come to think of Dr. Sartorius in Sartorian terms—that is, with the disinterest of a scientist. "I forgot what was personal," he said. "My father? An abstraction, an unsouled creature, beyond my caring. It was only his body as a field for scientific experiment that was of interest. . . . The doctor never tried to persuade me of anything, he wanted nothing of me, really. . . . Once we had made our gentlemanly agreement, I felt it was to my advantage to know him and hear him speak his thoughts."

"What was the agreement?" Donne asked.

"Only that I would make no attempt to leave, or interfere with the work. In return I could have the freedom of the place. . . . I'd be treated as a guest. Simmons was not entirely happy with the arrangement. Apart from understanding the . . . sensitivity of his work, Sartorius, as far as I could see, depended on others to analyze what was in his interest. He lacked cunning . . . he was not wily. I think there was just enough ordinary humanity in the man that he liked someone to understand what he was doing.

''Seven gentlemen were in that . . . league of immortals. One day one of them died, truly died, and Sartorius invited me to observe the autopsy. This was performed in his surgery . . . on an iron table with turned-up edges and a drainpipe at one end. A flexible shower fixture hung from the ceiling to keep the corpse cold with running water. He asked me to take the faucet from its cradle and direct the stream at effluvia . . . created in the course of his observations. I don't know if his procedures were those of a coroner, I doubt that they were. He opened the chest and examined the lungs and bronchia, and held the heart, and declared all of it normal, unremarkable. The corpse seemed serenely undisturbed by its dissection. The face was beardless, unlined, the expression composed and incorrupt. He was a man of middle age, younger than the others, which surprised me. Sartorius talked as he worked. 'When Mr. Prine came to me he'd been diagnosed as an epileptic. He was given to convulsions, and episodes of paralysis. I knew from certain signs on the scalp that he was, in fact, syphilitic.' Sartorius examined the scalp and then raised it away from the skull with his lancet. Then he applied the trephine and removed a portion of the skull. I was not made ill by any of this. In his presence you relinquished yourself to his state of mind—in this instance his keen interest in the post-mortem. The opened body released such fetid, foul stinks. . . . But I was somehow inured, I felt this was some sort of clockwork to be disassembled, the face after all remained at rest and indifferent, a mask, a machine's costume. I was avid only to know what the doctor would discover. . . . The whole inner table of the skull had a rough, eroded appearance. He pointed out three separate depressions where the bone had thinned, so that when he held it up to the lamp, light could be seen through it. These depressions corresponded to three hard and irregular coral-like growths on the surface of the brain—as if the brain itself had absorbed the bony material. He almost chanted his comments about what he found, talking either to himself or to me, it was not clear. . . . Though he used the terms of physical medicine, each reference was quite specific. I watched his long, delicate hands and was so concentrated in my attention . . . that I imagined at moments it was the hands that were speaking. 'These adhesions about the fissure of Silvius, see how they bind the anterior and middle lobes into one mass.' His accent was very slight, nothing more than an intonation, yet it was there. 'And the dura mater in this area adheres to the brain tissue.' I saw what he made me see. . . . The most awful thing was a suppurating, yellowish cheesy deposit, shaped like a pyramid, which he deftly cut out and laid with his bare hands on a small scale, to determine its weight. He put his instruments down and held his hands under the shower faucet. 'Yet you have noticed how much of the brain and the skull are healthy. Unfortunately I can't determine the extent to which we may credit the treatments he received here. All we can say by way of consolation is that Mr. Evander Prine, who was a terminal syphilitic, remained alive longer than he had a right to. But I confirm Ricord's *Treatise on the Venereal.* Under tertiary symptoms we must place nodes, deep-seated tubercles, tubercles of cellular tissue . . . caries necrosis. . . .' His diction was so unemotional that when he made a personal remark, it came almost as a shock. 'Too late,' he said, 'too late, even for Sartorius.'

"It was easy to misunderstand him—to perceive him as only a physician, with the interests and the regrets of a physician . . . to give him ordinary motives. . . . One day he asked if I'd permit him a small experiment on my person. I lay down upon his dispensary table and he attached two anodes of a small magneto to my head, one at each temple. These were connected by wires to a pair of needles with their points resting against a revolving wax cylinder set in a wooden box. He explained everything as he went along. The cylinder was turned by a gearshaft attached to a small brass steam engine. The entire

procedure didn't last a minute, and as he had prom-
ised, I felt no sensation at all—no pain or anything
else. Afterward he showed me on the wax drum what
he said was a graphic representation of the electric
impulsings of my brain . . . a fairly regular figuration
similar to the path of the sine and cosine in mathe-
matics. This remarkable picturing device was of his
own invention. He told me he was assuming for purposes of his inquiry that I was a mentally fit person,
though I might have my own doubts of this . . . and
then showed me by comparison another cylinder,
which recorded the activities of the brain of a man
afflicted with a terrible disease whom he had brought
into this place after having seen him wandering
about on the street. This was the unfortunate known
to us as Monsieur, a tic-ridden, stuttering spastic, full
of grimaces, grins, and wild-eyed faces, a continuous
hysteric whose presence you couldn't endure for
more than a few moments, he was so relentless in his
mimicking behavior, this poor soul, giving back to
you every fleeting expression on your own face, including, and especially, your repugnance or pity for
him. Every gesture, everything that caught his eye,
Monsieur gave back in compulsive imitation, and he
was never still a moment, it was a kind of helpless
raging theatrics of behavior that Sartorius said had to
arise from a defect of the brain tissue. . . . When you
analyzed it, he said, it was merely an acceleration
and intensification of normal human activity. The

cylinder showed a wild disarray of peaks and val-
leys, irregular, jagged, profuse.

"He kept this unfortunate in a dark room by
himself and maintained him as you would a horse in
a barn. The interest for Sartorius was not charitable.
He showed me what happened when Monsieur was
brought in among the fellowship of elderly gentlemen. He became calm, placid, and even allowed the
attendants to bathe him—but only so long as he had
in his field of vision the old men sitting about in their
vacant, expressionless way, indifferent to everything
around them. After a while, he took on their stillness.
And astonishingly, at the same time they began,
mysteriously, to stir, and show irritability, one or two
of them were even taken with small palsies of the
hand or foot. . . . No, this is no mere physician. . . .
You know, while I've always posed as an intellectual
. . . and am in fact well read and informed in the crucial questions to be asked . . . nevertheless, I have
never had that vitality . . . that marks a great intellect.
I make an invidious comparison here. I've never occupied the convictions of my thought but suffered
them as a man might pick up something that's too hot
to handle. You couldn't know this, Mr. McIlvaine,
because the attitude I always brought to you, along
with my work, was a calculated . . . arrogance. But I
was overwhelmed in the presence of this man's
mind. Dr. Sartorius is not a doctor . . . except as medicine engages with the workings of the world. He

thinks with pieces of the world. He sees into its structures. If he has one working principle, I think, it is to connect himself to the amoral energies human life in society generates . . . irrespective of its beliefs.

''As you know, I always felt like a foreigner in my own country . . . estranged, a born alien, dissynchronous with my times . . . so that every stone street of this city, and every stone mansion, I saw at times as a kind of Ptolemaic ritual of madmen . . . so that what you thought of as your homes, with their hearth lights inside, I could imagine as the temples of cruel and savage cults. And then you set these temples one next to another on avenues, and drove your iron engines between them and strung your wires overhead and set your wires humming . . . and I was no more than a phantom on this grid . . . born without the faith, the body, to make this obsessionally ruled, tracked, and wired . . . exchange . . . my native city.

''So I was . . . available . . . to his influence. It was like coming ashore on the freshened winds of a newfound land. The manifest thoughts of Sartorius were a field of gravity, drawing me to him. What I saw in him was an aristocratic dominance over men like my father. He was supreme . . . indifferent to everything but his work, so lacking in self-consciousness that he didn't even take the trouble to record his experiments—he knew what they were, and how they went, it was all written in his mind, and since he lived in himself as the sole occupant, he had no thought for Science, that he would contribute to its history—or for posterity, that he would even require a name on his gravestone, when it came to that. His marvelous brain was oblivious to its own feats.

"It was my idea that he should have a secretary, a personal historian, it was my idea, my initiative. Dr. Sartorius, lacking vanity, didn't think about these things.

"And what was this work, at least as I could fathom it? What was its driving principle? I saw him transfuse blood from one living being to another. I saw him with a hypodermic tube inject cellular matter into deadened brains. I saw first one, then another, of the orphan children begin to age, like leaves turning yellow. Was this the work? Though I saw some of it, I was in crucial matters kept ignorant. For all the freedom I was given, I was not admitted to the surgery for certain procedures, which took hours. And all the life in the building was presumed salutary, from top to bottom, everything for a purpose, for life's purpose, whatever the agency of man could do was done here.

"But the customs of New York, like the past life of the old men, were invoked, they were used, as everything was used, for their therapeutic value. There were dinners, dances. . . . What you must understand about Sartorius is that he was never committed to one therapy, he made corrections constantly, he was truly disinterested, and as ruthlessly critical of his own ideas as of others'. He sought out what was aberrant in brains and bodies, as if the secrets of living beings could be more easily exposed there. Normality obstructed the scientific vision, it suggested a self-assurance of form that life had no right to claim. But where existence was afflicted and grotesque, it announced itself as the truly unreasoning thing it is. He regularly examined people who made their living from their deformity. He went downtown to their museums of living wonders and freak shows on Broadway. Dwarfs, midgets, acromegalics, mermaid claimants, so-called wolfmen. Gynandromorphs, poor souls imperfectly participating in the anatomies of both sexes. He drew their blood. I came to understand the pure scientific temperament as it shone from this man. It produced a mind that was unshockable, a man for whom there was no sacrilege, a being whose life was not staked on any fixed or unchanging idea that he had therefore to defend for the value of his life . . . in the way, you'd expect, for example, from Dr. Grimshaw.

"So . . . similarly, and just as rides were given in charged weather in public transport through the active streets of the city . . . balls were held. And we all were elevated to the conservatory, lit green by the industrial sconces on the walls, and serving for a ballroom. While the orchestrion disc revolved and tined out its lumbering waltzes, boosted with automatic bass drum and cymbals, the creatures of the immortal fellowship danced in their black ties . . . with their caretaker women. It was a medley of the waltz tunes of the day, to which the old men, led by their cyprians, made their obedient slow shuffles . . . including my father, doing his dutiful dance in a way that absolved him in my mind of all his criminal cunning. He had forgone the dignity of death, as they all had. He was reduced to a vacant old man I could look in on. Augustus Pemberton, that cold, blunt brute of greed . . . it had never occurred to me that he could have had any unsatisfied desires, even megalomaniacal ones. But here he was, a mindless dancer enacting this ritual, this sacrament for a religion that did not yet exist.

''So everything was Sartorius's triumph. Though he scrupulously fulfilled his part of the contract, he was entirely without care or concern for his patients except as they were the objects of his thought. What he warranted was only his scientific attention. But this was all! And from it he was recomposing their lives piece by piece, swaddling them like infants, riding them, dancing them, schooling them in an assemblage of life's cycles, and with his emollients, and powders, and fluid injections from the children, reconstituting them metempsychotically as endless beings.''

Twenty-three

OF course I'm compressing everything
Martin said, or everything I remember of what he
said, over several days. We would go over there in
the afternoon and sit with him. He was always glad
to see us. He had the gratitude of the recovering inva-
lid. Sometimes he was silent for long minutes . . .
with his eyes closed . . . till we'd begin to wonder if
he was asleep. But these were reflective pauses.
Sarah Pemberton worried if it was wise to have him
relive his experiences to this degree. She asked us
not to encourage him to overtax himself, or to sit so
long with him. This was her way to deal with things
. . . by leaving them to swell the brain. Donne pointed
out to her the absolute necessity of learning everything we could . . . and I pointed out the benefits of
reliving every moment, if possible . . . that Martin
seemed to want to talk about what had happened
. . . and that there was nothing as good for him, for
anyone, as getting the story told, turning it into an
object made of language . . . for everyone to lift and
examine.

One day Donne felt he was able to ask Martin

when and why the gentleman's agreement with Sartorius was ended.

"I'm not sure I know," Martin said. "There was a woman assigned to look after me . . . who would bring me my meals when I was to eat alone . . . and provide me with the essentials and clean my room, and so on. She never said anything—none of them did—though she was friendly enough, with her smiles and nods. She was an odd-looking woman with sparse hair under her nurse's cap, she wore the nurse's gray, the uniform all of them wore. One day I asked her her name. I asked how many were on staff there. I was curious about everyone and everything going on. She didn't answer—she shook her head and smiled. The proportions of her face were not normal. It was a broad face with flattened features, but somehow overendowed with bone on the right side. On the left side her ear seemed smaller than it should be. I asked a few more questions, each of which she answered with small shakes of her head while she waited politely and shyly smiling until she could go . . . and I realized she was deaf and dumb. They were all of them on this staff, deaf and dumb, as if they'd been recruited from one of the institutes for these unfortunate people. . . . I realized that the only person who actually spoke in the place, to whom I could speak, was Sartorius himself. This, once I became aware of it, became oppressive to me. . . . I suppose I might have given him some indication.

"Then at one point Sartorius asked me if I would submit to another procedure. He had already, with my permission, siphoned off some of my blood. He warned me it was not quite as painless as that had been . . . or the recording of my brain electricity had been . . . and therefore would require anesthesia. The procedure involved the withdrawal of bone marrow from my leg. . . . I told him I'd like to think about it. This was not an answer in the scientific spirit . . . which he must have understood before I did. Perhaps the spell of him was wearing off . . . but I began at night to dream of that frowning nut-brown boy in my father's coffin at Woodlawn. . . . I was dreaming of him . . . but it was a kind of awakening . . . or re-awakening . . . to the specific therapies by which Sartorius contrived to exempt the old gentlemen from death. . . .

"I cannot explain it—how I had . . . known but not known. How I had conveniently . . . forgotten. As if I had performed on myself some excision of a portion of the brain. But the effect upon me now . . . of becoming aware of what I'd known all along . . . was overwhelming. I was sickened . . . so terribly self-traduced . . . I could literally taste and be nauseated by . . . my own moral rot. I'm not sure I actually considered trying to escape . . . from what? But I did begin to feel the need to . . . breathe. Like that child in the coffin, I was buried too. This was a windowless, gaslit place . . . with its machinery always humming . . . and a humidity in the air that made me feel sometimes I was underwater . . . or that this was a hermetic undersea vault I was sealed in. Perhaps Sartorius saw my disturbed state, and found it—I don't know—disappointing in some way. But he seemed to lose interest in me. He did not ask again to perform the procedure. I was not invited to watch or participate as often as I had been. I was left to my own devices. . . . I felt finally he had forgotten I was there . . . his mind had moved on without me.

"It was Eustace Simmons, I think, who took the initiative. He came in one day with the woman I'd asked all the questions of . . . and sat across the table from me as I ate. I had by then stopped taking my meals upstairs with the . . . community. I was spending most of my time in the library. I was surprised to see Simmons—you didn't see him that much. He chatted as if he was making a social call.

"The next thing I knew, I was in complete darkness, my head aching, and it was a different atmosphere, close, with the smell of burned air, of ashes and soot. . . . I could hear the sound of footsteps over my head. And when I stood to get my bearings I found my hands holding the bars of a cell. I thought, finally, that was just."

He'd been brought back to the orphanage . . . and could not tell us how long a journey it was . . . or what direction he'd come from . . . or anything else that would give us some idea of where this place was that was the heart of the enterprise.

"Why do you suppose Simmons didn't just . . . do away with you?" I asked him.

"It was probably what he would have preferred. Simmons is a kind of dark stepbrother to me, you know. Much older, just as I am much older than Noah, but spiritually . . . my father's son . . . and right hand . . . as I never was. He became the doctor's right hand. He has the utmost respect for Dr. Sartorius. . . . He has the soul of a factotum, Simmons, for all his cunning. He needs someone to work for. So . . . the doctor might conceive of another use for me. I had the time to think about this. How long was I down there before my mind began to . . . drift. But I heard the footsteps of those children over my head. I knew they were children—you can't mistake the footsteps of children. I shouted and screamed to them . . . to get away, to run . . . knowing they couldn't hear. I was one of them, you see. After all. I understood that."

Martin was more than a few times in these recollections on the verge of tears. I think this was a moment when he couldn't help himself. He put his hand over his eyes and he wept.

As I have said, we were well into the autumn of the year. Somewhere in the middle of October. And now several things happened, more or less simultaneously. I arrived one afternoon for my visit with Martin and found a policeman standing guard at the Tisdales' door. I had to identify myself in order to be allowed to ring the bell. Emily admitted me. Behind her, her white-haired father was coming down the hall. "Newspapers! Police! What next, what next! I'm an old man, don't you people understand? I am not used to this!"

Emily saw me into the front parlor and excused them both for a moment . . . and I heard their voices retreat upstairs, his louder than hers, but hers prevailing apparently . . . because in a few minutes she was back downstairs without him.

She said: "The man who was arrested has been found dead at the Tombs. The omnibus driver? Wrangel, is that his name? He hanged himself in his cell."

"Where is Donne?"

"He has gone to get Noah from school."

"Where is Martin?"

"He is upstairs in his room. His mother is with him."

My blood was racing now. One could anticipate a certain degree of desperation on everyone's part. The previous evening there had been the citizens' meeting I think I have mentioned . . . at the Cooper Union. A raucous meeting with calls for Tweed's scalp. Instead they formed a committee of seventy

. . . eminent men, to bring a taxpayers' suit against the mayor and his administration. This was to enjoin the Ring from issuing bonds or paying city money to any supplier until an investigation was held. I didn't know what judge would give them their injunction, but it was electrifying news that the attempt would even be made.

I waited anxiously for Donne. When he returned safely with Noah and had seen him upstairs, we were able to talk alone for a few minutes. Of course he had not believed Wrangel had hanged himself. He told me there were bruises on the driver's skull. He'd been struck unconscious before he'd been strung up.

"Who would be employed for that?"

"It's not an unknown practice . . . for the Municipals to save the judiciary the bother of an actual trial."

"Are the Pembertons in danger?"

"I don't know. It depends on who's attending to this. I have to assume they could have traced Martin through the hospital. They may not have. They may be thoroughly occupied with their other troubles. . . . Wrangel may be sufficient for them for the time being. Or he may not. Conceivably, they could be engaged in a general . . . extirpation of the evidence. Of course, you shouldn't go into this with the others."

"Of course. Though your police guard seems to have unsettled the whole household."

"Sarah and Noah should make camp here, if Miss Tisdale will have them. But I'll tell everyone these are simply precautions. I'm sure now 'Tace Simmons has not fled the country. That's all to the good, if we can get our hands on him. . . . What is really odd is that as of midnight yesterday, I was fully reinstated in my duties."

"What?"

"I'm as surprised as you are. Perhaps the Ring feel they want me where they can keep their eye on me. They have a lot to deal with."

Apart from the accelerating seriousness of all this, it was clear Donne was in his element. I envied him, being out of mine. What made matters worse, I was quite aware that I could, in the interest of protecting Martin and his family . . . I could give this story to a working reporter . . . or even do it myself on a free-lance basis for one of the dailies. If the account came out of Martin's imprisonment in the Home for Little Wanderers . . . on whose board Tweed and his colleagues had served . . . and which happened to be where the suicide, Wrangel, was employed . . . who had been arrested for the killing of a street tough . . . why, even that broken-off part of the thing, with promises of more of the story to come, would freeze them in their tracks. Getting the news out would be no problem. I had not lost my standing, only my job. My resignation was looking better around the trade, though I had done nothing to explain it or publicize it. I had received a note from Mr. Dana, the publisher of the *Sun,* asking me to come around for a chat. And one of my friends on the *Telegram* had told me the publisher thought the paper had gone down in quality since I'd left . . . and why would he have bruited that about unless he wanted me to hear it?

So there was every reason to go ahead . . . except that—I confess it here—it was despicable, but I felt I had . . . time. The more of the story I could get, the more it would be mine. Exclusively. Did that mean I found myself prepared to put the interests of the story ahead of the lives of the people involved in it? I'm not sure. Possibly it can't be rationalized . . . but there is some instinct that prefers . . . unintruded-upon meaning. That whoever tells our moral history . . . must run behind, not ahead of it. That if, in fact, there is meaning, it is not tolled out by church bells but suffered into luminous existence. . . . Maybe I felt that to print the story now, or what I knew of it, would be an intervention . . . a trespass of the reporter into the realm of cause and effect . . . that would change the outcome. Still secret, these events could unfold naturally or unnaturally. If you're not convinced, let's just say that I didn't think the story was reportable, accurately, until it was all in. That there was no story . . . until I saw Sartorius.

In fact, even when these matters were closed, and the events concluded and the issues resolved, and I had my exclusive, I never ran it . . . which may suggest I had a premonition that, even completed, the story was not . . . reportorially possible . . . that there are limits to the use of words in a newspaper.

Whatever the reason, I was a selfish son of a bitch and published nothing. I was everyone's friend on Lafayette Place . . . and their secret betrayer. I was in an adventurous mood and prepared to take chances with other people's lives.

It had not escaped my competitive notice that Martin himself had, from some profound chastening of his ordeal, lost his keenness for following things any further. He asked no questions of us. He only ruminated on his own experiences. This seemed to me a kind of proof of the soundness of my position.

And now Donne, in his researches for the collected money of the millionaires, came up with something interesting. He found an entry in the accounts of the city's Water Department for the previous year published in the *Manual of the Corporation of the City of New York*—some twelve million dollars attributed to an 1869 bond issue for the improvement of the Croton Aqueduct. Yet, as he discovered, there had been no such bond issued on behalf of the

Water Department. And why would the Ring let that glaring asset sit when their method over the years was to understate their receivables and pad their disbursements? Donne thought this entry was in fact a portion of the fellowship's investment. He thought he would look for similarly disguised entries in other city department accounts.

And then he had his brilliant and culminating insight.

We stood one morning under our umbrellas . . . on a gravel road, between the distributing reservoir and the waterworks of the Croton Aqueduct . . . on a high, flattened hill in Westchester, twenty miles north of the city. It was a miserable raw wet morning. The massive granite waterworks, with its crenellated turrets at the corners and cathedral entrance doors of oak, was stained and streaked black by the heavy rain.

Behind us was the reservoir, its dark water stippled with white. It looked like a natural lake except for the lack of trees around its banks. I noticed at the water's edge, not far from where we stood, the wreck of a toy wooden boat. It lay on its side and lifted and fell in the wavelets running against the embankment under the racing black clouds.

Donne had told me only to be ready to leave my house before dawn. I'd known nothing of where we were going. We had ridden by train up the Hudson to the town of Yonkers . . . and there a carriage met us that took us east through the country in the direction of Long Island Sound. When we'd come up the road to the waterworks, I was astonished to see a whole troop of Municipals spread out around the building.

The policemen had brought two of their Black Marias. There were several broughams besides. The vehicles were lined up in the road, the horses wretched in the rain, their feet planted foursquare, their heads hanging.

As I stood looking up at the waterworks Donne's realization slowly duplicated itself in my mind. Except for three bull's-eyes set high up near the roofline, the building face was uninterrupted by windows. The sky was tumultuous with billowing black clouds that took on a green cast as they sailed over the roof. It seemed to me everything was in motion except for the waterworks. Rain in striations . . . the clouds very low, very swift-moving. The ground under me pulsed like a heartbeat. But this was the pumping waterworks machinery. Or was it? I couldn't quite trust my senses because I thought I heard band music under all of this . . . agitated nature. Under the rainfall's hiss, the rumbling sky . . . something insistent, pompous, rhythmical.

Motioning to one of the policemen, Donne approached the entrance. I followed. We waited as the policeman pounded the doors. After a minute they opened. No man from the Water Department, but a woman in a gray nurse's uniform stood there. Her eyes went wide, not at the sight of the policeman, but in reaction, I thought, to Donne's height, as she stared up at him, his umbrella aloft. She didn't seem to understand him when he asked if we could come in . . . but she thought a moment and then she opened the door wide and we passed through.

You know, at moments when our attention is painfully acute, we notice peripheral things . . . as if to reaffirm to ourselves our basic irresponsibility. The moment I was inside this stone entry hall . . . poorly lit, like a mine, with kerosene lamps . . . I felt the chill of entombed air and I heard the power of ducted water hissing and roaring in its fall . . . and I was aware, too, of the rap of our heels on a flight of iron stairs rising circularly about a giant grease-coated gearshaft . . . but what I attended to most keenly as I followed her was the movement of this woman's uncorseted buttocks under her nurse's dress—a plain middle-aged woman of no beauty or station.

Donne and the policeman took their time coming up, as if they were memorizing every step of the way. Finally we reached the top, a narrow catwalk that passed into a cavernous chamber . . . at the bottom of which was a vast inner pool of roiling water . . . churning up a mineral mist, like a fifth element . . . so that I could see, growing everywhere on the blackened stone walls, patches of moss and lichen and bearded slime.

We passed through this . . . atrium to a corridor lit with gas jets . . . and through another door, which the woman held open for us . . . that led to a recognizable room. But the transformation was a shock, as in a magic trick. We were in an anteroom, or foyer, like any other, with painted white walls, parqueted floors, mirror and sidetables, and a decorative urn. The woman pointed to a group of upholstered chairs, inviting us to be seated. Instead, Donne strode past her, knowing somewhere up here he should find Dr. Sartorius.

At this level—the third story? the fourth?—the band music was audible . . . like a parade one hears a block away. Donne's head-bobbing long-legged glide down the corridor threatened to leave me behind. He ignored the closed doors of several rooms. One door I happened to see as I rushed by was open a crack . . . and I caught . . . a glimpse . . . the suggestion of a wall of books, a figured rug on the floor, a gas lamp, and a man sitting in a chair reading. I did not for some minutes register the intelligence of this . . . but rushed on after the policemen.

I followed them up a broad flight of polished wood stairs with a carved banister. At the top of the stairs was a small landing . . . and double doors of steel with a wheel lock. Donne's man turned the wheel, pulled open the doors, and the music rushed out at us like the wind.

Shadows of the storm clouds loomed and faded

like a passing armada on the translucent green roof. The steel ribs of the roof shot out like flying buttresses. The orchestrion of oak and glass, as monumental as a cathedral organ, shuddered with its own music. The great golden disc revolved that beat the drum and shook the bells and plucked out the chords of a robotic waltz.

In the central terrace, women in gray nurses' uniforms were dancing with one another.

Our presence interrupted nothing. Here and there, stretched out on a bench, or slumped across a garden table, or, in one case, lying across a gravel path under a tubbed tree, were fully dressed old men. Donne went methodically to each one and felt the pulse. They were all dead—five there were—but for one rasping out his death rattle.

The nurses . . . or nurse-cyprians . . . waltzed slowly around. Their faces were immeasurably sad. I thought their cheeks were wet with their tears, but as I looked more closely I saw this was the humid atmosphere on their skin, as it was on my own when I touched my face . . . the atmosphere that was produced from the vents in the slate floors . . . a suspension of droplets that adhered to the skin like an oil.

I felt the oppression of a universe of water, inside and out, over the dead and the living.

The old men were shrunken, unnaturally darkened and sunken in on themselves, like vegetable husks. I looked at each face carefully, but I did not find one I recognized as Augustus Pemberton.

We searched the suites where the old men had slept and the rooms where they had been ministered to . . . doctor's surgery, treatment rooms, dispensary. All unoccupied.

I said to Donne that on the floor below I had seen a man reading in what looked like a library.

Donne's expression was puzzled. It was not that the music had drowned out my voice but that my voice itself, which I could hear, had a peculiar, gargled quality to it. I repeated what I knew as he bent his head to listen. A moment later he was rushing back down the stairs. Halfway down the corridor that door was still ajar. Donne's policeman flung it open, slamming it against the wall.

Sartorius looked up from his reading. He closed his book, stood, adjusted his tie, tugged the points of his vest. . . . A slender figure, not tall, but military in bearing, unhurried, with a supreme authority about him. He wore a black frock coat, a fashionably wide, loosely tied cravat with stickpin. The dark hair was close-cropped, the gaunt face clean-shaven, but for black burnsides framing his jaw and continuing under the chin to cover the neck and throat like a fur collar. The dark implacable eyes with a kind of desolation of knowledge in them . . . the thin-lipped, abstemious mouth . . . He regarded us . . . with his rigorous impersonality . . . and removed his watch from his fob pocket and glanced at it . . . as if to see if we had arrived more or less at the time he thought we would.

Why hadn't he tried to run? I have thought about this for many years. Society, as I've said, made no impression on him. He did not see himself in any relation to it. Certainly not to its laws. He had marched and ridden through the worst of our Civil War unscathed . . . either by its cannon and shot or by its issues. The seemingly endless carnage ended upon the table before him in his field surgery . . . as one continuously fascinating . . . wonderfully torn and broken and dying body . . . with endless things to be fixed. . . . He may have thought that whoever in the city had backed him would protect him now and see to it that he was restored to his work . . . so that, though his experiments had been disrupted, they would be . . . resumed. Or he may not have thought that at all.

But I'll tell you here . . . it is the nature of villainy to absent itself, even as it stands before you. You reach for it and close on nothing. You smash your hand on the mirror. Who is this looking back at you? Perhaps you're aware by now of the elusiveness of my villains. This is a story of invisible men, dead men or men indeterminately alive . . . of men hidden, barricaded, in their own created realm behind the thick walls of the brownstones of New

York. . . . You have not seen them, except in the shadows, or heard them speak, except in the voices of others. . . . They've been hiding in my language . . . men who are only names in your newspapers . . . powerful, absent men.

I remember as we drove away from the waterworks I was the one who turned and peered through the oval window of the brougham . . . streaming with rain . . . for a last glimpse of this hideous industrial monument . . . so utilitarian, and yet penthoused for a voluptuary consciousness. A few policemen had been left on watch. We made a parade of our wet, plodding departure, one of the Black Marias behind us filled with the cyprian-nurses and odd attendants and personnel of the waterworks, and the other . . . now a kind of hearse . . . policemen ahead of and behind us in their carriages . . . a procession in the name of crime and punishment . . . except that Sartorius, sitting between Donne and myself, might have been talking to friends and admirers at a dinner party.

"When young Pemberton first arrived at my laboratories he was outraged . . . whether because I had kept his father alive or had not kept him alive enough, I couldn't determine. In either case, he was blinded by his own moralism. But after a while he began to understand. There was no integrity in the lives of my patients, they were self-submitted to me for my use. They are notable for proving to me so far only how terribly membranous the mind is, so easily breached, with a drug, with a kind of light, or a degree of heat or cold. . . . They did not agree to give themselves to my care in a uniform condition, you understand. The illnesses varied, the ages, the prognoses. Though all the illnesses were fatal. Yet I had them conformed to a degree of existence I could lower or raise by my application, as you quicken or dampen a gas flame with a turn of the wrist. I reached only this early stage, that I could keep them biomotive, that is, where they did not stop breathing, to the extent that I did not overendow them with self-sustaining energies. This, of course, was not what they had dreamed of for themselves. On the other hand, they had, in this state, all the time in the world, didn't they? All the time in the world . . ."

Donne said: "We did not find Augustus Pemberton."

"I think Mr. Simmons must have taken him away . . . when it became apparent that . . . the experiment could not continue. Apart from my vitalizations," he said in his surprisingly boyish voice, "the interesting truth is in the great losses that human life can sustain—its individuation of character, its speech, its volition—without becoming death. You learn this first as a surgeon in terms of what can be cut away. It is possible that a working familiarity with the mechanics of the human body engenders cynicism. More likely it cleanses the natural scientist of ennobling sentiments, pieties which teach us nothing. The old categories, the old words, for what is, after all, a physically very modest creature, though self-impressed . . .''

I was sitting shoulder to shoulder with Sartorius . . . and felt his own physical modesty through the cloth of my coat.

''He is alive, then?'' Donne said.

''Who?''

''Mr. Pemberton.''

''I can't tell you if at this moment he is alive or not alive. . . . Without treatment his time is limited. I find your concern amusing.''

''What does it matter, after all?'' I said to Donne.

Sartorius apparently mistook my meaning. ''Whatever their state of being, they were hardly more pathetic than people you will find strolling on Broadway, or shopping in Washington Market, all of them severely governed by tribal custom, and a structure of fantasies which they call civilization. . . . Civilization does not fortify the membranous mind, or alter our subjection to the moment, the moment that has no memory. . . . The person who grows old, or halt, has no past in the eyes of others. . . . The gallant soldier on the battlefield one day is the next day the amputated beggar we would rather not look at on the streetcorner.

''We live subject to the moment according to cycles of light and dark, and weeks and months. Our bodies have tides, and flow with measurable impulses of electric magnetism. It may be that we live strung like our telegraph wires in fields of waves of all kinds and lengths, waves we can see and hear and waves we cannot, and the life we feel, the animacy, is what is shaken through us by these waves. . . . Sometimes I cannot understand how these demanding questions of truth do not impel everyone—why I and a few others are the exception to the mass of men so content with their epistemological limitations that some even make poetry of them.''

And so we made our way through the rain back to the city.

Twenty-four

HERE is Sartorius as I dream of him. . . .

I stand on the embankment of a reservoir, a vast squared body of water cratered in a high plain overlooking the city. The earthen embankment rises up from the ground at an angle that suggests the engineering of an ancient civilization, Egyptian, or perhaps Mayan. The light is bad, but it is not nighttime, it is storm light. The water is sea-like, I hear the violent chop, the insistent slap of the waves against the embankment. I'm watching Sartorius, I have followed him here. He stands out a ways in the darkening day, he is gazing at something on the water, my black-bearded captain, for I think of him as that, as a man of the sea, the master of a vessel. He holds his hatbrim. The wind takes the corner of his long coat and presses it against his leg.

He knows I'm watching him. He acts on the presumption of partnership, as if he were on watch for our mutual benefit. What directs his attention is a model boat under sail, rising and falling on heavy swells, disappearing and then reappearing at an alarming heel, water pouring off her deck. She rises on a crest, dives, and rises again. I am lulled by the rhythm of her shuddering rises and swift, pointed descents. Then it happens that I wait for her to reappear and she does not. She's gone. I am as struck in the chest by the catastrophe as if I were standing on a cliff and had watched the sea take a sailing vessel.

Now I am running after him across a wide moat of hardened earth that leads to the waterworks. Inside I feel the chill of entombed air and I hear the hissing and roaring of water in its fall. The walls are stone. There is no light. I follow the sound of his footsteps. I reach a flight of iron stairs rising circularly about a giant gearshaft. Around I go, rising to a dim light. I find myself on a catwalk suspended over an inner pool of churning water. The light drifts down from a translucent glass roof. And I am standing next to him! He is bent over the railing with a rapt expression of the most awful intensity. . . .

Below, in the yellowing rush of spumed currents and water plunging into its mechanical harness, a small human body is pressed against the machinery of one of the sluicegates, its clothing caught as in some hinge, and the child, for it is a miniature, like the ship in the reservoir, slams about, first one way and then the next, as if in mute protest, trembling and shaking and animating by its revulsion the death that has already overtaken it.

I find myself shouting. Then I see three men poised on a lower ledge as if they have separated from the stone or made themselves from it. They are the water workers. They heave on a line strung from a pulley fixed in the far wall, and by this means advance a towline attached to the wall below my catwalk where I cannot see. But then into view comes another of the water workers, suspended from a sling by the ankles, his hands outstretched as he waits to be aligned so that he can free the flow of the obstruction.

And then he has him, raised from the water by his shirt—an urchin, anywhere from four to eight, I would say, drowned blue—and then by the ankles and shoes, and so, suspended both, they swing back across the pouring currents, rhythmically, like performing aerialists, till they are out of sight below me.

Outside, at the entrance doors to the waterworks, I watch Sartorius load the wrapped corpse into a white city stage, leap onto the driver's perch, and lay out over the team of horses a great rolling snap of the reins. He glances back at me over his shoulder as the carriage races off, the bright black wheel's spokes brought to a blur. He smiles at me as at a complicitor. Above him the sky is a tumultuous rush of billowing black clouds shot through with rays of pink and gold. . . .

Finally you suffer the story you tell. After all these years in my head, my story occupies me, it has grown into the physical dimensions of my brain . . . so . . . however the mind works . . . as reporter, as dreamer . . . that is the way the story gets told.

Here is the dream's conclusion: The rain begins. I go back inside. It rains there too. The water workers are dividing some treasure among themselves. They wear the dark blue uniform of the municipal employee, but with sweaters under their tunics and their trousers tucked into their boots. I imagine in their lungs the same fungus that grows on the stone. Their faces are flushed, their blood urged to the skin by the chill, and their skin brought to a high glaze by the mist. They break out the whiskey for their tin cups. I understand there is such a cherishing of rituals too among firemen and gravediggers. They call out to me to come join them. I do. . . .

Or else I began suffering this dream long ago, years before these matters I've been describing to you . . . before I knew there was a Sartorius . . . when . . . on the embankment of the Croton Reservoir . . . I think now . . . I imagine . . . I'm convinced—is it possible?—he rushed past me with the drowned boy in his arms. There are moments of our life that are something like breaks or tears in moral consciousness, as caesuras break the chanted line, and the eye sees through the breach to a companion life, a life in all its aspects the same, running along parallel in time, but within a universe even more confounding than our own. It is this other disordered existence . . . that our ministers warn us against . . . that our dreams perceive.

Twenty-five

SHORTLY after reaching Manhattan, Captain Donne found a judge through the local precinct house and procured a court order remanding Dr. Sartorius, for observation, to the Bloomingdale Asylum for the Insane on 117th Street and Eleventh Avenue. The rest of the procession continued south into the city but Donne and I were driven by carriage to the New York Central station at Inwood, near the Spuyten Duyvil, and caught a train that would take us to Tarrytown, thirty or so miles up the Hudson. We had risen before dawn but Donne showed no sign of weariness. In fact he could barely sit still. He walked the length of the train several times and finally came to rest standing on an open platform between cars and inhaling the wet wind.

I didn't know what a capture felt like to a policeman. My own sense of things was that we had drummed the prey into the net. . . . The undeniably brilliant intellect of Dr. Sartorius rendered him, paradoxically, a wild animal in my mind, a pure unreasoning product of nature. But Donne seemed not even to be thinking of Sartorius. He would not talk about the morning's work. He'd decided that he knew where Simmons had taken the dying Augustus Pemberton. He was supremely confident, as why should he not be? He said: "Even they have sentiments. Their sentiments parody the normal person's . . . but I suppose, after all, it makes them human."

I felt worn down with gloom. After seeing the inside of the waterworks I grieved for Martin Pemberton. . . . He had been awed by Sartorius and then repelled by him . . . and then subjected to slow starvation in solitary darkness . . . which he saw as a kind of penance. I wondered if it was a mistake to expect of him anything more than a continuing and deep state of shock.

By now, midafternoon, the rain had stopped, but the heavy black clouds were still with us, moving low and seeming to keep pace with the locomotive on its journey up the Hudson. In Tarrytown we boarded the river ferry to Sneeden's Landing, where we hired an open carriage and asked directions of the livery boy . . . and in a short while were making our way uphill through the forested road, and then along the western bluffs of the river to Ravenwood.

The Hudson is a magnificent wide silver river at this point . . . and riding along the sheer bluffs with a view of the river southward, and the enormous black agitated sky rushing up from Manhattan, I found myself thinking not that this was the home territory of Augustus Pemberton. I thought instead of Tweed—I

felt these excursions out of the city limits were trac-
ing Tweed's beginning campaigns against the larger
nation.

At Ravenwood you came in off the road onto a
wide gravel path that went along a quarter mile or so
through the woods . . . very dark that afternoon, like
the cavernous inside of something . . . past some
shadowy outbuildings . . . to a curving drive that circled around enormous hedges . . . to the entrance
steps at the foot of the portico. Here, when the horse
was reined and stood still with a soft shudder, and we
no longer had in our ears the sound of its footfalls or
the crackle of the carriage wheels on the gravel path,
the silent presence of the Italianate mansion made itself felt. It was unlit. Every window was boarded.
The great greensward leading down to the river was
overgrown with grass that had fallen over on itself.
The light was bad—it gave us none of the detail of
the house, but only its extent, its length of porch, and
. . . as we sat in the carriage, not realizing that neither
of us was in a hurry to get down . . . a sense of commanding wealth.

I imagined Sarah Pemberton and Noah in residence here. I saw them in the lighted rooms, appear-
ing in one window . . . and after a moment in another.

Perhaps Donne was thinking along similar
lines. . . . I could not ignore the energy of his pursuit
. . . that it had to do with Sarah. It was really a ro-
mance they had made for themselves out of this un-

holy matter . . . and I saw an intrepid spirit in it, I suppose, a human means of resistance to the darkest devilishness, the way people have of combining for strength, through their feelings, though I doubt that their understanding of their feelings had been expressed in many words or included, as yet, any declared intentions.

Donne had bestirred himself and was now on the deep porch, walking from one end to the other. I heard him try the front door. I heard his footsteps. It was getting dark rapidly. I got down from the carriage on the river side, and looked down the long, dark slope to the peculiar implication of a river in the lighter sky between the bank and the far bluffs. But then I thought I saw something in the grass about two thirds of the way down the slope.

After a few feet my pants legs were soaked. The rains had left the grounds swampy. It was some consolation that after sloshing my way down there, I found the corpse of Augustus Pemberton propped on a rattan chaise that was faced toward the river. He, or it, was soaked too, with his bony legs ridged in his trousers, his large bluish feet bare, the toes pointing to heaven, his hands folded, his fingers intertwined . . . a man at peace . . . who had lived in the limbo of science and money. The head was turned to the side, as if from its own weight, and I could see the wen on his neck, which had apparently maintained its health amidst the general wasting away. I was not repelled, only curious, and in the fading light was able to see that the bonework of his large head had stretched the skin so taut . . . and it was so empurpled . . . that this was no longer a human face possessed of character . . . and I could not believe it to have been the source of any kind of affection in the heart of a woman of the quality of Sarah Pemberton . . . or obsessive fascination in the heart of the young Martin Pemberton. I tried to perceive the tyrannic will in these remains, but it was gone, just part of the estate.

With the encroaching darkness the wind began to pick up. I called to Donne. He came down and knelt beside the body, and then stood and peered in every direction, as if something of Augustus Pemberton that should have been there was missing. The wind seemed to be blowing the darkness in upon us. ''We need light,'' Donne said, and strode back up the slope.

I stood for some minutes beside the body on its chaise, as if it were my orientation in this . . . wilderness. My camp, my base. I had always made a distinction between what was Nature and what was . . . City. But that was no longer tenable, was it? The distinction was between all of God's endless provision . . . and the newsroom. I longed to be back now in my newsroom, sending the story up to the compositors. Not in this wild—I was not one for the wild.

I felt a perverse admiration for Mr. Pemberton . . . and for his colleagues of the mortuary fellowship,

Mr. Vanderweigh, Mr. Carleton, Mr. Wells, Mr. Brown, Mr. Prine. I saw Sartorius, for all his imperial achievement, as . . . their servant. They, not he, had ridden up Broadway with the news . . . that there was no life, no death, but something that was a concurrence of both.

Actually, when the hearing was held to decide if Sartorius should be permanently committed to the insane asylum or put on trial, this same idea, his servitude to wealth, was brought up by Dr. Sumner Hamilton, one of the three alienists on the Commissio de Lunatico Inquirendo. But I will get to that. Donne came running back with a kerosene lamp he had found by breaking into a gardener's shed. In the light of the lamp I saw Augustus's gray hair receding at the front of the skull but rising in a billow at the crown. "Someone had to close the eyes," Donne said, and holding the lamp over his head, he made his way to the land's edge.

Now, as I have said, there was a narrow cut downward to a scaffolded wood stairs that had been built down the sheer bluff to the beach several stories below. In this bad light, from the top platform, we did not at first see the broken railing halfway down. What we saw below was a skiff blowing about at anchor a few feet off the shore, its unfurled sail dragging in the water.

While I waited there, Donne went down the stairs. I watched as the light descended, growing brighter in itself but casting less and less illumination for my benefit with each of his steps. Then he called, and telling me to tread cautiously and stay to the wall side, he bid me come down . . . which I did. We stood on a platform perhaps two thirds of the way down: the railing here was entirely gone, and resumed, jaggedly, halfway down the next flight of steps.

We got down the rest of the way and found a man on his back with his head almost entirely pounded into the sandbank by a seaman's footlocker, which, nevertheless, he continued to hold in his arms as the object of his love. Donne said quietly it was 'Tace Simmons. There was a great mess of blood and matter around the head, which had struck some sort of rock under the sand. One of the eyes had been dislodged from its socket. When we pulled the footlocker out of the stiffened arms, the latches, which had no padlocks, fell open with a clink. Donne opened the top of the chest back on its hinges . . . and there, filling it from top to bottom, were stacks of greenbacks, federal gold certificates of every denomination . . . and even shinplasters, notes for amounts less than a dollar. Donne remarked that apparently not all of Mr. Pemberton's fortune had been turned over to the enterprise of endless life. ''Cunning to the end'' was what he said by way of eulogy, but with respect to the factotum Simmons or to the old man up on the bluff, I could not tell.

Twenty-six

THE laws of New York State held—for all I know they still do—that a person committed to an insane asylum by anyone other than a legal relation has to be examined by a board of qualified alienists . . . to determine if the commitment is appropriate. Sartorius had no living relations. The doctors at the Bloomingdale facility having recommended his confinement in the New York State Institution for the Criminally Insane on Blackwell's Island, a state-appointed Commissio de Lunatico Inquirendo, as the alienists themselves so delicately put it, was called into session. All this in a matter of weeks. It was unseemly haste on the part of the medical community! The Commissio was not a court and had no obligation to make its hearings public. I was beside myself. Try as I might, I couldn't sit in. At one point, I know, they adjourned to the waterworks to examine Sartorius's facilities. They called on Martin Pemberton for his testimony . . . and somehow Dr. Grimshaw, terribly exercised by the thought that Sartorius might not stand before a court for his crimes, arranged to be heard before them. Donne was not called, nor was I.

No written record was made of their delibera-
tions. The report of the Commissio was sealed by
court order and to this day has never been released.
But let me tell you about institutional thought. Whatever the institution . . . and however worthy or sub-
stantive . . . its mind is not an entirely human mind
. . . though it is made up of human minds. If it were
really human it would be capable of surprises. . . . If
it were wholly human it would be motivated by all
sorts of noble or ignoble ideas. But the institutional
mind has only one mental operation: It abhors truth.

The head of the Commissio was Dr. Sumner
Hamilton, a leading psychiatrist of the city. He was a
stout, heavily jowled man who waxed his mustaches
and combed his thin black hair crosswise, ear to ear.
He loved good food and wine, as I was to learn, after
footing the bill for our dinner at Delmonico's years
later . . . when he was quite willing to talk.

"I had of course heard rumors of a scientific orphanage." Hamilton's voice was a very deep, reso-
nant bass. "Somewhere up on the East River, or
north of the Central Park, or in the Heights. . . . I
didn't know exactly what *scientific* was supposed to
mean. On the other hand, an orphanage presumably
set up to test modern theories of behavior or health or
education seemed likely, even inevitable, given everything going on in New York . . . everything
changing, modernity driving all before it."

"Had you ever met Sartorius?"

"No."

"Had you heard of him?"

"Never. But I'll tell you, I knew he was a good doctor the minute I laid eyes on him. I mean, you would trust him to do what had to be done. Not the personality. No bedside manner there. But the quality of mind. Very strong, powerful. He answered only the questions he felt deserved an answer. We ended up trying to formulate questions he respected! Can you imagine? I thought . . . if I poke around his disinterest, the pure science he seems to . . . exemplify, I might get a rise out of him. Crack him a bit, see what's underneath. I suggested that he was one of those doctors who attach themselves to the wealthy. There are not a few like that, who take their practice to the money, I can tell you. I was deliberately rude. I asked if, after all, he was no more than a kind of . . . medical valet.

"He said—and I can't give you that accent . . . it was so slight, vaguely European, but he might have been a Hungarian or a Slav as easily as a German— he said: 'Do you imagine, Dr. Hamilton, I would have as a purpose merely to keep certain wealthy men alive? That that end would interest me, of itself? I maintained them in the context of my larger interests, not as a physician but as a natural scientist. Whatever their own desires, or grandiose intentions, I told each of them exactly what I would endeavor to do . . . that might, incidentally, be to his advantage

. . . and that is just what I have done. . . . Whether this one hoped for a normal recovery, or that one for extended life, or another cherished a vision of eternal life, that was their business. I offered them something they understood quite well . . . an investment. They were qualified for my attention not by their wit or the importance to mankind of their continued life, the gifts they had to give for the benefit of society, or the fact that they were good and kind . . . but precisely by their wealth. This work cannot be done unless it is endowed. It requires money. They were qualified subjects by reason of their wealth and self-qualified by their rapacity—these seemed to be the essential things, and not at all in short supply in the city of New York. But in addition, each one of my gentlemen was given by nature to secrecy, to conspiracy, they were ultimate conspirators, this amiable circle, they not only wanted what I offered, they wanted it only for themselves.'

''Put me in my place, I can tell you. He was . . . impressive. He'd spent a couple of weeks up there in Bloomingdale. It showed in his suit, which was somewhat the worse for wear. He'd not been permitted to shave . . . and so on. But it didn't matter. He had this upright horseman's posture. He didn't plead, needless to say, or attempt to sway us one way or another. He didn't choose to demonstrate to us, however subtly—and I know how subtle some of these maniacs can be—that he was sane, or for that matter insane. We were there to commit him . . . or to hang him. Since neither alternative was desirable, he didn't seem to care which it was.

"But I kept pressing the point . . . in vain, of course. He couldn't be shaken. He said the proof of a scientific proposition was that it was universally applicable. If an experiment of his was valid, it could be repeated by others to yield the same results. He said that in the war he had devised surgical procedures for the wounds of high-ranking officers . . . that were now standard medical corps procedures for all ranks. When I asked him, pointedly, if he was saying someday his researches would be to the benefit of . . . street children . . . he smiled and he said: 'You're not suggesting, Doctor, that I am to be distinguished from you or your colleagues . . . or indeed anyone else in the city . . . in observing the laws of selective adaptation . . . that ensure survival for the fittest of the species.' "

I said to Dr. Hamilton: "How can a procedure be repeated if no one knows it exists? Martin Pemberton told me Sartorius kept no records of his work."

"It's not true that he kept no records. We found his notebooks, stacks of them, locked in a cabinet in his dispensary."

"What happened to them? Where are they?"

"I won't tell you that."

"Did you read them?"

"Every word. He wrote in Latin. It was breathtaking. We were able to understand some of his . . . equipment only by referring to the notebooks. I will say this to you: He was a man ahead of his time."

"So you didn't think, then, he was truly insane?"

"No. Yes. My profession was implicated. There was something in this . . . quite crucial to all of us. It happened in our midst. The behavior in question appeared to be criminal, at least. Let us say it was. But it was . . . consistent with the man's whole medical achievement. He was a brilliant practitioner. He kept going! That is the point—he kept going . . . through, beyond . . . sanity, whatever that is. Or morality, whatever that is. But in a perfect line with everything he'd done before.

"Good God . . . as to what is sane or insane . . . I'll tell you about the state of knowledge in the profession of psychiatry: Give me an old man making his will and let me ask him a question or two and I'll tell you if he is competent. I am sufficient to the task. I know in a lunatic asylum to instruct staff to stop punishing the poor souls. To give them good food and clean beds, and fresh air. To get them doing things with their hands, knitting, or weaving, or drawing their mad little pictures. There you have the level of psychiatric knowledge today. And no less culpable for the handsome living I make from it. The degree of the man's behavior was—what?—excessive? Whatever the system of thought behind it, the behavior was excessive. Insanely excessive. The deeper question was—should we let the public know? This city had recently suffered several shocks to its spirit, if I may call it that. There was some question as to whether it could suffer another. The district attorney all but said to us . . . If he is sane a charge is drawn, the legal machinery begins to move. A preliminary hearing is held in a courtroom. In the courtroom are members of the press . . .''

''He was under Tweed's protection.''

''Tweed was finished anyway.''

''So you knew Sartorius was sane?''

''No, by God, I'm trying to tell you. We knew no such thing. Can you call the things he did . . . sane? *Sanity* is a term about as useful as . . . *virtue.* Will you give me a clinical definition of *virtue*? This wine in my glass is a damn good wine, a virtuous wine, virtuously . . . winy. It exemplifies the best behavior of wine. It is a good and sane and virtuous wine!''

''You went up there—to the waterworks.''

''Yes.''

''What was your impression?''

''My impression? He had machines there we had never seen before . . . that he'd invented. Apparatus for the transfusion of blood. We are just coming around to knowing how to do that. Apparatus to measure brain activity. Diagnostic uses of fluid drawn from the spine. . . . He operated on those men. He cut away their malignant organs and connected them to machines which performed the work of those organs. He'd devised a method to distinguish different types of human blood, he injected bone marrow to arrest malignancies of the blood. Not everything . . . There was a lot of foolishness . . . drifts into metaphysical nonsense . . . cosmetic therapies. . . . He had so many things going on for those old men, he couldn't always have known which was working and which was not. No, it was not all triumph. . . . The last things in the notebooks . . . he was doing animal experiments, I think . . . actually trying to transfer a heart from one animal to another.''

''Did you burn his notebooks? You did, didn't you?''

''You asked for my impressions. I sat down on a bench in that indoor . . . park of his and . . . I couldn't be sure that I wouldn't have willingly committed myself to his . . . genius. To have one of those women minister to me . . . to my every need . . . in that pastoral . . . scientific heaven . . . to live there in a kind of dumb, mindless happiness in the belief that I was being rejuvenated for . . . eternal life. I sat there in that conservatory . . . in that quiet, civilized industrial paradise—I'll tell you what it reminded me of . . . the very quiet, pleasant railroad-station café of a small European city—and thought, yes, if I had the courage, I would do just what they did, those old scoundrels. I would do just what they did.''

I said: ''Dr. Sartorius extracted the blood . . . the bone marrow . . . the glandular matter . . . of children . . . to continue the lives of these elderly, fatally ill men . . .''

''Yes.''

''. . . who gave him their fortunes in hopes of . . . denying their own mortality.''

''Yes.''

''Children died in their place.''

''Never by his hand.''

''What?''

''Not from any of his procedures. Either he took them after an accidental death . . . or, if he worked with living . . . donors, as he did subsequently . . . those who died, died of fear. Of an undetectable . . . infirmity in their spirits of the . . . survival instinct. Physically, the children's health was never impaired. That's what he said. And it's a matter of record . . . how well they cared for them in the Home for Little Wanderers.''

Dr. Hamilton's eyes were bloodshot and baleful. ''You tell me, McIlvaine, since you're feeling so righteous. What we did worked out, didn't it? Civilization was avenged, was it not?'' He sat hunched over in all his bulk, resting his elbows on the table, his arms bulging in their sleeves, his hands crossed at the wrist. "I believe you're something of a historian. You remember the doctors' riots . . . when the mob chased those Columbia medical students and wanted to lynch them for dissecting cadavers in their anatomy classes?"

"That was a hundred years ago."

"You're not telling me we're that much further along, are you?"

Twenty-seven

I'M fully aware that you may think what I've been telling you is no more than an elaborate rendition of my . . . insanity. That's reasonable enough. I'm an old man now and I have to acknowledge that reality slips, like the cogs in a wheel. . . . Names, faces, even of those close to you, become strange, beautifully strange, and the commonest sight, the street you live on, appears to you one sunny morning as the monumental intention of men who are no longer available to explain it. . . . Even words have a different sound, and things you knew you relearn with wonder before you realize you knew them well enough once to take no notice of them. When we're young we can't anticipate that what is so matter-of-factly there for us in life is just what we'll have to struggle to hold on to as we grow older. . . . And time estranges us from the belief we are all given—the pious and the blasphemous alike—that we are born to live in pleasure or pain, happiness or despair, but always in great moral consequence.

For all of that, I've had this apartment in Gramercy Park for many years now, and I'm known to people in the neighborhood as a sane and responsible citizen, if sometimes difficult or cranky. I'm not unduly modest . . . certainly insofar as I've lived much of my life in the satisfaction of the results I've had from the insecure trade of newspapering. If I were crazy, wouldn't I want something? It seems to me madness is a kind of importuning, a clutching at the sleeve. I seriously question the value of this account to my madness, if it is that, since I require nothing of anyone who will hear it. I need nothing and ask for nothing. My only worry . . . my only worry . . . is that I've given myself so completely to the narrative that very little of my life is left for whatever else I might intend for it . . . and that—it's really an uncanny feeling—when the story ends, I will end.

Now by way of coming round to the end, I'll say here that when Sartorius was remanded, for life, to the Asylum for the Criminally Insane, I felt a peculiar sort of injustice had been done . . . that the man deserved a trial. Of course some of my reasoning was self-serving: If there had been a public record, I would have had corroboration for my exclusive . . . although I was by this time thinking even more ambitiously of not merely breaking the news but telling the whole story within the pages of a book. Let the daily papers cover the trial and I would be able to amplify it with everything I knew, in all its detail, from the beginning. The papers would provide my preamble. But beyond that . . . to undertake the ritual by which we could . . . acknowledge ourselves . . . for what we were. I'll grant you, perhaps it is sentimentalism to think a society is capable of being spiritually chastened . . . in some self-educative way . . . of pulling itself up just one . . . rung . . . toward moral enlightenment. That we would, as a kind of municipal congregation, drop to our knees and gather our children to us. What really happens is that we shunt off our evil, embody it in . . . our defendants and turn away. Still, I had these uncharacteristic sentiments . . . to the point of wondering if I had been cast, myself, into some mental state of—God help me—sympathy for Sartorius, an echo of Martin Pemberton's.

I also found myself in an unlikely alliance with Dr. Grimshaw, who went about trying to muster up public support for a court proceeding. He was not interested in ritual edification. He wanted the man to hang. The difficulty was . . . Sartorius was by now a condemned inmate in a mental asylum. That was his identity, that was who he was . . . and it seemed to have the effect of erasing everything else about him. Such people are without a past, so . . . definitive is their present circumstance. The whole thing had been wrapped up very quietly . . . cooperatively. The doctors and the Municipals and the district attorney's office had all agreed, though for their own reasons, that the resolution should be this . . . quite unconstitutional resolution. Even to those others who heard the story, or part of the story, it seemed incidental to

the political fireworks: Tweed's right arm, the comptroller, Connolly, had offered to cooperate with the
public inquiry. Other Ring members had fled the
country. And a grand jury had been empaneled to
hear evidence and draw up indictments.

I will say here that the esteemed Captain Donne
was in this matter a disappointment to me. He was by
now situated back behind his desk at the Mulberry
Street headquarters, and receiving petitioners with
his hands folded before him on the desk, and his long
face lowered between the flying points of his shoulders. I joined our friend Grimshaw in appealing to
him to side with us filing for a writ of habeas corpus
. . . that would be the beginning of a legitimate legal
process. He would not do it.

"I think justice has been done," he said.

"How, sir," said Grimshaw, "if the man is left
alive to do more murdering evil?"

"Have you ever been to Blackwell's Island,
Reverend?"

"I have not."

"What we have done may be unconstitutional
. . . it is not due process . . . but it is all the justice you
could wish for."

I said: "Except that the rights of the society are
scanted."

Donne said: "If you have a trial, he will have to
be heard. Any lawyer would see that the only hope of
a defense would be in taking his testimony. He could

argue in his perversity that our interruption of his work cost the lives of his patients. And our proofs, you know . . . are largely circumstantial. At the least his ideas will be heard . . . his . . . genius will be on view. I can't think that would be of any benefit to a Christian society,'' he said, turning his gaze on Grimshaw.

You will not hear from me that Edmund Donne had his limits. Perhaps he felt, after all, that the rights of society had been honored . . . that from the blundering ad hoc constituency of our frail selves . . . somehow, by hook or by crook, we had managed to rid our city of this . . . horror. We had worked it out. There was a degree of satisfaction to be taken. A young man's life had been saved. A family had been restored to itself. And in the course of things Donne had found a face to look upon that he had loved once before . . . or was newly in discovery of . . . but, in either event, was in hopes of seeing every day and night for the rest of his life.

So I will not say Donne did not appreciate the depth of the conspiracy—that it was not only a concordance of wealth, and government, and science but a profound . . . derangement of the natural order of fathers and sons. There was a more fathomless threat there than to Christianity . . . that left my eyes blasted to peer into it.

I went across to Blackwell's Island one day from the pier at Fifty-ninth Street. The ferry was no more than an open boat fitted up with side-wheels and powered by a small coal-fired steam engine mounted on the deck. It barely kept its course against the powerful scalloping currents of the East River. The weather was raw—this was November, when the chill winds huddle you in your coat and give clear, icy indication of the age of your bones. I should also say, in abhorrence of suspense, that I think now, if I wasn't the only person to visit Sartorius, I was certainly the last before his murder at the hands of a colleague in criminal insanity a few days later.

He wore the gray beltless robe they dressed them in. His eyes were sharp and clear black behind the incongruous pince-nez affixed to the bridge of his nose . . . but his head was shaved, he was beardless . . . and in this freezing catacomb his legs were bare . . . so that I was put in mind of some . . . garden creature . . . something hairless . . . and all eyes. I saw him through a meshwork screen bolted, floor to ceiling, to iron bars. He sat quite still on a bench in a constantly moving, muttering, moaning, outraged population of maniacs, some in restraining jackets, others in shackles. They kept these people not in rooms but in what seemed to be a succession of hall wards with high clerestory windows and vaulted ceilings finished in ochered brick. The great volumes of space above the inmates mixed their screeches and shouts and cries of despair into a cathedral of prayerful sound. But it was an institution, you see, and so he seemed quite comfortable in it . . . this doctor who had run field hospitals and operating rooms and institutes of his own design. He sat and watched. . . . Even had I not known who he was, my eyes would have fixed on him because he was the only one not moving . . . not shuffling about, or pacing an imaginary cell, not lifting his eyes to heaven, not twitching, shrugging, or giggling or dribbling over himself, not lying on the floor and waving his arms like a swimmer, not hideously laughing, not endlessly crying.

A large fire hose was mounted on the wall in the narrow corridor in which I stood. The asylum smell was pungent—from the ammonia wash that was periodically sent over the floors and walls. The guard, who had led me here, rapped his club on the bars to get Sartorius's attention. What was unsettling about our subsequent exchange was the doctor's unfaltering poise. He asked me why I had come. I found myself ridiculously flattered that he had recognized me. I said: "I would like if possible to give you your day in court."

"That would only be hypocrisy. I respect the self-interest behind this expedient," he said, indicating the hall. "It is more in character with the society. Besides, I don't intend to remain separate from these people. I intend, as soon as I understand them, to share their rituals . . . so that a month from now, if you return, you will find me indistinguishable from everyone else here.''

''To what purpose?''

''I have no other means of experiment than my person.''

''What sort of experiment?''

He didn't answer. Behind the close mesh he was crosshatched, like a steel-point etching. He turned his back and folded his arms, so that we were looking at all the madmen together, he from the inside, I from the corridor. ''You see the profusion?'' he said. ''Nature reaching out everywhere, endlessly rooting, making more of itself than it needs . . . profligate, supremely wasteful, and, of course, inured to the agonies of its . . . specimens. Always willing to transform, to experiment, to propose itself into a new shape, a new way of being, a new mind.''

''I intend to write about the . . . experiment just concluded,'' I said.

''As you wish,'' he said. ''But it will not be possible for a long time.''

''Why?''

''Until you have the voice for it. And that will only be when your city is ready to hear you.''

I said: ''I'm glad I had some small part in halting your work. Do you have anything to say about that?''

He shrugged ''It's past.''

"Yet I don't think you know my name."

"It's of no use to me."

"Did you know that we found the body of Augustus Pemberton?"

"He could not have survived for long."

"How did people come to know of your work? It was kept secret. How did a sick and dying Augustus Pemberton hear of it?"

"I am not the one to ask. They are all in communication, these men of the city. It was through the city. Mr. Simmons is well placed. He had heard, I suppose."

"Simmons is dead as well—did you know that?"

"I think I did. He was a capable fellow. He approached me on behalf of Pemberton. I was impressed with him. At that point I was in need of administrative assistance. The city trustees suggested him as someone who could provide it."

"Do you regret his death? Do you regret the deaths of your colleagues—Wrangel, certainly, who served under you in the war?"

"I won't speak of this."

"Am I right in supposing you feel morality is . . . atavistic?"

He was silent for a good minute. I heard in the meantime the Blackwell's Island birdhouse symphony of shrieks, cries, caterwaulings, trills, shouts, and pealing laughter. Then he spoke along the following lines: ''I believe all life is contingent, from the first autonomous springings of the organism itself, to the accidents of its changing form. This is what we know of our biological history, that it is accidental . . . beginning from an arbitrary circumstance. So, we must rid ourselves of our poetic . . . conceits. We have now the periodic table of elements to think of, but as the crudest beginnings of our understanding of what is invisible in the composed life-forms. We have the work of the descriptive naturalists, looking always for organizing principles—that this creature is like that creature, that they exist in groups or families—which begins to simplify the seemingly unending diversity of vitalities upon the earth. But this is merely to picture our own limits as perceptive beings. The unifying morphology of living things may be nothing more distinguished than what we are lately identifying as the cell, something that can be seen only with a microscope. And when we have the structure and function of this, it will still be a journey to the truth. The truth is so deep inside, so interior, it operates—if that can be said to be the verb—in total blindness, in the total disregard of a recognizable world that would give us comfort, or in which we might find beauty or the hand of God—a point where life arcs into its first sentient glimmerings . . . from clashes of inanimate things so small as not to be even things . . . but where entity is very hot or very cold and gaseous and flam-

ing and senseless and unalive, and quite . . . mindless
. . . as it is in black space. Philosophy poses the right
questions. But it lacks the requisite diction for the
answers. Only Science can find the diction for
answers.''

''It is only a matter of the right diction?''

''Finally, yes, we will find the language, the
formulae, or perhaps the numeration . . . to match
God.''

''And God himself cannot be relied upon for the
answers?''

''Not as God is now composed.''

Not as God is now composed. I should say . . .
in those days the interview was not a defined journalistic form. . . . It would not come into being, as such,
for a few more years . . . not until the telephone made
people more accessible to reporters and we could
take statements routinely without having to run all
over the city for them. So I doubt if, as I questioned
Sartorius and he answered, I thought I was practicing
a particular form of journalism . . . but I did know
enough to write down as much as I could remember
of this . . . interview as soon as I was out of there.
Everything I could hear in that din, at any rate.

By contrast now I'll tell you something I remember verbatim because I was able to read it and
commit it to memory—it was too tasty to do otherwise. . . . I've recited it at parties over the years . . .
the deposition of a Cuban provincial, a fisherman

named Merced, taken by Ensign Forebaugh, of the U.S. Navy, who commanded the river gunboat *Daniel Webster.* They were chasing Bill Tweed through the Cuban jungle, you see. . . . Tweed had escaped from jail and had fled to Cuba.

This is in translation, of course: ''I see him wading ashore, a white man of girth, with an unkempt beard, and clothes all torn. On a rope he pulls his pirogue up on the bank. He slaps at the mosquitoes and hops about. He has no paddle or provisions, no shoes, but from his pocket he removes a wet and wrinkled green American dollar and asks for a drink. I give him water. In his eyes writhe the snakes of desperation. He takes the name of the Lord in vain. What kind of country is this, I said a drink, you ignorant black person of no ancestry. I do not countenance his bad behavior and go to my house and make my children stay inside. He sits out on the sand all day and we hear him wail from time to time and it is clear to my wife he is a poor afflicted soul. She is a gentler spirit than I, and after crossing herself, she brings him some fish and rice and beans and her good flatbread. In his ragged pants he finds another wet dollar, which he presents to her. Every time we tend to him he produces another wet dollar. The man is not a Christian. And what besides will I do with such worthless currency? He says, You know who I am? He shows interest in our birds. He sees the egret on the bank, he sees the parrots in the trees, and the white sandbirds and diving little big-headed birds who fish in the river, and the red-blue birds who hang by their beaks on the blossoms to drink, and these are of great interest to him, because he strides back and forth, calling to them their cries, though badly, tweet tweet, he says, over and over, I am tweet, which has no meaning, but then he is clearly crazy. He is impoverished of language but with grand ideas. Of the egret he says in his city they are worn as hats by women of sport. I do not wish my wife to hear this and send her inside. Oh yes, he says, my city is the city of God. And these women are beautiful who wear the hats of birds. And he tells mad stories. That in this city of his god, they make burning gas explosions to light up the darkness of night so the ladies with the hats of birds may walk there and call out to men their birdcalls. And they have burning wheels that do the work of men, and pull vast weights of cargo on silver paths without the need of oxen or mules . . . and others to cut the crops, and weave the cloth, and sew like tailors, all of these burning wheels. And the houses are not like mine, of poles and thatch, but of a substance harder than stone that is made out of fire. And with this substance they build houses high as mountains and bridges to cross rivers. He is a wonderful madman, and he says he is the god of this city where there is no darkness and the women wear birds. He speaks in such a manner. My children play around him and I have no fear because he sees them and laughs and does tricks for them and then he cries, he so loves children. He gives them a wrinkled dollar too. So he is a poor madman. He says he is going to Santiago and then across the sea. Before he leaves he produces another dollar, which he throws on the water, and he waves from his pirogue as he drifts away downstream . . . which of course is not the way to Santiago!

''And the last thing I remember . . . he says . . . in his city of God they have learned the secret of eternal life . . . and when he returns to it he will be anointed to live forever.

''And he waves and once more says he is the bird calling tweet tweet, except now this bird is roaring like a beast and we hear him roaring even after he disappears from sight down there where the river turns. He was a wonderful madman.''

Twenty-eight

FINALLY, after all, I have been talking about our city. Sartorius's head was one day smashed against the asylum stone floor with such force—the strength of his attacker the strength that is given only to maniac rage—that the skull caved in like an eggshell and the brain . . . there is no other word for it . . . ran. The precise nature of his offense was never determined . . . perhaps the attempt to treat . . . but he, like all his artwork of immortal dead men, was forever stilled. He was buried in the potter's field on Hart Island, which is in the Sound, off the shore of the Bronx.

Augustus Pemberton was buried on the sward at Ravenwood where he had died. This required the permission of the absentee owners, a commercial firm that bought and sold real estate . . . and was the idea of his widow, Sarah, who was able to feel as no one else could the pitiable nature of her husband's brutally selfish life.

Eustace Simmons was committed to a public grave in Rockland County. Like Sartorius, he apparently had no living relatives. Nor did the loyal, oxlike Wrangel. One way or another, these were all single, unrelated men . . . as were Donne, and Martin Pemberton, and I, for that matter.

I don't know whether the cast-off families of the mortuary fellowship were ever informed . . . or where the old men were buried or, indeed, if any of the collected funds they had contributed for their eternal welfare were ever recovered.

The footlocker that had killed Simmons held a fortune—something in the neighborhood of one and a half million dollars. This was presented to Sarah Pemberton as her due—please don't be shocked— with no overexacting concern for the laws of probate.

That winter I was a guest at two weddings held within a week of each other. Martin Pemberton and Emily Tisdale were married, by their preference, in the open air, on the garden terrace of the Tisdale home on Lafayette Place. Dr. Grimshaw, who, in the course of these events, seemed to have simplified his spiritual life into a steady and perpetual disapproval of everyone and everything on earth, conducted the ceremony with his little neat nose red from the cold and with a bead of clear liquid hanging from its tip. The bride, typical of her practical nature, wore a white satin gown with a lace shawl about the shoulders . . . very simple in its lines, with no undue embellishments, and the simplest of veils, which lay like a celestial white leaf over her hair. Real remnant leaves from the earth, in orange and yellow and brown, blew about our feet, and the only music was the wind coming off the dormant garden. As Grimshaw read the service in his high thin voice, I saw from behind how the bride held the arm of her groom, from elbow to clasped hand, and tight to her side, to prop him up, or herself, or perhaps both of them. They were matched in height and in youth and in the history of their childhood lives . . . a perfect match, and consecrated in the appropriate place, overlooking their small walled park, hidden from the city . . . which is the way nature hopes to survive in New York.

I was circumspect in my examination of the bride's figure, though angered by what I imagined were the similar longings of the large wheezing fellow who stood beside me . . . even though, in what I supposed was a capitulation of sorts, he had brought as a wedding present the portrait of Emily he had painted for himself. When the bride said her "I do," her voice cracking in her joy, my heart, I like to think, was broken forever.

Sarah Pemberton was in attendance, of course, radiant to be resolved in her widowhood, Donne by her side . . . and the elderly Lavinia Pemberton Thornhill, back from her annual general inspection of Europe. Mrs. Thornhill was exactly as she had been described to me, a fussy old woman of wealth who wore an old-fashioned hoop gown and a wig that didn't sit quite straight on her head. She had a peremptory way about her . . . a family trait . . . and seemed to be satisfied only by the conversation of Emily's father, Amos Tisdale, who was roughly her own distinguished age and thereby deserving of her attention. Of course she had not been told anything at all . . . and since her connection to Martin all his life had been tenuous, at best, in the great tradition of this in-name-only family, she kept looking at him as if trying to assure herself that he was indeed her late brother's son.

Noah, dressed in a short-pants suit with his hair combed back and his shoes shined, served as best man, a role he performed with a solemnity no greater or less than his everyday solemnity. He handed the ring up in its little velvet box on the palms of both his hands to his stepbrother, and it was this moment . . . seeing in his hazel eyes as he glanced up at Martin the manly compact that he made with him . . . that secured for me the revelation of our rituals . . . this old lapsed Scotch Presbyterian, his suppressed tears swallowed in his throat . . . that they are made holy truth by the children.

The ceremony done, we all got ourselves inside to the parlor quickly enough, where there were mulled wine and cocoa and plates of wedding cake. Amos Tisdale had graciously refused to express his misgivings . . . and sealed his determination by bestowing upon the young couple a six-month Grand

Tour of Europe in the following spring. When this was announced, to congratulatory applause, Harry Wheelwright was inspired to recall to me his own trip abroad. He spoke with that reflective self-assessment people are given to at weddings. "I went to Europe," he said, "to stand before the work of the Masters, and so I did . . . in Holland, in Spain, and in Italy. I would have done better . . . just to drop to my knees and touch my forehead to the cold floors in front of them."

"You didn't learn anything? You were not inspired?"

"Yes, I was inspired. I was inspired to run through my capital until I had left only the price of a decent second-class passage home. . . . My inspiration was to forget art . . . and simply paint the faces and figures of my fellow citizens—at least those who would pay me. To find the character in the eyes, the mouth, the chosen posture—wasn't that, after all, what this Rembrandt had done, this Velázquez? I would be a fellow tradesman, however obscure. I would share the intent, at least, to paint human faces unlocated, with nothing behind them . . . alone in the universe."

He drank off his wine. "But, you know, they loved every ruffle of the collar, every line of the chin, every brown shadow in the corner. Nothing was scanted, it was all light of one kind or another, and they loved light . . . whatever it fell on. They were helpless to do anything but render it. I knew I had that . . . love of light. But if it was to be called art, what I did, others could think about it, I would not . . . ever again. And that is what I've done.''

I could not decide if Harry deserved my congratulations for conceding . . . in the history of western art there might have been a better painter or two. But I would have preferred to go on listening to Harry if I had known Martin Pemberton would collar me to express his gratitude. Martin was overheard, unfortunately, and in another moment the others had gathered around . . . all of them apparently dedicated to embarrassing me to the utmost.

My freelance said with an awful earnestness: ''You saved my life, Mr. McIlvaine.'' I found this remark almost frightening, like a confirmation of his permanent mental decline. It was the same pale fellow with thinning blond hair and penetrating gray eyes and intensity of expression . . . but the thought was banal.

Then Emily, my dear Emily, stood on her toes and kissed my cheek. . . . This was intolerable to me, although none of them understood why . . . and then they all laughed because I had turned red.

''Captain Donne found your fellow,'' I said to her.

I looked up at Donne, standing behind everyone and towering over them. Well understanding my discomfiture, he said: ''Mr. McIlvaine saw before anyone else that something was . . . amiss.'' Can you imagine? He used that word for everything I've been telling you! ''Amiss''! ''He came to see me—it was he who brought in the Municipals.''

''Mr. McIlvaine has done us all a great great service,'' Sarah Pemberton said, placing her hand on Donne's arm and gazing at me with her Mother of God composure.

I don't even know why I'm repeating this—so that you'll forgive them, perhaps. The way people, the best people, must go spiraling off in the resolution of things. As if there would be no memory. No carriage coming up Broadway that will forever be the white stage with the nodding old men in black.

I can't tell you how deeply I abhor our custom of steadfast carrying on . . . in the manner of people of our sort. The women are mostly responsible for that. In the obituaries we speak of survivors. ''Mr. Pemberton is survived by . . .'' I want you to understand the devastation . . . I felt was in that parlor . . . among Augustus Pemberton's survivors. I could feel it in myself . . . like a bit of indissoluble ash on the tongue. Nevertheless I made some cheerful remark about the future. The young couple would be abroad for a year. I told Martin that when he returned I expected to have an assignment for him. I had gotten a new job, you see, as assistant city editor on the *Sun.* He said with a wan smile: ''I will be willing and able.''

And I think finally that's why I never wrote up the story—not because it would not be heard but because it was his . . . his patrimony. . . . For a writer the story is his patrimony . . . and he might, someday, come into it . . . my freelance. My freelance.

I did go to the other wedding, on the Sunday following, in the afternoon, at St. James Episcopal on Laight Street. We were in the December of the year. It had snowed in the interval, leaving the entire city white . . . and then in brilliant sunlight the air had warmed, and then turned bitter cold, coating everything in an icy glaze.

The wedding party was augmented by a number of policemen in uniform, as well as parishioners who had elected to stay after the service to see who was getting married. In their sight of the bride they were well rewarded, Sarah being a creature of uncompromised grace, regal in a pale blue gown . . . that matched her eyes. She did not seem ever, that I remember, to hurry . . . and now, coming down the aisle on Martin's arm to the soft measures of the organ, she seemed to flow, this great beauty, surely one of the most beautiful women I had ever seen . . . the wide full mouth in a smile, the unveiled head slightly tilted.

Donne stood in terror at the steps to the altar. Before him was the Reverend Charles Grimshaw in his best-laundered white surplice and a white stole embroidered in gold, his chin raised, his determinedly cheerful gaze on the empty balcony at the rear of the nave. Perhaps the rector was thinking of the first time this woman had married—a far grander occasion, when it was a far different church . . . filled with the names of the city . . . and the only policemen were those on guard outside.

So there, with the organ playing, and the roof beams of St. James in a kind of perpetual dusk, though the winter light came planing through the clerestory windows, and the stained-glass *Deposition* behind the altar glowed with the colors of the sun . . . was God as he is now composed.

And Donne and Sarah were married. I did not stay long afterward. The reception was in the parsonage, with a red punch from a cut-glass bowl, and cocoa, and the small round cakes with pink icing that were then very fashionable—not really my native kind of revel. Sarah Pemberton Donne told me they had found a house on West Eleventh Street, a red brick with french windows with wrought-iron balconies and a front yard with a tree in it and a wide granite stoop . . . a quiet street with all the houses set back and little traffic . . . though Noah would have to change schools. Donne curved himself downward to shake my hand and admitted to what I had heard around town, that he had been approached by reformist elements in the Republican party who had it in mind . . . if all went well in the elections . . . to

offer him the post of police commissioner with a
mandate to clean up the Municipals.

I remember how still the city was that afternoon
as I walked uptown from the church. It was brilliantly sunny and terribly cold and the streets were
empty. The footing was treacherous. Everything was
thickly glazed. . . . Horsecars were frozen to their
rails, as were the locomotives on their elevated rail-
way of ice. . . . The masts and sheets of the ships in
the docks were ensheathed in ice. . . . Ice floes lay in
the viscous river. . . . The ironfronts on Broadway
seemed in the sun to be burning in ice. . . . The trees
on the side streets were of crystal.

Of course it was Sunday, the day of rest. But my
illusion was that the city had frozen in time. All our
mills and foundries and presses were still . . . our
lathes and our boilers . . . our steam engines and pul-
leys and pumps and forges. Our stores were shut
. . . our carriage works and iron works and sewing-
machine and typewriter factories . . . our telegraph
stations . . . our exchanges . . . our carpentries . . . our
electroplaters . . . our stoneyards and lumberyards
. . . our abattoirs and fish markets . . . our hosiery
mills and garment shops . . . our smithies and stables
. . . our manufacturers of tool dies and turbines and
steam dredges and railroad cars and horse collars
. . . our gunsmiths and silversmiths . . . our stove-
works and tinware stampers . . . our coopers and

clockmakers and ship chandlers . . . our brickworks
. . . our makers of ink and our paper mills . . . our
book publishers . . . our mowers and harvesters and
sowers and reapers—all still, unmoving, stricken, as
if the entire city of New York would be forever encased and frozen, aglitter and God-stunned.

And let me leave you with that illusion . . .
though in reality we would soon be driving ourselves
up Broadway in the new Year of Our Lord, 1872.

(continued)

Judith Krantz, *Dazzle*
Judith Krantz, *Lovers* (paper)
Judith Krantz, *Scruples Two*
John le Carré, *The Night Manager* (paper)
John le Carré, *The Secret Pilgrim*
Robert Ludlum, *The Bourne Ultimatum*
Robert Ludlum, *The Road to Omaha*
Cormac McCarthy, *The Crossing* (paper)
James A. Michener, *Mexico* (paper)
James A. Michener, *The Novel*
James A. Michener, *The World is My Home* (paper)
Richard North Patterson, *Degree of Guilt*
Louis Phillips, editor, *The Random House Large Print
    Treasury of Best-Loved Poems*
Maria Riva, *Marlene Dietrich* (2 volumes, paper)
Mickey Rooney, *Life Is Too Short*
William Styron, *Darkness Visible*
Margaret Truman, *Murder at the National Cathedral*
Margaret Truman, *Murder at the Pentagon*
Margaret Truman, *Murder on the Potomac* (paper)
Donald Trump with Charles Leerhsen, *Trump: Surviving
    at the Top*
Anne Tyler, *Saint Maybe*
John Updike, *Rabbit at Rest*
Phyllis A. Whitney, *Star Flight* (paper)
Lois Wyse, *Grandchildren Are So Much Fun
    I Should Have Had Them First*

The New York Times Large Print Crossword Puzzles (paper)

Will Weng, editor, Volumes 1–3
Eugene T. Maleska, editor, Volumes 4–7
Eugene T. Maleska, editor, Omnibus Volume 1